First published in Great Britain in 2008 by Comma Press
www.commapress.co.uk

ISBN: 1905583184
ISBN-13: 978 1905583188

The publisher gratefully acknowledges assistance from the Arts Council England
North West, and also the support of Literature Northwest.

literaturenorthwest ◉

Set in Bembo 11/13 by David Eckersall
Printed and bound in England by SRP Ltd, Exeter

THE NEW
UNCANNY

Edited by
Sarah Eyre & Ra Page

Contents

CONTENTS

Introduction

I had a dream last night (but then I have it most nights) in which I found myself back home. Standing on the front lawn that's now a patio, or in the bushes now cleared to make a widened drive, or from some other angle, I gazed trying to take in the usual four-square comfort of the sight: my parents' house. Somehow though, for all its reassurances – the well-worn doorstep, the re-pointed wall – its familiarity saddened me. I knew it was a fake.

Beyond the obvious, certain features began to stand out as altered, their deformations almost spreading as I looked. The back garden seemed flatter, lower, quarried away somehow. Old familiars like the toolshed were left on stilts of bedrock, like museum pieces. Nothing about it was mine or belonged to the house I grew up in. The walls themselves seemed to thin and dry in front of me, mortar dropping from their cracks.

In happier versions of the dream I stay under long enough to realise it's not all bad; this place is a duplicate. The real house remains preserved, some miles behind this one, in someone else's keeping. But even knowing this, and having no sense of danger or threat to point to, I would still call it a nightmare.

In and of itself, this may not be an uncanny dream. In his famous essay of 1919 – the reason we're all here – Freud listed eight officially uncanny tropes, that is to say eight irrational causes of fear deployed in literature:

(i) inanimate objects mistaken as animate (dolls, waxworks, automata, severed limbs, etc.),

(ii) animate beings behaving as if inanimate or mechanical (trances, epileptic fits, etc.),

(iii) being blinded,

(iv) the double (twins, doppelgangers, etc.),

(v) coincidences or repetitions,

(vi) being buried alive,

(vii) some all-controlling evil genius,

(viii) confusions between reality and imagination (waking dreams, etc).

What were these manifestations of exactly? To paraphrase, the uncanny is that which may be familiar, or ordinary, but somehow disturbs us, makes us uncomfortable, and in some cases gives us the full on willies. A murderer leaping into view unexpectedly in a horror film is not uncanny. The fear that we, the audience, feel is perfectly rational, empathetic fear for the character's safety (and *through them* for our own). Nor is straightforward gore or gruesomeness uncanny – again our aversion to it is rational, natural. The uncanny is rather that subtler, added texture in a film or story (in the best cases, the *only* texture) specially applied to instil an inexplicable air of unease, a cognitive dissonance that mounts and mounts until we are almost literally 'unnerved'. Freud, being a self-confessed interloper in the realm of aesthetics, grabbed what literary precedents he could, added a handful of his own experiences to flesh the list out, and then threw a single tarpaulin-theory over all of it: that these phenomena or situations scare us because they remind us of repressed belief-systems; either from childhood (like the belief that dolls can come to life, or the yearning to return to the womb), or from primitive stages of human development (like the belief in a protective twin-spirit accompanying us through life and death). Being reminded of these old, repressed ideas by an uncanny event or object, sends a shudder of recognition through us which we instantly revolt against. The fear of losing one's eyes is a sublimation of the childhood castration complex. The fear of being buried alive indicates a repression of the childhood desire to return to the womb, and so on.

Each item on Freud's list offers a kind of literary template, and together they provide writers and filmmakers with an ever dependable shopping list of shivers, a 'goth-kitty' to keep returning to indefinitely. Freud, and fellow psychoanalyst Ernst Jentsch, drew the beginnings of the list from the work of just one writer, E T A Hoffman, and largely from just one short story, *The Sandman*. But the vestiges of Freud's list can be traced backwards or forwards in time, far beyond this one story. Clarence's famous nightmare speech, in *Richard III*, chalks up three uncanny archetypes in almost as few lines with its talk of jewels lying in skulls on the sea-bed, crept 'where the eyes did once inhabit [...] as 'twere in scorn of eyes'; there being much of Freud's fear of being buried alive in his ensuing, sub-aquatic inability to 'yield the ghost.' Likewise, ninety years after the publication of Freud's ideas, cinema's love affairs with science fiction writers like Isaac Asimov and Philip K. Dick, and indeed the zombie genre, are all still in bloom, carrying forth an undiminished obsession with automatons, doubles and the living dead. Parallel to this, film's fixation with the eye and its mutilation could be used to tell the story of cinema itself; from the eye-slitting of *Un chien andalou,* to the eye-gorging of Hitchcock's *The Birds*, to the eye-replacing of *Minority Report*. It's hard to find a sci-fi flick these days or a technologically assisted thriller that doesn't have a retina-scan popping up in it. And every month a new film seems to arrive to play the uncanny card ever more explicitly: David Moreau and Xavier Palud's *The Eye* (2008), Alexandre Aja's *Mirrors* (2008), etc. There are even uncanny comedies like Graig Gillespie's *Lars and the Real Girl* (2007).

But to get back to my dream for a moment – as the narcissistic patient might say. The homestead remains central to all this. The haunted house is iconic in the oldest and newest of ghost stories (Freud confessed he would have made it number one in his list if it weren't that, so often 'the uncanny in it is too much intermixed with what is purely gruesome'). And away from horror, SF writers like Asimov and Dick always knew that robots aren't all that menacing, until you invite one home.

But it's more than this. The home is not just the setting and target of the threat. The uncanny is somehow *of* the home, or *under* it. It squats in the very word Freud used for 'uncanny' in German, 'unheimliche', meaning literally 'un-homely'. It lies beneath the house, under that heavy architecture of habit and belief, buried. And for a reason. As for my particular dream, there remains something peculiarly uncanny about the anxiety in it – I'm convinced. Indeed this act of interpreting my own dreams – splitting the self and subject, with half of me climbing off the couch to look down – is also uncanny. Even more so, the facsimile of Freud that I, and so many other self-diagnosers, habitually refer to: that 2D cut-out of Freud, the blow-up effigy of him we call upon at parties or in the pub when making our almost evangelic deference: WWFS? ('What Would Freud Say?').

Some claim that we live in a uniquely uncanny age. Computer games and the internet provide more and more opportunities to duplicate ourselves – Facebook profiles, Flikr accounts, Second Life avatars – not to mention more opportunities to find ourselves duplicated by others: spoofed emails, identity theft, and so on. Other critics insist that the uncanny cuts much deeper than current fads and neuroses, and is timeless. The uncanny is a 'crisis of the natural,' argues Nicholas Royle (the literary theorist, not his uncanny namesake featured here). The uncanny destabilises 'the reality of who one is, and what one is experiencing.' It disturbs any straightforward sense of what is within and what without, and alerts us the 'foreign body' within us. Or worse, makes us regard ourselves *as* a foreign body, a stranger.

INTRODUCTION

Seeing as Freud took a single short story as his case study, rather than a patient, it only seems right for the editors of this anthology to test his theories on a sample of similarly unassuming short stories. This was our plan. Fourteen established writers were sent copies of the original essay (though many were familiar with it) and asked to respond directly and consciously, in any way they wished, with a new story. We were curious to see which archetypes still rang true and which, if any, paled. As it transpired, the earlier items on Freud's list proved the most popular (dolls/automata, sleepwalking/epilepsy, blindness and doubles). As expected new technology provided plenty of confusion between the animate and inanimate, not just through computers, but also tactile, mechanical devices like Jane Rogers' Ped-o-Matique. The eye found itself new spectacles – like the all-seeing 'i' of the internet in Ian Duhig's story. But there were almost as many un-technological stories here too. Further down the list, the responses thinned. No stories came back about confusions between imagination and reality, or being buried alive. Only one writer explored the idea of a greater, controlling intelligence – namely Christopher Priest in his exposition of that seemingly modern threat, the stalker. And one writer, Etgar Keret explored a cause rather than a symptom of uncanny anxiety: Freud's 'fear of sex'.

Our sample size is too small to prove anything of course. But it's interesting all the same to note the overwhelming emphasis here on two phenomena in particular: the double and the doll. In conversation with several authors, it transpired that another essay, by a contemporary of Freud's, came to bear heavily on their story, this being Rilke's exhibition-review-cum-thesis, 'Dolls: On the Waxwork Dolls of Lotte Pritzel' (1913). For Rilke, dolls weren't so much a reminder of that time in childhood when we did 'not distinguish at all sharply between living and inanimate objects,' as Freud puts it, or when we might have fancied that the doll 'would be certain to come to life [if looked at] in a particular, extremely concentrated way.' For Rilke, it was more personal. To see an old, familiar doll, as an adult, provokes a layered reaction in us. Firstly, he claimed, we feel anger – at the doll's betrayal and its 'horrible dense forgetfulness' of that 'purest affection' we once squandered on it. Secondly, it scares us, for it reminds us of the first time we had to assert our own identity, rather than let our identity be steered and lost under the overcoat of others'. We had to be ourselves, that is *invent* ourselves, when left alone for the first time with a doll.

Thirdly it saddens us, because it reminds of the time we first learnt of the non-responsiveness of the world, the first time our questions and demands were met only by silence – an answer we grew all too used to as adults – and of the wider hollowness of things (including ourselves). Finally, the sight of such a doll in adulthood fills us with a feeling of estrangement, Rilke claimed. We no longer recognise it as this protagonist of our imaginary world, nor do we recognise 'the confidences we heaped over it and into it,' nor the child that did the heaping.

There is nothing in Rilke's rich and moving essay that speaks of repression or denial. His subject is the re-evaluation of objects with which we now have a different relationship; and the realisation that the identity of both parties has shifted, drastically. As a child, Rilke hardly seems to have believed his dolls would awaken and come to life, as Freud claims. His sense of betrayal is rather that the doll no longer awakens something *in him*: the passion, the engagement they once had. Rilke's reaction is a projection of a disappointment in himself, for *his own* 'dense forgetfulness', not a suppression of some old belief.

As for the double, Freud is again frustratingly cursory. Citing fellow psychoanalyst Otto Rank, he compares the double to that immortal twin-spirit of ancient mythologies, the 'ka' accompanying us through life and transporting our soul after death. Carl Jung – deferring to mythology, but one can't help thinking buoyed up by Dostoevsky's *The Double* and Stevenson's *Dr Jekyll and Mr Hyde* – constructed a more elaborate thesis for the double, calling it 'The Shadow'. This he claimed was one of the first 'archetypes' to reveal itself in psychotherapy: a subconscious embodiment of a lesser, more imperfect version of oneself, a vessel for the shortcomings and baser instincts one hopes or pretends one does not have.

Looking at the stories collected here, though, there seems to be much more synergy between the dolls and doubles than can be found in the diametric opposition between what Rilke said about the former (lost friends) and what Jung said about the latter (concealed, darker selves). In these stories they almost overlap. Take Adam Marek's beautiful 'Tamagotchi'. At first glance this is a technological update of the doll story, deserving to sit on the same bedroom shelf as A. S. Byatt's collectible antique, echoing its function. But told from the father's point of view (not dissimilar from a psychanalyst's), the toy also becomes a repository for a more dangerous, contagious version of the child's malady, that is it becomes Jung's Shadow. Come the end of the story, however, it switches back to a simple doll, that which only a child can release, only a child can betray. A similar synergy unfolds in the 'imaginative play' of Frank Cottrell Boyce's story, where the 'doll' in question – the computer game The Sims – invites a doubling from the off. In some stories, like Nicholas Royle's 'The Dummy', the double remains pure Jungian Shadow, but more often it is grafted on in childhood, beginning life with a doll-like speechlessness, such as the chilling companion in Sara Maitland's 'Seeing Double'.

The doll and double are two faces of the same coin, these stories seem to suggest. The former reminds us of the person we no longer are, and of that first identity we asserted in a doll's presence. The latter, or rather that tingle of unease we get from a double (receiving a spam email from ourselves, for example) makes us shiver for a moment and ask, Who is this? Who am I? In both cases, identity slips, becomes fallible. To take my house dream: the older version of the house, the original, feels more sturdy in the dream than the flimsy present-day duplicate, no matter how inaccessible the former has become. The house we grew up in, or the dolls we played with as children, though lost to us, are still more real. As are, perhaps, the people we were growing up with them. There are two versions of the doll, or the house, and two of us.

Crucially, Freud is right when he talks of the division of the self, as necessary for the development of a conscience – that agency able to 'stand over the rest of the ego,' observe, criticise and censor the self. The fallacy of a split-self is something that must also accompany the acquisition of language and its progression into thought. Here, we see the double as much the same thing as the doll: an older, disembodied inheritor of the doll's role in our mental universe; that is to say the addressee of our thoughts. Whereas once the doll enabled us to play the language game to ourselves, and create worded, spoken thought, now the double sits speechless in the fallacious dialogue of adult consciousness, the audience of our internal speech. To see a doll is to be reminded of the fallacy's beginning, to see a look-a-like of oneself is to be jolted into the fallacy itself.

But it's fun, this fallacy, with its various triggers – doll or double, eyeball or living machine. As the stories commissioned here will attest, it quickens the heart, raises the neck hair, makes us squirm, writhe, or even feel physically sick. In a good way. It puts us on edge – that place we really should be from time to time – and reminds us: it's us that's alive.

Ra Page
Oct, 2008

Double Room

Ramsey Campbell

'You aren't with us, are you?'

'I'd like to be.'

'What's your name?' the other girl said, looking impudently quizzical. 'You've seen ours.'

He was glad if they assumed he'd been squinting in the dimness of the hotel bar only at the badges pinned above their long slim thighs. Each badge bore the image of a winged young woman dressed in a chain-mail bikini and a virtually transparent robe, an outfit both girls had copied apart from the wings. The sword in her hand indicated their names, Primmy and Barbaria. 'Edwin Ferguson,' he said.

'That's an old name,' Primmy commented.

'You need to be old to know all the tricks.'

'I like a good trick, don't you, Primmy? Are you going to show us yours, Edwin?'

However guilty he couldn't help feeling, he thought he might feel worse if he let the opportunity pass. 'I only give private performances,' he said.

'Is it going to be all for us?' Primmy cried.

Barbaria bent her head and an eyebrow towards her, prompting Ferguson to assure the girls 'It's all right, I didn't think you were angels.'

'Why not?' Primmy demanded.

He pointed at her badge – at least, he hoped it was clear that was where he was pointing. 'No wings.'

'Sometimes we are,' Barbaria said. 'We can be all

1

kinds.'

'Depends who we're with.'

'I'm looking forward to finding out. What roles you like playing, I mean.'

He made the sudden silence the occasion for a sip of Scotch followed by a larger one. 'You're looking at them,' Barbaria said.

'And they're all you'll be seeing,' Primmy said.

He was able to mistake this for a promise until they turned away as a man strolled into the bar. He was at least as old as Ferguson and even stouter, with greying hair that Ferguson thought far too long for his age. Nevertheless the girls stood up eagerly, although Primmy lingered to say 'Thanks for the fun.'

'Is that all?' When she tried to appear prim instead of primitive Ferguson was provoked to add 'Maybe you shouldn't come out in public dressed like that. You might give some people the wrong idea.'

'We were at the masquerade.'

'You've been doing some of that all right.' Loud enough for her to catch he said, 'And what do you get up to the rest of the time?'

Barbaria turned long enough to inform him 'We're social workers.'

'Is that what they call it these days?' he might have retorted except for feeling obsolete. As the girls each took the newcomer by an arm Ferguson saw that the man's badge depicted a bronzed bruiser in sandals and loincloth and crown, who was brandishing a blade at a lengthy name Ferguson felt expected to recognise. He drained his Scotch and murmured to the barman 'Who's he?'

'One of their writers.'

In his sleeveless denim outfit the fellow didn't look much like one, or his age. Was being a writer all it took to have girls hanging on your arms? Perhaps now Ferguson had time to write the book he imagined he contained, the rest would follow. The idea seemed so variously disloyal that he felt his face glow like the light of a brake he'd applied too belatedly to himself, and he hurried not much better than blindly out of the bar.

He hadn't reached the lifts when the lobby grew loudly crowded with people emerging from the conference suite. While a few were fantastically costumed, most struck him as not much less anonymous and awkward than himself. The hotel notice-board identified their event as a Fantasy Weekend, but it didn't mean the kind of fantasy he'd yielded to imagining. At least, it certainly didn't for him.

He kept his back to the mirror in the lift once he'd jabbed the button. On its way the lift opened to admit a view of the second-floor corridor, where badged individuals and their noise and drinks were spilling out of a room. For a moment he wished he were in there, but the room sounded too small for the revellers who were. That was one reason why the wish fell away before the corridor did.

The adjacent lift had just delivered someone to the third floor. Ferguson glimpsed their shadow vanishing around the corner ahead as he made for his room. From the corner, he saw the door next to his standing ajar. 'Good night,' he called as it shut, because the clinically pallid corridor with its equally colourless doors separated by timid abstract pastels made him lose all sense of himself. His last word was echoed in such a muffled voice that he couldn't be sure of its gender.

Once the lock on his door had given his card the green light he left the card in a slot inside the stubby vestibule to drape the room with indirect lighting. The word flat might have been invented for the accommodation: the boxy wardrobe and dressing-table, the single angular nominally padded chair, the double bed tucking nothingness up tight. Perhaps the midget television might provide some company – distraction, at any rate.

A fat old man with a threadbare grizzly scalp met him in the bathroom. The sight fired up the taste of his Indian dinner, the taste of which rose in a volcanic belch. 'Pardon,' he said almost as inadvertently, rousing a muffled echo. He wasn't apologising to his reflection; he didn't even watch the old fool mouth the syllables. He lifted the toilet seat and its lid with the toe of his shoe, and the plastic ovals rapped the tiled wall. The small room seemed to have an echo for everything. He dragged his baggy zip down to fumble himself forth, and had hardly started pouring when the noise became a duet. The other performer was in the adjoining bathroom.

Urinating in company always made Ferguson feel like a shy child, and he faltered to a dribble that trailed off to a drip. Was his neighbour suffering from the identical problem? Straining never helped, and the silence aggravated his inhibition just as much. He could only hum to lessen his awareness or pretend it wasn't troubling him. 'Let's Do It' always came into his head on these occasions, and he might have added words − one of his rhymes for bees, 'People who have finished having pees' or 'Women who are down upon their knees', that used to amuse Elizabeth whenever he sang them at random − if his neighbour hadn't joined in.

He still couldn't identify the gender from the voice. His own was shriller than it had any right or need to be. Perhaps his fellow guest was borrowing his solution to the urinary annoyance; they hummed louder once Ferguson did. He squeezed his eyes shut and then managed to relax them, and was rewarded with activity where it mattered. Something had worked for his neighbour as well. The streams dwindled and fell silent simultaneously, and he was shaking himself dry when he heard a clink through the wall.

His neighbour had put a glass down, but it was ridiculous to fancy they'd been using a glassful of water to imitate his sounds. He pulled a tissue out of the box by the sink to blow his nose. As he dropped the wad in the toilet he heard a nasal trumpeting in the adjacent bathroom.

If it sounded very much like his, did it have much leeway to sound different? Hooking the toilet seat with the side of his shoe, he let it drop along with its lid on the pedestal, and was unsurprised to hear an echo through the wall. Both toilets flushed while he turned back to the sink. He had barely started brushing his teeth when the sound was imitated in the other bathroom.

The old wreck in the mirror let his wrinkled mouth hang open, displaying all his front teeth and the gap one had left last month. How could such a tiny noise be audible through the wall? How could his? He decided he'd heard an echo until another bout of brushing was copied beyond the mockingly blank wall. His neighbour must be making the noise in some other way, unless they were attacking their teeth with a savagery that sounded demonic. 'Hope they all drop out of your head,' Ferguson spluttered and spat in the sink.

The answering spit was fierce enough for an insult. The words that followed were repeated in exactly Ferguson's tone, as far as he could distinguish the qualities of the voice. Was it deliberately muffled? Perhaps the speaker was obscuring it with a hand, hiding their ruined teeth from the other mirror, a notion that prompted Ferguson to blurt 'What must you look like?'

Although he thought he'd only muttered it, the question came back through the wall. The idiotic trick must be affecting him more than he realised. 'I know how I look,' he couldn't help retorting as he wiped foam off his lips. 'I think I'm better off not knowing how you do.'

He was unable to imagine a sufficiently grotesque costume for them. Perhaps they passed for normal until an event like this weekend's gave them licence not to be. Well before they finished echoing his latest remarks he was sick of the joke, if it could be called one. 'Very funny,' he responded, wondering why he'd waited for the mimicry to finish. 'Thanks for the laugh. Just what I needed. I haven't been so entertained since —'

He didn't know. When the partial sentence came back

neutered through the wall, he had the uneasy idea that the imitator was about to complete it for him. It faltered as he had, but he wasn't about to finish it off. He couldn't just blame the clown beyond the wall for the whole asinine situation; there was a clown in here too, looking foolish and pathetic, not to mention incapable of controlling his own behaviour. If he didn't make any more noise, the other would have nothing to mimic. He turned off the light, muting the switch with his hand, before tiptoeing out of the room.

For the duration of a couple of prolonged but silent breaths he was able to enjoy the possibility that his neighbour might be lingering in the bathroom for another noise to echo, and then the enforced hush set about troubling him. It emphasised the anonymity of the bedroom, which felt close to empty even of him. He wasn't going to be forced to act as if he weren't there. Grabbing the remote control from the shelf that enthroned the dwarf television, he threw himself on the bed.

Did he just hear the springs yield beneath him, or was there an answering twang in the adjacent bedroom? He supported his shoulders with a pillow and awakened the television with a shrill whisper of static. Dismissing the Frugotel information menu, he began to search the channels: a comedy film teeming with teenagers even louder than the party he'd seen from the lift, a report of a polo game where all the players were in wheelchairs, a documentary about a drug that was meant to retard ageing, an episode of a reality series called *Fostered for a Fortnight*, another by the name of *From a Previous Relationship*... He hadn't reached the second channel when, with barely a second's delay each time, a television beyond the wall behind his head commenced dogging his progress.

His neighbour was entitled to watch television too. The order of the browsing needn't be significant, since it was the obvious one. Ferguson felt irrational for wondering what would happen if he reversed it — at least, until he did so and heard the other television copy him. Changing channels at random produced the same result, and he had to struggle not to shout at the wall. How could he watch the programme he'd been tempted to? Without the sound, of course.

He buttoned it before poking the keys to summon the Frugrownup channel, where he came in some way through an act of the kind the channel offered the no doubt solitary members of its audience. The rhythmic activity was as noiseless as it was vigorous, so that he couldn't help fancying that the participants were all straining to produce a sound. At least he'd called up silence in the next room too, and his body had begun to show signs of emulating that of the man on the screen by the time he heard a noise through the wall.

Somebody was panting. It grew louder and more dramatic, keeping pace with the efforts on the television. His neighbour had given in to the same temptation, Ferguson tried to think, but weren't the gasps too theatrical even for this sort of film, and oddly androgynous? Was the other guest producing them to taunt him? Without question there was just a solitary voice, and he could hear faint laughter too. It was muffled by distance, unless there were more people in the next room, covering their mouths so as to titter at his situation. That was beginning to seem as contemptible as his attempts to pick up the girls in the bar. He switched off the television, and the panting stopped at once.

He lurched away from the bed and stumbled to the window. The hotel was indeed reflected across the deserted downtown street, where the front of a building was largely composed of glass. He could see his room and his faint self in the elongated window of an unlit office, but no sign of the next room. Could its occupant really have seen the reflection of the programme Ferguson had been watching? Perhaps they were using binoculars, or their eyes were keener than his. He dragged the dun curtains together, to be rewarded by a clash of curtain rings on the far side of the wall. 'Show's over,' he mouthed and saw the old man beyond the dressing-table risk a triumphant grin. 'Try and get to me now,' they both said silently as he began to undress. He heard no further sound through the wall as he dumped his clothes on the chair and wriggled under the sheet and the dishevelled quilt before darkening the room.

The silence in the other one felt so frustrated that he nearly laughed aloud, but he wasn't about to invite an imitation. He closed his eyes and edged the quilt over his exposed ear and sought the dark. It swarmed with thoughts, of which the most bearable was the book he'd imagined writing. Even this seemed potentially troubling now – the idea of a couple who fell in love at first sight only to be separated for the rest of their lives. When at last they met again they would be too changed and too senile to recognise each other. In their final moments one would regain the memory, which would seem to keep them together for eternity. Who would have it, or could it somehow be granted to both? The more Ferguson worried the idea the less likely it felt, and he was glad when the Scotch and the bottle of wine he'd had at dinner conspired to sink him in the dark.

A voice wakened him. He thought it was his own, despite its lack of shape. 'Elizabeth,' it repeated, or more accurately 'Livadeth.' It was talking in its sleep – no, replicating how he must have talked in his. 'Weary of you,' it said.

He wouldn't have said that, ever. He must have been asking where she was. 'I bloody am of you,' he informed his imitator. As soon as the remark started to be echoed he thumped the wall above the rudimentary headboard. 'Enough,' he yelled. 'Enough.'

The thumping was mimicked, and so was every repetition of the word. He might have been competing for the last one. He groped for the light-switch above the ledge that was Frugotel's version of a bedside table, and was marching or at any rate limping at speed towards the corridor before he grasped that he shouldn't leave the room while he was naked. Grabbing his trousers, he danced an ungainly impromptu hornpipe to don them, accompanied by echoes next door of the thuds of his bare feet. This enraged him so much that he almost forgot to retrieve his key as he stalked into the corridor.

It was deserted. If there was muffled laughter, surely it was downstairs. He pounded on the next door with both fists, so hard that the plastic digits of its number seemed to tremble. No doubt that was partly because of the pounding that answered his. 'Stop this bloody game right now,' he shouted. 'Normal people need their sleep.'

He was echoed so closely that they might as well have been speaking in chorus. 'That's all. You've had–' he said and felt idiotic for attempting to catch the imitator out by stopping unexpectedly, all the more so when it didn't work. 'You've had your chance,' he declared and shoved his face at the spyhole in the door. The darkness beyond it only convinced him that he was being observed. Having dealt the door a final thump, he tramped to grab the phone from the ledge by his bed.

The receptionist hadn't finished announcing herself when he said 'Can you do something about whoever's next door?'

'What seems to be the problem, sir?'

'They're–' He might have demanded whether she could hear the echo of his side of the conversation, but he didn't want to seem irrational. 'They're making all sorts of noise,' he said. 'I've asked them to stop but they won't.'

'Which room is that, sir?'

'They're in 339.'

'Just a moment.' After several of those the phone rang in the next room. It was answered immediately, but only by a childish imitation. 'Ring ring,' the voice said in falsetto. 'Ring ring.'

The phone fell silent, and so did the mimicry. As he strained to hear more than the labouring of his heart, the receptionist said 'Is that Mr Ferguson?'

'There's just me here, yes. Why?'

'I'm afraid you're mistaken.'

'What do you mean?'

'We've got nobody in 339.'

'Don't give me that. You told me you were full. You couldn't change my booking.'

'It was a late cancellation.'

'Well, someone's in there. I can hear them. I've heard them all the time we've been talking. Maybe some of this weird lot you're full up with have managed to get in.' The muttered repetition of his protests had begun to madden him. 'Don't take my word for it,' he urged. 'Go and see.'

There was silence at his ear and beyond the wall. Eventually the receptionist said 'Somebody will come up.'

Ferguson replaced the receiver and was devoting his energy to making no further sound when he wondered if his complaints might have warned off his tormentor. Suppose the person fled and left him looking like a fool? He sprinted to the door despite the twinges of his heart and leaned into the corridor. It was empty, and his neighbour hadn't had time to dodge out of sight along it. He glared towards 339 until he heard a lift hum and stop humming, and a large man in the yellow Frugotel uniform appeared around the corner.

Other than frowning at Ferguson, he refrained from any comment. Once he'd finished peering through the spyhole he rapped on the door of 339. 'Staff,' he called. 'Can I have a word, please.'

Ferguson wouldn't have been surprised if the man had received every one of them back, but apparently the prankster wasn't so easily tempted. The man knocked harder and then slid a card into the lock. Brandishing the card like an identification and a threat, he advanced into the room. Ferguson mostly heard his own heart, but there were also the click of a light switch and the scrawny rattle of a shower curtain. He waited for the sounds to be followed up, and then he snatched his key card out of the slot on the wall and padded heavily into the corridor. 'What's the hold-up? Who—'

He faltered, not just because the next room was almost indistinguishably similar to his. The Frugotel employee was staring at him across the tucked-in bed. 'It's like Reception told you, sir. Nobody's in this room.'

'You are,' Ferguson thought of retorting, but demanded 'Have you looked in the wardrobe?'

The man lingered over looking at him, so that Ferguson wasn't far from opening it by the time the employee did. 'Nobody,' he said at once. 'Nobody's been here. Now if you wouldn't—'

A woman's peevishly sleepy protest interrupted him. 'What's going on now?'

She was in the room opposite Ferguson's. From the threshold her husband or a man performing some of the functions of one informed her 'It's the old hooligan that was making all the row out here before.'

Ferguson was sure he recognised one of the rowdy drinkers from the floor below. 'That's more your style, isn't it? I thought people were meant to keep their drinks in the bar.'

He wouldn't have minded if the hotel employee had asked what he meant, but it was the man across the corridor who spoke. 'You know, he looks like the old reprobate Primmy said was trying to get off with her and Barbaria when they just wanted a quiet drink.'

'I don't think any of you know how to be quiet,' Ferguson retorted and might have said more if the man hadn't called 'Good God, he's showing everyone what it sounded like he wanted to show them.'

Ferguson glanced down to find his flies gaping wide. While his member had the grace to hide its head, its mat as grey as dust was well in evidence. 'Forgive me,' he gasped, yanking up the zip so fiercely that it came close to scalping his crotch. 'I'm a bit distracted. It's not long since I lost my wife.'

'Then what are you staying here for?' the offstage woman across the corridor wanted everyone to know.

'We'd already booked. I didn't want to let the hotel down. I thought it'd be better than staying at home by myself. We often used to come here,' Ferguson added as best he could for a nervous belch, which he tried to explain by saying 'It was one of our favourite towns to eat in.'

None of this seemed adequate, but before Ferguson could think of a further excuse the man said, 'We can tell.'

'We're sorry to hear of your tragedy. Please accept our sincerest condolences.' It was unclear whether the employee was speaking for Frugotel or on behalf of the couple opposite. Having locked 339, he said 'Will you be all right now?'

'I haven't been hearing things, if that's what you mean. That's to say I have. I certainly have.' Ferguson folded his arms in case this lent him some authority and to hide his hirsute obese breasts. 'I've lost my wife,' he said, 'not my mind.'

He had time to interpret the awkwardness of the silence in various ways before the uniformed man said, 'We don't want any more of a disturbance. Most of our guests are asleep.'

'I don't. I'd like to be,' Ferguson said and backed into his room. He'd managed not to slam the door when he wished he'd left his listeners a better image of Elizabeth. Perhaps they imagined an old woman as overfed as he was, not the girl he'd carried over a stream and to a gate a quarter of a mile up the sunny slope beyond it, or the mother who'd perched their daughter on her shoulders when they'd returned for the same hillside climb, or the grandmother who'd continued to outdistance him on their countryside walks even once those had grown shorter and more effortful. He bruised his forehead against the door as he peered through the spyhole. If anyone was out there he was going to let them know that he and more importantly Elizabeth had come here for the countryside, not just the food. The corridor was deserted and silent, however. 'It's all your fault,' he almost yelled at the next room, instead mouthing the words. He tiptoed across the prickly carpet to stand by the bed, where he unbuttoned his trousers and eased the zip down and stepped clumsily but silently out of them. Once they were heaped on the floor he sat so gradually on the bed that the springs stayed as quiet as he was. He inched under the bedclothes and stood a pillow on end to support his raised head while he waited for some sound from the next room.

Could the imitator have gone away? Might they have fled as soon as he'd had the receptionist phone the room? He was convinced that he'd heard them imitating his subsequent protests, but if he was left alone at last, surely it was all that mattered. He listened to the hush until it let him breathe freely and slowed his heart, and then he reached to lay the pillow down. His knuckles bumped the headboard, and he heard an answering rap through the wall.

He might have grabbed the phone to demand another visit from the staff or, better, have dashed into the corridor to cause uproar outside 339, ensuring that the intruder couldn't escape unseen this time. Instead he spoke, quite conversationally. 'I know you're there.'

'I loathed her hair.'

He wanted to believe he'd misheard or imagined the voice, which was more muffled than ever. Even when Elizabeth's hair had grown so thin her scalp showed through, he'd stroked it in the hope she would forget about its state. He hardly knew whom he was addressing as he objected 'I never said that.'

'I never said fat.'

'That's right, I didn't.'

'That's right, I did it.'

'No, not that either.'

'Oh, what a liar.'

'That's just not true.'

'That just stopped you.'

13

Ferguson had begun to feel trapped in an infantile game by someone who'd succumbed to their second childhood, if not worse. He could hardly wait for them to finish echoing or rather misrepresenting him before he responded – he was becoming desperate to think of an answer they couldn't turn into a gibe. He might have imagined he was being tricked into selecting words his tormentor found it easy to mishear. Although he tried to take his time, the best he could produce was 'What a lie.'

The indefinite voice didn't bother imitating his pause. 'Watched her die.'

While there was no denying this, he didn't need to admit 'That's true.'

'Not you.'

He was afraid his words might take him unawares. 'All right,' he mumbled, 'let's have silence.'

'All right, let's have slyness.'

He found his mouth with a hand, flattening his lips to keep in any further inadvertent speech. He ached to sleep, but suppose it released his voice? Even the notion of dozing made him feel threatened by a dream – an ill-defined image of somebody wakening in a dark place and struggling to communicate by whatever clumsy methods they still had. His mind recoiled, but staying awake was no refuge. Soon the voice in the next room began to speak.

He bore it mutely as long as he could, and then he tried to deny all it said. No, he hadn't ever even slightly wanted her to die. No, he hadn't grown tired of holding her hand as she lay in bed open-mouthed as a stranded fish. No, he hadn't wished as her hand grew slack yet again that this time it had slackened for good. No, he hadn't been disgusted by having to dab at her drool and deal with her other secretions. No, he hadn't sneaked out of their room to pray for an end to it all. By now he was striving to blot out the voice, but it went inexorably on until he lost any sense of which of them was trying to contradict the other. 'All right,' he cried at last. 'I did, but only for her sake.'

If this was echoed, it was by the flatness of the hotel room. He felt abruptly far too alone in the dark. When he switched on the light, the room looked as impersonal as a hospital ward – the kind of ward where Elizabeth hadn't wanted to spend her last weeks. His scattered belongings were at best pathetic attempts to make some kind of claim for his presence. 'I shouldn't have come,' he whispered. 'There's nothing here.'

He didn't know who was supposed to overhear this, or perhaps he did. 'It didn't mean anything with those girls,' he tried saying. 'They wouldn't have wanted me. Nobody would.'

He was hoping to be contradicted, but the only sounds were his – the creak of the bed as he shifted his weight, the intermittent urgency of his heartbeat. 'You're still there, aren't you?' he said louder. 'Say you're there. Say anything you like.'

His voice made the room sound as small and flatly featureless as a cell. So did his rapping and then knocking on the wall. It was too late to wonder what he'd done to earn the answering silence. If he caused much more noise the hotel staff might intervene again and drive away for good whoever had been there. He could still use the phone, and he keyed 339, though his fingers were so unsteady that their fat tips almost added extra numbers. He heard the other phone ring in the dark, and continue ringing and at last fall silent, because he'd laid the receiver to rest in its cold plastic trench. After that there was silence – for all the long night, silence.

Possum

Matthew Holness

I picked it up by the head, which had grown clammy inside the bag, drawing to it a fair amount of fluff and dirt, and pushed the obscene tongue back into its mouth. Then I blew away the black fibres from its eyes and lifted out the stiff, furry body, attached to its neck with rusted nails. The paws had been retracted by means of a small rotating mechanism contained within the bag handle itself, and I detached the connecting wires from the small circuit pad drilled into its back. Forcing my hand through the hole in its rear, around which in recent years I had positioned a small number of razor blades, I felt within for the concealed wooden handle. Locating it, and ignoring the pain along my forearm, I swerved the head slowly left and right, supporting the main body with my free hand while holding it up against my grubby mirror.

I'd come home to bury it, which was as good a place as any, despite my growing dislike of the mild southern winters. Yet, having stepped from the train carriage earlier that afternoon and sensed, by association I presume, the stretch of abandoned line passing close behind my old primary school, up towards the beach and the marshes beyond, I'd elected to burn it instead; on one of Christie's stupid bonfires, if he was still up to building them.

Despite my plans, I'd felt inclined to unveil it mid-journey and hold what was left up against the compartment window as we passed through stations; my own head concealed, naturally. But I'd thought better of that; I dare say rightly. In any case the bag concealing it drew inevitable attention when, entering the underpass on my way back to the house, one of the legs shot out, startling two small boys who were attempting to hurry past. Years of adjustments to the inner mechanism had enabled the puppet's limbs to extend outward at alarming speeds, so that when operated in the presence of suggestible onlookers, it looked as though the legs of some demonic creature, coarse and furred, had darted swiftly from an unseen crevice. Then, as happened rather beautifully on this occasion, the perturbed child, or children, more often than not would catch sight of a second, larger hole, carefully positioned at the rear of the bag to capture peripheral vision, and glimpse, within, its eye following them home. The effect, I am pleased to say, was rather stunning, yet, like any great performance, had taken me years of practice to perfect.

Christie had not been at home when I'd arrived, although as usual the front door had been left unlocked and the kitchen table crammed with large piles of rubbish awaiting destruction. Stacked among the old comics and clothes I'd found the familiar contents of my bedroom drawer, along with an old tube of my skin cream and a skull fragment I'd once dug up at the beach. Having retrieved these, I'd drunk a large measure of his whiskey, tried the lounge door, which, unsurprisingly, was locked, then taken my bag up to the bedroom. The walls had been re-papered again with spare rolls from the loft, familiar cartoon faces from either my sixth or seventh year. The boards were still damp, the floor slimy, and a strong odour of paste hung heavily in the cramped room. I'd opened a window – the weather was indeed horribly mild – and switched the overhead bulb off, favouring darkness for what I was about to do.

Although the body was that of a dog, Possum's head was made of wax and shaped like a human's, and I could not have wished for a more convincing likeness. Capturing even my old acne scars, yet with hair less neat and a gaunt quality reminiscent of the physical state I had embodied when the mould was made, the eyes were its greatest feature. Belonging to what had once been a bull terrier, both were former lab specimens, heavily diseased, preserved together for years in an old jar of formaldehyde. Several minor adjustments and refinements made by a past colleague, a long-dead teacher of science to whom my work had strangely appealed, had turned them into hard, bright, unique-looking decorations for Possum's face. Deceptively cloudy until caught in the correct light, these two vaguely transparent orbs were the key to Possum's success, and, despite patent similarities in our appearance, evidence of his own distinct personality.

My most recent addition to his look, nevertheless, had proved extremely effective. Having attached coloured flypaper to the tongue, which, like the body, was canine in origin, over the previous summer the mouth had accrued a large cluster of dead insects that dropped abruptly into view whenever the puppet licked or swallowed, usually scattering one or two dried bluebottles into my spellbound and horrified audience. A tiny battery-powered mechanism in the concealed handle allowed me to control rudimentary facial movements, although I had never once bothered learning how to throw my voice. Possum's wide-eyed, open-mouthed stare penetrated well enough during his sudden appearances, without the need of vocal embellishment. Only ever revealing him at points in my plays when his presence was a complete surprise, his unnerving silence merely served to exacerbate his subsequent chaotic behaviour. Whether I had him devouring other characters without warning, perhaps even my hero or heroine, bursting through concealed walls or destroying with unrestrained violence my neat but tedious endings, Possum's soundless, sudden presence held sway over my young audiences like no other puppet I'd ever built. He was a rule unto himself, and now he was beginning to do things I couldn't allow.

I leaned closer toward the mirror, reflecting on my most recent performance, and watched the sinking sun darken Possum's face with shadow. I observed how his head continued to stir subtly of its own accord as my body's natural rhythms gradually made their way into his, and I tried in vain to freeze his movements. Then, before it was fully dark, I took Possum outside.

There was no sign of frost, but the earth was suitably wet. I dropped him in the stagnant water tank behind the old shed, where he couldn't get out, and threw mud and stones at him from my vantage point at the rim. I pulled faces at him until I could no longer see anything below me, then went back into the house. I considered waiting up for Christie's return, but instead went straight to bed.

I awoke to find it beside me, the long tongue hanging out like a vulgar child's. The head had been turned to face me in my sleep, and its eyes in the dawn light were a pale, milky yellow. As I sat up to scratch the tiny bites covering my legs and ankles, several dry houseflies dropped from the pillow onto my bed sheet. Later I found a dead wasp tucked inside my pyjama pocket. I pushed Possum to the floor, realising that his head had been wiped clean and his body scrubbed. Sensing that the parlour games had begun, I dressed quickly. I could hear Christie clattering about in the kitchen below, and I took the puppet with me when I went downstairs.

'Good morning and thank you,' I said, dumping Possum on the cluttered table. 'Now please burn all your hard work.'

Christie, moving slowly with the aid of a stick, handed me a mug of strong tea and the ancient biscuit tin.

'Good morning,' he said, smiling under his thick, nicotine-stained beard. 'The head is expertly made.'

'As are the legs,' I said, sipping my drink. 'A perfect job.'

'*You* wired them in?' he asked.

I looked out at the garden. A huge bonfire had been piled ready.

'I want it burned,' I said. 'That's why I threw it out. You wasted your whole night. Now that's funny.'

Christie laughed, which made me laugh.

'I'm going for a walk,' I added. 'What are you doing?'

The old man hobbled slowly across the room, into the hallway.

'I'm going to bed,' he said, and began climbing the stairs. I waited until he was halfway up, then called out loudly.

'Wasn't your best.'

His prolonged silence I interpreted as a subtle joke, and went out into the garden. I inspected Christie's mammoth bonfire, rummaging through the piles of ragged clothes and compost until I located some more of my old possessions buried within. I wasn't upset to see my gloves there, but I rescued an old watch my father had given me on my eighth birthday and decided that I'd try and fix it. Deep within the piled rubbish was the inevitable road-kill, including a mangled fox. I sensed that this was the second of Christie's seasonal parlour games and dragged it out by its tail. As I passed back through the house on my way to the front door I slung it halfway up the stairs, hoping that Christie might fall when he bent down to remove it. Then I zipped Possum up in my black bag and walked to the school.

I didn't stop once along the lane, although I saw enough to know that my old classroom, the scene of Christie's little stunt, had long since disappeared. An extension to the central building almost blocked my view of the playground, where the brick wall, over which I'd escaped, had been painted over with a large smiling face. I passed the second of two remote mobile classrooms, decorated with nativity displays, and continued on towards the familiar stone steps leading down to the abandoned station. I followed these onto the empty platform, examining the shelter on the opposite side of the track. Despite an abundance of thick spray-paint and several smashed windows, the place was abandoned. I stepped down quietly onto the disused line. The metal tracks had been ripped up long before I was born, and the banks on each side of the route, beyond the declining platform, were heavily over-grown. The ancient trail turned sharply to the left before reaching a small, concealed footpath that snaked off into the trees. I brushed aside overhanging branches as I forced my way along it, pausing several times to pinpoint exactly where I'd once built my secret camp. Further along I found the old tree I'd climbed to impress friends, and the small slope we'd raced down. Beyond these, hidden beneath the thickest trees, was the place I was looking for.

I crouched down on the approaching path and located a suitable vantage point. I made my way over to a dense row of bushes and knelt behind the leaves. The ground around me was littered with empty crisp packets and crushed tins. Nearby lay scattered the feathers of a dead bird. Sooner than I expected to I developed cramp, and, making as little movement as possible, shifted weight to my hands. Then I settled down to wait, keeping absolutely still.

When I finally heard someone approaching, I unzipped my bag. Possum's face looked up at me as I drew back the black leather, his eyes twinkling beneath the overhead sun. I gave him some muddy leaves to eat and was in the process of extricating the rest of his body when I heard other sounds coming from behind. Someone else was approaching at speed and I barely had time to conceal Possum when a tall man appeared from within the trees. He wore walking shoes and a fashionable winter coat, and carried a school rucksack under one arm. His face was hostile and suspicious.

'Good morning,' I said. Without replying, he moved off swiftly in the direction of the approaching child, calling loudly. I stood up, finding myself unable to move due to the numbness in my legs, and grabbed the handle of my bag. I waited, suspecting that I might require the use of Possum's limbs in order to effect a diversion worthy of pantomime. But no one else appeared, and the man did not return. As soon as I could, I walked home through a great many winding streets.

'Tell me again about the fox,' Christie said.

'We were in the woods one day and saw a fox. It was panting at the mouth and its whole body was shaking. We thought it had swallowed something bad. When we came back later it was dead. So we played with it a while... stuck things in it. Then, as we left for home, the fox stood up. It had been playing with us.'

'I mean the fox you dropped on my stairs,' Christie replied, smugly. Another game won. And putting the dead animal in my bed and laying it out on the kitchen table before me as I ate my breakfast equalled three victories already that morning. 'You shouldn't have stolen from my bonfire,' he said. 'That was misbehaviour.'

I sipped my tea and ate a stale biscuit. 'Merry Christmas.'

'Not yet, it isn't.'

Christie rose slowly from the table and put on the jacket he'd hung on the back of his chair.

'Not staying?' I said, examining the local paper spread out before me.

'Drinks with friends. The house is your own.'

'I know it is,' I countered. 'And don't you forget it.' One parlour game to me.

'I'll be back at six to start my bonfire.'

I followed him out into the hall, trying the handle of the locked lounge door as I passed, loudly enough for him to hear.

'What happened to our decorations?' I asked. 'We used

to have several boxes.'

The old man was struggling with his shoe-laces. I didn't help him.

'And what's this with the old caravan site?' I said, indicating the article I'd read.

'Deconstruction,' he replied, eyes focused on his feet.

'It's hideous. What are they putting in its place?'

He stood up, wheezing, and limped forward into mild sunshine.

'Nothing.'

I followed, handing him his walking stick.

'Nothing at all?'

'Not if they start finding things.' He unearthed a strange-looking plant, exposing a huddle of pink, swollen tubers.

'These shouldn't be ready this time of year.'

I walked back to the house.

'I'll have something else for you to burn later. My puppet.'

'Not working any more?' he said, over his shoulder.

'Retired,' I replied, and shut the door on him.

The bleak monotony of the muddy shoreline was lifted only by the distant dance of little red Wellingtons far behind. Echoes of light laughter overtook me on the breeze as someone closer, concealed on the far side of the approaching breaker, kicked pebbles repeatedly against the wooden barrier. I refrained from operating the bag in this exposed area, progressing instead along the coastal path toward the strange sunken mast that bordered the marshes. This tall concrete post stood out bleakly against the horizon, as it had done ever since I was young, a rusted sign nailed to its front stating 'keep out'. I was still unsure what purpose it had once served, but thought perhaps it could have formed part of an electrical generator servicing the nearby caravan site. Unchanged, it stood grim and obsolete while I leaned against it and watched the trail behind me, cradling my bent cigarette from the wind.

Ahead, the path grew slippery as it rose toward the crest of a wide ridge overlooking a large, artificial crater. Formed by a jettisoned wartime bomb, this enclosed ravine was broken only by the slow progress of a shallow, man-made stream through its centre. The path, dipping sharply as I continued toward a low wooden bridge, crossed the green and stagnant water, disappearing again over the opposite rim.

The bridge itself retained most of its original slats, yet one or two had fallen away over the years, exposing foul silt gathered beneath. I stepped across, looking down at the clay bank rising from the water's edge, noticing several holes in the mud that looked like the work of small animals. I considered planting Possum inside one so that my half-buried likeness could surprise the unwary children following behind, but then I thought of a better plan. Removing Possum from the bag, I left the bridge and stepped down with him into the stream, my feet sinking deep into the thick, oily mud. Using the roll of tape I always carried with me, I manoeuvred myself beneath the bridge and fastened Possum's body securely to the rotting planks above, directing his face so that the eyes stared back up through the slats. Returning to the bridge, I was pleased to find that the effect was quite disarming, and would prove so, I hoped, to any of my approaching billy goats.

I left Possum to do his work and moved onward, out of the ravine and across an expanse of wet marsh towards the abandoned caravan site beyond. As I approached, cleansing the mud from my boots in deep puddles, I heard the resounding thud of electrical machinery. The approach to the site involved crossing a stile situated halfway along an elongated hedge, concealing the cabins beyond from view. I was surprised to find, however, that this had now disappeared, along with many of the caravans I had still expected to find on the other side. Some distance away, a slow mechanical digger was grouping piles of rubble into a large mound. Across what remained of the park stood a few of the older cabins, built decades before to capitalise on a short-lived tourist trade. Many were blackened by what must have been a recent fire on the site, their walls and doors plastered with offensive graffiti. On one, a small naked doll had been tied to the remains of its twisted television aerial.

As I walked around the site, away from the digger, I encountered a 'no trespassing' sign posted up by the local council. Rain began to fall in large, heavy drops, and the ground grew rapidly sodden. I sat down on an old tyre and watched as the man operating the digger closed it down and wandered off towards a small truck parked at the far edge of the site. The vehicle moved away into the main road and headed back towards the town, leaving the site deserted.

I felt around in my bag for my tool case. Opening it, I removed a small chisel I kept with me for repairs and began to sift through the mud around my feet, smelling the yellow earth gathered upon its metal blade. I carved a large smiling face into the muddy ground and watched as the rain slowly destroyed its features, then walked back to collect Possum.

At first I thought the tape must have worked loose in the rain, but then I saw how far the puppet had been moved from the vicinity of the bridge, and decided that something must have dragged it there. It could have been one of the children, but closer examination of the muddy bank behind Possum revealed the small paw marks of a dog, almost completely eroded by the sudden downfall. His head had been mauled at the ears, and one of the eyes was protruding slightly more prominently than usual. I kicked him around in the wet mud for a while and stamped hard on his face, wondering whether it was worth burying him permanently beneath the mud. Then I remembered the digger, packed him up in my bag and walked home.

'I'd like a demonstration before I burn him,' said Christie, opening two tins of cheap beer for us. 'Nothing special, but I want to see how the legs work.'

'Trade secret,' I replied, lighting the candles. When this was done he finally removed our meals from the oven.

'What other puppets do you use?'

'Several, but I want this one burned.'

He served me the larger dish, which I realised was the dead fox.

'I heard about your last performance,' he said, popping an olive in Possum's mouth, whom I'd sat on the spare chair between us. 'One of my old teaching colleagues wrote to me about it. An unpredictable affair, by all accounts.'

I ignored the comment and jabbed at the sticky burnt carcass staring up at me from my plate.

'I don't like this,' I said. 'Care to swap?'

Grinning, my host tucked greedily into what looked like a small bird.

'You forgot party crackers,' I said, sipping my beer.

'And grace,' he replied, removing a small shred of bone from his upper lip.

'They'll have me back, once *he's* gone.' I poked my fork at Possum.

'We'll need gloves to get rid of it,' Christie said. 'It's diseased.'

I examined my hands, which were peeling terribly and beginning to bleed, and felt my face. I was covered.

'Eczema,' I said, hiding my wrists beneath the table.

'Remember,' said Christie, his mouth full. 'A demonstration.'

The front half of the cabin was severely smoke-damaged, although in places I could still make out graffiti beneath the charred remains. The place stank of urine and petrol, and I sat at the back with my black bag, near to where the bathroom had once been, and watched the remains of the site through the van opposite, which retained one unbroken, though heavily-stained, window.

I sat there for about an hour, thinking. It was about midday when I crouched down on my knees so that I could not see out and crawled across the cabin floor. I examined where the cupboard used to be and touched the far side of the rear wall with my hands, feeling for the faint words scratched somewhere on its surface. I leaned closer, sniffing at the floor, then withdrew. I stood up, returned to the seat, and unzipped my black bag.

I pulled Possum out and sat him on my lap. His body felt softer on one side. When I pressed my fingers against the fur, the insides gave a little, and I assumed they must be damaged in some way. His protruding eye, too, had broken open. A crack to the outer shell had caused a small leakage that ran down Possum's face, looking like dried egg yoke and smelling vaguely of chemicals.

I pulled his tongue down and tucked stray hairs behind his mauled ears. The wiring mechanism now broken, I extended, manually, each of his legs, until he sat astride me. I lay back against the seat, stretching my body lengthways, pulling him on top of me so that his face rested inches from my own. I slung his two front paws over my shoulders, opened my own mouth to mirror his, and stared back into his contaminated eyes. Then, with my tongue, I removed one of the dead flies from his.

'Don't,' I said, and swallowed it. One by one, I ate them all. When Possum's mouth was clear, I lifted him from me, very gently, and sat myself up. I resisted the urge to retch and removed the tool case from my black bag. Having selected a blade, I picked up Possum, bit his ear without warning and threw him roughly to the floor. I knelt down on top of him and sawed at his nose, slowly and methodically, until I had sliced off its tip. I stuffed the severed segment inside his mouth and angled his limbs against the floor. With my boot I snapped each joint in turn and threw the broken legs out of the open window. I seized Possum's torso and thrust my arm into its rear. Wincing as the razors bit deeply again into my wounds, I smashed the puppet against the wall, rocking the unstable cabin, before scraping the mutilated face against every sharp and jagged surface I could find. I removed my arm then, which was bleeding heavily, and took the scissors from my tool bag. I snipped off Possum's hair and jammed the tattered clumps between his teeth. I stabbed his eyes repeatedly with both blades until the weak one gave way entirely, spurting a glob of liquid over my fingers and up the scissor blade. I spat back at him, attempting to gouge a channel from one eyehole to the other, across his nose. The wax proved too strong, and instead I cut my own fingers. Grabbing a blunt wooden pole from my bag, I struck his head several times before shoving the blunt end of the pole into his mouth. When I'd finished thrusting, his head pinned and useless against the cabin wall, I gathered what was left of him beneath my arm and threw him into the corner. I kicked his stomach repeatedly until it caved in, exposing the stained wooden handle inside. I stuffed the belly with junk and threw Possum through the broken doorway, out into the yard beyond. Then I sucked the blood from my fingers, picked up my bag and left the cabin.

I stood as close to the flames as I could bear, hoping that my clothes would retain the smell of smoke. Christie shovelled in another heap of rubbish, momentarily stifling the blaze. I opened my bag and pulled out Possum's head, which I'd severed from his body with a spade while Christie had ransacked the last of my bedroom cupboards.

'Season's greetings,' I said, tossing it across the grass towards him. 'Too late for a demonstration.'

'You should let me fix it,' he said. 'I like fixing things.'

I lifted up the headless body of the stuffed dog and threw it on the bonfire. Smoke curled around the bent, twisted nails wrenched incompletely from its neck as a sharp, sulphurous odour burned my nostrils. Flames snapped loudly against the coarse, brown fur as Christie held up the decapitated head and laughed.

'A broken toy,' he said. 'You shouldn't have.'

'Soon as I saw it I thought of you,' I replied, which made him laugh even more. I lit us both cigarettes while Christie perched what remained of Possum on an old wooden stool. He placed his cigarette inside the mouth and begged another for himself. When we'd finished, he lifted up the head ceremoniously and dropped it on the bonfire, along with my watch, smiling to himself as he jammed them deep into the blazing compost with his pitchfork.

'How will you spend the rest of Christmas day?' he asked.

'Exercising,' I replied.

'Exorcising?'

'Past the school, if you must know.'

'The school.' Christie's face was a mischievous grin. 'I taught you there once.'

'I know. You died while reading us a story.'

'I came in especially, the day after that business with the fox. To teach you all a lesson.'

I watched Possum's face blacken and bubble, collapsing gradually into soft clear rivers of molten wax.

'Now that was a game to remember,' Christie continued. 'The looks on your faces. You should have seen them.'

'I'll be out all day,' I said, zipping up my coat.

'Children talk such rubbish.' The flames began to rise again as he turned over a pile of burning rags. 'When there's no one around to reassure them.'

The eyes fell out together, exposing two pallid-looking sockets. Soon, these, too, would disappear.

I had meant to purchase my return ticket, but realised upon reaching the station that there would be no trains leaving until the following day. I wandered for an hour or so until I summoned up enough courage to enter one of the few pubs that were open. There I stomached a strong whiskey and some fatty sandwiches as the sun went down, before heading out once more, away from insufferable partygoers, into the darkness of the surrounding streets.

I gazed into people's houses through open blinds as I passed. The gaudy house-fronts, plastered with coloured lights and cheap decorations, one after another, left me feeling lost, so I sought darker avenues as I fled the town centre in the direction of my old school.

The ground through the adjacent lane was slippery, as if many people had been rushing along it during the day, and I found myself slowing involuntarily and glancing across at the disparate group of buildings that made up the school. A single lamp lit the area of the playground, exposing the large painted face that marked the area where Christie had chased us, full of life having feigned his sudden heart attack. Someone, I assumed a janitor, was watching television in a small hut on the far side of the concrete field. I stopped for a moment to stare at the small alley in which I had sat alone many times during my final year, attempting to make sense of all that had happened to me. When I heard something enter the lane behind me, I moved on, quickening my pace.

I raced down the stone steps, crossed the old platform and dropped down into the abandoned line, pausing only to adjust my vision once more to the surrounding darkness. I moved off carefully, the noise of my footfalls interrupted only by the soft rush of wind moving through the nearby treetops. It took me longer than usual, but I eventually found the small hidden pathway into the trees and walked along it, noting that the ground here, like the school lane, was wetter and

31

more broken up than before.

I found the place again instinctively, clear as the event still was in my memory, and stood up straight upon the spot, making sure I didn't slouch or bend my back in any way. I unzipped my coat and drew out the small lunch box I'd filled secretly after Christie had left the house, having failed once again to force open the lounge door. I removed the lid and, one by one, thrust my peeling hands into Possum's ashes, noting the sharp, unpleasant smell my skin now emitted. Once I was satisfied that the remains were truly soiled, I tipped the powdered mess onto the ground where the man had first shown himself to me, and smeared what was left into the earth, tossing the empty box into a nearby bush, where he'd dragged me.

It was while I was wiping my hands clean with my handkerchief that I heard the dog. It had followed me through the empty station and was nosing through the bushes behind, tracking my scent. I thought of playing dead, but instead strode out into the footpath, holding out the diseased hands he had hated touching. I shrieked loudly at the top of my voice and this time the dirty creature stalking me ran a mile.

I mouthed words into the receiver as my fingers tapped nervously on the dull, metallic surface of the dial pad, flashing blue lights from the distant caravan site reflecting against it. When I looked up again, the policeman who'd come over to watch me hadn't moved.

'He put me in his bag,' I said aloud, to the faint electric buzzing of the dial tone. 'And took me to his caravan.'

The rain had returned. I peered out across the grass slope, trying to look preoccupied, as he began walking towards me.

'Always had something on his face,' I said, starting to sweat. I nudged the door ajar to inhale the fresh sea-air.

'...he never took it off.'

I hung up.

Foolishly, as the officer reached me, I smiled.

'On your way,' he ordered, studying my face. As I walked back to town, one of the their cars followed me home.

Christie was drunk when he opened the door, and laughed openly at the state of my hands.

'That won't help you this time.'

I snatched the bottle from him and wandered through into the kitchen, swigging heavily from it as I sat down.

'I'm leaving tomorrow,' I said.

'Are you now?' he replied.

'Thanks for putting me up.'

'Always a pleasure.' He grinned inanely, performing an awkward, drunken dance. 'Always was.'

He began to sing an obscene song.

'Why don't you go to bed?' I snapped, taking another swig from the bottle. I stood up, swaying, and put what was left back in the cupboard beneath the sink.

'Your present's in the lounge,' he said.

I felt like I'd been hit.

'The lounge?'

'Sorry everything's so late.' He stopped moving long enough to light a cigarette. He appeared to be gasping for breath.

'They've found something up at the site,' I said.

'They have indeed.' He inhaled heavily, and blew the smoke back into my face. 'I'll have a car collect you tomorrow.'

Suddenly sheepish, he stumbled off in the direction of the stairs, moving up them much faster than I'd thought he was capable of.

I didn't go in immediately, as the whiskey had made me feel nauseous. I smoked a couple of cigarettes and listened for a while to Christie crashing about in my room above.

When I did finally venture into the lounge, unlocked for the first time in thirty years, I noticed that our tree remained in exactly the same position it had stood on the day Christie first arrived. It was still bare, all its decorations having been burned ceremoniously by him in the weeks following my bereavement. Now, instead, something horribly familiar sat at the top, where my Daddy had once lifted me to place the fairy.

It was the man's dog mask, and although all I could now see through its cruel eyeholes was the damp wall beyond, I realised that it belonged to Christie, and that he'd worn it here with me all these years, waiting for my courage to awaken.

And below, beneath the tree, was my present, wrapped up in newspapers and tied at the top with an ancient ribbon. It was a large, odd-looking object, bearing an old gift tag addressed to me that hung, quite still, from a small thread of dull, red cotton.

As I got down on my knees and crawled towards the parcel, the thread began to twitch and twist. A faint rustling noise sounded from the wrapping, where the taut sheets had begun to bulge gently back and forth, as though something trapped beneath them were beginning to breathe. When its long leg burst through the paper and pawed violently at the carpet in front, teeming with life, I rushed forward, eager to unwrap the rest.

Seeing Double

Sara Maitland

His mother had died when he was born. His mother had been young and at the end of a long and very hard labour, made more exhausting by the size of the baby's head. The mid-wife had acted promptly, gathering in the baby and carrying it away. She had washed and dressed it, before bringing it back to the mother, with a delicate lawn and lace bonnet framing its sweet little face. The mother had taken the child in her arms and smiled, though wearily; but she had made no apparent attempt to count its toes, fingers, eyes and mouths, and after a moment the midwife had turned away to her immediate duties. When she turned back the mother was dead; her face was frozen in a strange rictus, which might have been the consequence of a sudden sharp pain or might have been terror. The midwife, a woman of sturdy good sense and addicted to neither gin nor gossip, deftly massaged the mother's face back into a more seemly expression and closed her large blue eyes forever.

His father, a hero of the nation, loved admired and honoured, but now retired to his family home in the mountains, grew gentle and sad. He spent most of his time walking in the high hills above the forest or in his library where he was slowly but steadily compiling a taxonomy of the local flora and fauna. He took tender but perhaps slightly distanced care of his only son. He created a pleasure palace for the child – his own small suite of rooms, opening through large airy glass doorways onto a pleasant shaded portico and beyond that a delightful secluded garden with high walls, climbable trees and a pool designed for swimming in. At considerable expense, and to the irritation of the local community, he employed the midwife as a permanent nanny and found a blind but nimble servant to assist her.

The child grew, grew strong and straight and healthy. When he was old enough his father would sometimes take him up into the forests and the mountains beyond the forests where he learned the names of all the butterflies and many of the flowers. Sometimes at night they would climb together onto the roof of the house and watch the stars, and his father taught him to trace and see the patterns of the noble constellations and told him the ancient Greek stories that gave the patterns their names.

The Christmas that he was eight, his father gave him a train set and together they built and developed it. When it grew too extensive for the nursery floor, his father opened up the attics and they created a whole little world there, with electric signals and tiny model towns; and model mountains with tunnels through them, so that the boy could wait in eager anticipation for the engine to emerge from the darkness and sound its miniature horn. They made and remade ever more complicated timetables and were anxious that the trains should run on time, and not crash into each other at the points.

Each evening, after his bath, and when he was all clean and warm and ready for bed, his father would come to tuck him up and give him his good night kisses, one on each cheek and one very gentle special one on the back of his head. Then his father would pull up the hood of his pyjamas, tie the strings and say, 'God bless and keep you, little dark eyes,' and the boy would snuggle down scarcely conscious of his own happiness.

He was twelve when he found out. One morning Nanny woke up sick – not very sick, but with a feverish headache and heavy eyes. When she did not go to the kitchen to collect the breakfast the housekeeper foolishly sent one of the younger maids through with the tray. The boy was already up, hungry and eager, though of course properly concerned about nanny. He was sitting cross-legged on the sofa reading a book. The maid plonked the tray down on the little table by the window and then stood there, fidgeting. The boy did not often see people other than Daddy and Nanny and the blind servant, and he was not sure how to behave. He smiled at the girl. He had a very sweet smile, like his father's but younger and more carefree. She smiled back. She was not much older than he was and the differences between them, obvious to grown ups, were nearly invisible to them.

He said, 'Hello.'

She bobbed a sort of half-curtsey and said, 'Hello' back.

There was a pause, in which he smiled some more and she fidgeted some more.

But in the end she could not resist. For fourteen years she had heard the talk and the secret murmurs, because no respect or even love for their Squire is going to keep his tenantry from gossip about him and his, from speculation and a mild mannered sort of malice. She was curious on her own behalf, and more tempted yet by the stir she will create in the servants' hall at dinner. And he looked so sweet, with his huge dark eyes and a smile like his father's. And she might never have another chance.

'Go on,' she said, 'show us.'

He almost turned his book towards her, assuming she wanted to see the picture, but there was something, something else; even with his negligible social skills he knew there was something else.

'Show you what?' he asked, but still pleasantly, almost in his father's kindly style, which unfortunately made her bolder.

'You know,' she said, 'it.'

The new pause was longer; he really did not know and she, better attuned, as all servants are, to the nuances of social meaning realised that he really did not know. She had gone too far. She was embarrassed. But her shame made her even bolder.

'You know,' she said again, 'The face, the other face; the back of your head.'

Instinctively he lifted his hand to the back of his head. Through the soft flannelette of his pyjama hood, he felt the back of his head lumpy, then moving. His hand was frozen for a moment. Then he felt something bite sharply into the fleshy pad at the bottom of his thumb.

He screamed.

Suddenly Nanny was standing in the door, her hair down, grey and straggling as neither of them had ever seen it, her face flushed with her fever and fury.

'Be quiet,' she said in a commanding tone, and then losing her grip on her anger, 'Be quiet, you evil, wicked girl. Go away. Go away.'

Sobbing, the little maid ran from the room and the boy and his nanny listened to her clogs go rattling going down the passage.

'Nanny?' he said, and had she been well and wakeful it might yet have been alright; she might have given him a cuddle and he would have shown her his hand and she could have magicked a pin out of his pyjama hood and told him she was a silly old nanny for leaving it there. But the headache was stronger than her wisdom and all she wanted was her bed.

'It was nothing, darling,' she said quickly, 'nothing at all. Just a silly girl. A very naughty little girl, probably trying to be funny. We won't be seeing her again. Now eat up your breakfast and go and play in the garden.'

He ate up his breakfast and went into the garden but not to play. He had so seldom been lied to directly that he did not understand it. Thought and speech were one in his closed world. But he knew, he knew that nanny had made a deliberate gap between her thoughts and her words. He went into the garden, but not to play. There was playing, which was not relevant; there was hearing, which was not trustworthy; there was seeing which was not possible. There was touching and feeling. He looked at the little red mark at the base of his thumb, which was beginning to bruise and very tentatively, very, very carefully, using only his finger tips and ready for sudden attack he began to explore the back of his head.

After an hour he knew. And knowing, he knew that he had always known. There was another face: he could feel its nose through the flannelette of his hood, shorter perhaps than his own, though hard to tell, but with two indentations for nostrils, certainly; he could feel its lips though carefully with the flat of his hand so as not to get bitten again. He knew already it had teeth. He thought he could feel the hinge of its jaw moving just behind his ears.

He could not untie the string of his hood, but after some effort he worked it loose enough to pull it back from his head. He placed his two hands delicately on the back of his head, either side of its nose, and could feel the hollow underneath his palms. He waited and felt a flutter, like a butterfly's footfall. It was blinking. He pulled his hood back on and wriggled the knot tight. He went inside and sat on the sofa again and chanted his times tables, all the way from one-two-is-two to twelve-twelves-are-one-hundred-and-forty-four over and over again, all day long.

Later on, just as the day began to fade, he left his room very quietly so as not to disturb nanny and went along the passage to find his father. After he had passed the bottom of the stairs that went up the attic he did not really know the way. He opened various doors into various rooms all heavy with dust and cold. A huge cold dining room with twelve empty chairs and faded red velvet curtains; a room with an even bigger table covered in green cloth; there were no chairs and the edge of the table was turned up – he did not know what it was for. There was a long passage, a huge hall almost dark, and a room with little uncomfortable sofas and lots of little tables with lots of little things on them – that room was lighter, with long windows looking out over the shaggy field that his father called 'the lawn'; he had only ever seen it from high up on the hillside. That room seemed a strange thing to him because it was both beautiful and pretty. He had not known that something could be both. But his father was not there.

He came to a door with light coming out underneath it. He opened it very softly. The room was warm and clean and wonderfully untidy, with precarious piles of paper and books stacked up or lying on the floor, as nanny never let him leave his. His father was sitting with his back to the boy; his bald head inclined forward over a large desk. The boy could see that he was writing. He watched him, watched the smooth back of his skull and the slight movement of his elbow.

His father was unaware of him. After quite a long while the boy said, 'Daddy.'

His father raised his head, apparently without shock or surprise and said, 'Hello, what are you doing here? I was just going to come for you. It must have been a boring day for you with Nanny *hors de combat*.' He often had to guess what his father meant, and it did not worry him. 'But you must learn not to be impatient.'

'I am not impatient,' he said with dignity. 'I have come to ask you something of grave importance.'

'And what is that?' His father smiled at the formality of the announcement.

'I need to ask you why there is someone else on the back of my head.'

The boy was aware that the warm peace of the study was broken. It made him wary – his father was a hero of the nation and should not be afraid of anything. He said nothing, awkward now. After a pause his father said, 'How did you find out?' He sounded weary.

'It bit me.' The boy walked towards the desk holding out

his hand.

He was almost too big to climb into his father's lap but the older man held him close, kissing the small bruise. He sagged there for a while exhausted by the long slow day, but it was not enough,

'But why, Daddy?'

'I don't know,' his father said, 'no one knows. It is a strange and mysterious thing.'

'Couldn't you take it away?'

'No, no, I'm afraid not. But it is not a someone, it is a part of you.' The boy could hear a strange insistent urgency in his father's voice; and he thought it might be fear. So his father was afraid of something. The boy's world shivered, threatened. Perhaps it was his own fear that made him daring, because even as he asked, he knew it was a dangerous question. He asked, 'Is it what killed my mummy?'

'No.' But the no was too loud, too strong, too resolute. It was like Nanny's 'naughty girl'; it was true but not true; the speaker chose it to be true although there were other choices which the speaker did not choose. Grown-ups, he learned far too suddenly, spoke with double voices, cunningly, so that true and not true weren't like white and black, like either-or, like plus and minus; they were like the bogs on the hill side, shifty, invisible and dangerous.

His father's revulsion from the boy's deformity was very strong. Because he was a man of self-discipline rather than courage he would never admit this even to himself; this was why, each evening, he obliged his often reluctant lips to kiss the secret face so tenderly. This was why, too, he missed the boy's curiosity and tried to offer him consolation instead of information.

'Look,' he said, 'have I ever shown you a picture of your mother?' He turned the boy's head very gently towards a miniature set up on a filigree easel on his desk. She smiled there, all pink and blond and blue-eyed. She was pretty. But it was a picture, a painting; the boy knew that paintings did not always look like the thing they were paintings of. He could never be sure. And he did not much care; he had other things on his mind. But he understood that his father had let him into a secret place of his own and deserved some sort of thanks. He tried, slightly experimentally, to say the right thing, to do that grown-up speaking which makes a gap between the feelings and the thoughts and the words.

'I don't look much like her, do I Daddy?'

He had got it right. He felt his father smiling. 'No, you look more like me, and bad luck to you, except that men should never be that pretty.' Their dark eyes met in what the father thought was a sweet moment of male complicity and bonding. And a little later they went upstairs, hand in hand, to play with their train set.

But the day had been too difficult and his need had not been met. What he had learned was not about the other face, but about the way grown-ups did not want to talk about the other face. There was something dark and horrible about it. They were ashamed. They wanted him to keep it secret with them and from them.

But alone, alone in the darkness of night, and the deeper darkness of its invisibility, with delicate and attentive fingers, he began to explore the back of his head. He learned that what hurt it, hurt him, so he had to treat it tenderly; he learned that it blinked when he blinked, but did not smile when he smiled, or weep when he wept; he learned that its nose never dribbled, but if he pinched its nostrils closed, it did not breath through its mouth, but he became breathless; he learned that he could make it happy or angry, but that it seldom bothered to be sad.

In the end fingers were not enough. He needed to see. He could not ask.

It took him nearly two years to work it out. Then one day while the blind servant was in charge, he stole into Nanny's bedroom and borrowed the mirror from her dressing table. He took it into the bathroom and began to experiment.

His father had by now taught him both some physics and how to play billiards. There had to be a way of angling the light, like angling a delicate in-off with the ivory billiard balls. If he looked in a mirror into another mirror at the right angle, he calculated that perhaps it might be possible. It was awkward. The bathroom was not designed for the purpose and its mirror was fixed to the wall.

Then, almost unexpectedly, with Nanny's mirror propped a little precariously on a tooth-mug on the windowsill, he turned his head a little and he saw what it was he was trying to see. The face was paler than his face and had no proper chin so that the mouth was angled slightly too much downwards; but he could see that its nose was very like his and its eyelashes were longer. It was prettier than he was, and it was not a painting or a picture; it was real. It opened its eyes and they were blue, as blue as the summer sky, as blue as his mother's were in her painting. Its eyes met his and it smiled, a cunning triumphant smile. It was not an it, but a She.

All women have double mouths, he thought and then he thought that he did not know where the thought had come from.

After that he could hear her voice. She whispered to him. She used his brain to think her thoughts. She used his breath to be alive. He was never alone. And he could not tell anyone.

Sometimes it was fun – She was his friend and he had never had a friend before. They played games together, and usually he won because their feet and hands were under his management; but when he tried to run away She would come with him, following close behind, though looking in the other direction, and he could never get away.

Sometimes it was not fun – She thought thoughts he did not want to think; She said words he did not want to hear and he could never get away.

He could not have any secrets. He made his life a secret

from Daddy and Nanny, but they were not real secrets because She always knew and he could never get away.

Adolescence. That was what Daddy and Nanny called it, affectionately usually, even proudly. But She called Daddy 'Papa' in a sweet little voice, which Daddy would have loved if he could have heard it; and She was mean about Nanny and refused to understand how much he needed and loved her. She complained when he wore a hat; She would wriggle and protest if he tried to lie on his back, to sleep or to look at the sky; She loved the light, and the sunshine, to which he did not like to expose her.

She hated it when he masturbated. His fingers, now well practised in delicate explorations, had new plans of their own, plans which sometimes he found appalling and sometimes found intriguing and occasionally found absolutely the most fascinating and delightful and demanding and consuming ideas in the whole wide world. She would distract him with loud noises, silly giggles, filthy words and a scathing contempt at his ineptitude, both physical and manual. He was to her both pathetic and disgusting. She was always there, and he could never get away. She had to be kept secret but he was allowed no other secrets, or privacy or silence.

When he was seventeen he fell in love. A new maid came who sang like a bird in the early morning and was soft and round with dimply cheeks, big breasts, orange hair and a merry smile. He never spoke to her, but he watched and yearned and dreamed and hoped. He wanted without knowing what he wanted. Sweet first love, or first lust without knowing the difference. But She was having none of it. She was jealous and mean and set up a shrieking in his head. Over and over again she shouted, 'Freak, freak, freak. That one will never love you – she'll only want to see me.'

When he tried shouting, 'freak' back at her like a little boy, she giggled spitefully and said, 'No, no. I don't exist. I am just the freak in you. I don't have a me. I have a you. I'm not a someone. I'm a part of you. Ask Papa.'

She said, 'That little trollop won't love you; she won't spread her legs with a Lady watching.'

'Never?' He asked her plaintively.

'Never,' She said with undisguised glee.

'I'll kill you,' he threatened.

'You can't,' she said, 'You can never get away.'

So one evening, just as the day began to fade, he left his rooms very quietly so as not to disturb Nanny and went along the passage, but not to find his father. As he passed the bottom of the stairs that went up the attic he remembered the train set with which he and his father had not played for years. It was not enough. He opened various doors into various rooms all heavy with dust and cold. Then he went downstairs to the gun room, wrote a short note for his father and shot Her through the mouth; his mouth because he couldn't get the shot gun into the back of his head.

The Underhouse

Gerard Woodward

I first got the idea for The Underhouse when, as a child, I would stand on my head in a corner of the living room, and thereby find myself in a different house entirely, one where the furniture hung from the ceiling rather than stood on the floor, where light bulbs grew at the tops of tall, thin trees, and where doors had to be passed through like stiles, one leg at a time. I desperately wanted to explore this exotic house, and was profoundly disappointed every time I uprighted myself (at the behest, usually, of my exasperated parents, 'the blood will pool in his head!') to find that it had vanished.

Then, as a grown-up with my own house, I noticed how the cellar, which was underneath only one room (the living room), exactly matched, in shape, the room above it. And then I thought how the horizontal boundaries of rooms, unlike their vertical counterparts, change their essential nature depending on which side you are viewing them from. To put it more simply, a wall is a wall no matter which side of the wall you are. But a floor, when viewed from underneath, becomes a ceiling, which is a very different thing. Do you follow?

Standing in my cellar one day, looking up at the boards which provided a floor for the living room, I had the turn-around thought; what if I refused to regard this thing above me as a ceiling – what if I decided to call it a floor also? The thing is, it looked like a floor. It was made of wooden boards supported by joists. The only difference was that the joists were foremost, and the boards were rough, dirty wood, whereas on the floor above they'd been varnished and draped with rugs. Dimensionally the only real difference between the cellar and the living room above it was to do with height. The cellar was a much lower room than the living room. I had to stoop whenever I went in there, though in fact this was an unnecessary precaution, for when I measured it it turned out to be six foot five inches from floor to floor boards (i.e. ceiling), and six foot exactly from floor to joist. At five foot eleven I had plenty of headroom, but still I felt the need to stoop.

The dissimilarity in height between the cellar and the living room became something of an obsession, and eventually I had to do something about it. It was a very simple thing. All I had to do was to lower the floor of the cellar by exactly thirty-seven inches, and the two rooms, above and below, would be perfect spatial mirror images of each other. I suppose it was something to do with symmetry.

So I took a pickaxe to the floor of the cellar. It hardly needed it. The floor was a ropy thing made of asphalt under a thin layer or concrete. A garden fork could just as well have done the job. It yielded, under its crisp shell, thousands of sticky, black grains that I had to scoop into a bucket and carry upstairs and out into the back garden. Beneath the asphalt I was into the raw earth of the world under my house, which I dug down into. Then when I had gone far enough, I leveled off and finished with a layer of good cement. It was hard, aching work, and took me several weeks (I'm not as strong as I was). But at the end of my work I had a room, below my living room, that was its proportional twin.

It occurred to me then to set about duplication of the room above in other ways. Firstly I bought floorboards to nail over the joists of the cellar ceiling to form a perfect replica of the floor above. In effect I now had two floors back to back. Onto this upside-down floor I tacked rugs identical to those in my living room, and in the same position. I bought furniture identical to the furniture in my living room, and placed it on the upside down floor of the cellar, in identical positions once again. This was a harder task, and one I could only just manage on my own. Bolting a settee to the ceiling of a cellar is work for a strong man. I will not go into details about how I managed it, except to say that I adapted techniques I read about in an account of the building of Salisbury Cathedral. Nor will I detail the many journeys I had to make in order to find chairs identical to those that furnished the living room. But the exquisite delight I felt when I achieved my aim, when I found my replica suite, my coffee-table's double, the lamp-stand's long lost and long-forgotten twin, in some distant junk shop or car-boot, was indescribable. Though perhaps it is not unlike that experienced by an actual twin, who has been deprived of the knowledge all his life, to find himself reunited with his brother from the womb.

I now had everything on the floor of my living room reproduced exactly upside down on the ceiling of the cellar, bolted fast, the cushions of the seats stitched to them, and all other precautions taken to make a convincing upside-down room, identical to the original.

And so I began work on the walls. Bare brick in the cellar, I plastered them as best I could (I'm no handyman, really), and after a reasonable period of drying out, papered them with the rose pattern I had so long lived with (and which was very, very hard to find). The paintings that hang on them were also difficult to reproduce, and I had to try my hand at copying one of the simpler ones myself, the result of which endeavour surprised and pleased me. It took me several years of hard work to reproduce everything in the living room. One thing I couldn't reproduce, of course, was the view from the front bay window. I had to satisfy myself that drawn curtains would do. Eventually I worked out how to make them hang convincingly, which involved a hidden rail at the bottom of the curtain, so that in reality the curtains hang downwards into the pelmet. I succeeded very well, I think, in giving them a convincingly unfastened look.

The most enjoyable touches were the two light fittings (one a chandelier) that in the real room hang from the ceiling on thin lengths of flex. Again, trompe l'oeil was involved in producing flex that would hang upwards and support a shade; moreover, I fashioned a modest chandelier, just like the one above ground, and managed, with glue and solder, to make the crystals hang upwards instead of downwards. I think if there is any true crowning glory to my upside-down room, it is in the upside-down chandelier, with all its crystals pouring casually upwards as if there was nothing untoward in their world at all. Of course, I wired the lights up to work just like the lights in the real living room.

Completed, my project gave me many moments of unspeakable joy. Just sitting in my arm chair, knowing that beneath the floor there was another armchair, hanging, in a room where everything else hung that should have stood, and which stood that should have hung, just knowing it was there, was enough to cause delight. It was as though my life was a reflection in a pool, into which I could actually enter. It was as though narcissus could indeed embrace his own reflection.

The experience of descending the cellar stairs into the inverted world below, to suddenly find oneself the only upright thing in a room turned upside-down, to be given the sense that gravity pushes upwards rather than downwards, to feel oneself floating, in fact, was an experience of delirious, dreamy delight.

And one I had to share.

So that is how I came to bamboozle acquaintances I met at The Earl of Chatham, the rather innocent, almost destitute young men who frequented that once family-friendly place, and who could easily be bought drinks. I would invite them home, after many reassurances that I was not an old queen, and they would accompany me back, usually because they had nowhere better to go, and not much prospect of a roof over their head for the night. I would sit them in the armchair, plying them with Jim Beams and playing Count Basie on the record player, until they passed out in a drunken swoon. Then I would carry them down to the cellar, lay them down on the floor (the ceiling), and leave them alone to wake up, but still with Count Basie playing on the now upside-down record player. I would return to the right-way-up-room, and wait. It could take a long time, but eventually there would come a cry from downstairs. 'Jesus Christ' they might say, 'Holy Jesus, get me down, get me down,' and I would go downstairs into the cellar, peep at them from round the corner and see them writhing on the floor (the ceiling), petrified at their weightlessness, terrified at their defiance of gravity. At first I would hang from the stairwell and peek at them upside-down, as if I too were part of the upside-down world, to increase their sense of being on the ceiling.

'What's the matter old chap,' I would say, 'feeling a bit light headed?'

They would stare at me with about-to-be-shot eyes, hyperventilating, unable to find words, pressing themselves to the floor (the ceiling).

'You should be pleased, old chap,' I would say, 'you've learnt how to fly. Aren't you the clever one?'

I would then reassure them that it was simply something they'd drunk. I would tell them to close their eyes and let me take care of them. Then I'd carry them back upstairs, plonk them down in the right-way-up living room, tell them to open their eyes again. From their perspective they had not left the room at all, merely descended from its ceiling to its floor. The look of tender alarm on their faces, as they felt about the arms of the chair, and the floor with their feet, to ascertain whether they really were back on the ground, and the way they looked up at the ceiling, apprehensive of the horrible notion that they might, at any moment, plummet towards it, was something to cherish.

I have plans for extending my underhouse, so that the whole house, every room including the loft, should be duplicated. It would be a work of many, many years, and one I may not live long enough to complete. To open up so much empty space beneath my own house could be dangerous. I have this peculiar thought that, having completed my duplicate upside-down house, and having weakened the foundations of the right-way-up house, the latter will eventually collapse into the former. If the right-way-up house fell down into the upside-down-house, one must suppose that the two would cancel each other out, and that both houses would simply disappear. And if I happen to be asleep in my bed (right way up or upside down – how would I know?) what would become of me? I would have folded myself out of existence. A rather attractive thought. I'd better start digging.

The Dummy

Nicholas Royle

The featureless road. The driving rain.

White lines, empty fields.

The endless rhythm of the stop-go shunt, a Newton's cradle of cars on the motorway heading north-west. The occasional church spire in the distance piercing the dark grey wadding of the clouds. The monotony is relieved by a fizzing spot of fluorescent yellow up ahead. You squint, peer through the windscreen, rub with your sleeve at a stubborn patch of fog on the glass. The view clears. The fluorescent spot grows, elongates, becomes a figure.

The motorway narrows from three lanes down to two. The traffic slows accordingly. The man in the high-visibility clothing moves his left arm up and down, telling you to slow down further. He's standing hard by the crash barrier on the central reservation. He's either suicidal or insane or both. There has to be a better way to warn drivers of impending hazards, you think. Sure, he's completely covered in hi-vis gear, from the hood of his jacket to the turn-ups of his trousers, but you can't imagine this man's UK counterpart happily standing that close to moving traffic on the M1. Maybe the Belgians pay danger money, or perhaps, as seems likely from the standard of the driving, all Belgians are clinically insane. Admittedly this may be the birthplace of surrealism, but still.

You twist your head for a closer look as you roll past. The planes of his face seem abnormally severe, his skin unnaturally smooth. Do motorway maintenance workers really shave every morning?

★

'Tell me where it comes from, this love of our country.'

Asking the question was a striking young woman of slender build and average height, her irregularly cut mahogany-coloured hair framing a face shaped like a warning sign. Eyes that glittered; a short, sharp nose, pointed like the bill of a goldfinch; lips painted a vivid red. When she leaned forward across the hotel breakfast table, peripheral vision gifted me a view down the front of her top.

'What's not to love about it?' I said, careful not to let my eyes drop. 'Beer, chocolate, medieval architecture.'

'In that order?'

She flashed her teeth; one was chipped at the corner. Either her lower lip was uneven or she twisted it unconsciously while she spoke. I remembered reading somewhere that beauty was all down to symmetry. I'd thought it was rubbish at the time and now here was proof.

'Definitely.'

'No, but…' she started, signalling the switch to serious interview mode by picking up a sachet of sugar and turning it end on end on the tablecloth. 'The Eddy De Groot novels are bestsellers. You're not telling me his creator is inspired by nothing more than a desire to sit drinking Duvel at pavement cafés in the Grote Markt.'

'With a view of the Stadhuis.'

'Exactly.'

'No. In fact, just between you and me,' I said, lowering my voice to a conspiratorial whisper, 'I don't actually like Duvel.'

She sat back, eyes wide.

'I know, I know,' I said, hands in the air. 'The man who didn't like Duvel. I don't like tripels either. I like blond beers. I've always been partial to blonds.' I gave her my winning grin.

'Only blondes?' she asked, sitting forward again.

'As you probably know if you've read the books, I like

the brown beers best.' My eyes flicked down momentarily. 'Westmalle, Ename, Chimay – but only the red or the blue.'

Around us, hotel staff were discreetly clearing tables.

'So, Eddy De Groot, your Flemish detective, is you?' she asked, bending the sugar sachet in half.

'It's easier than making stuff up.'

'Your alter-ego?'

'If you like. All I know is he's not Poirot and he's not Maigret, but he's not Van der Valk either. I saw a gap in the market for a Dutch-speaking Belgian detective. Written by an Englishman.'

Now it was my turn to sit back in my chair. I took my eyes off her for a moment and looked around the breakfast room. She had described my Eddy De Groot novels as bestsellers. Which of course they weren't, not in the UK, but they did OK in Dutch translation. In addition, they probably sold as many English copies here in Belgium and in Holland as they did back home, there were that many English speakers in the Low Countries. In any case, the figures obviously added up, or I wouldn't get this treatment: five-star hotel, a reading slot at the Antwerp festival, a round of interviews with local and national media. The girl with the sexy mouth had come up from Brussels to do a piece for *De Standaard*. I wasn't kidding myself it was going to last for ever, but I might as well enjoy it while I could.

'It goes back to when I was a kid,' I said, leaning forward and taking the sachet of sugar from her hand. 'My dad used to bring me stamps off the ships. He was a customs officer and he used to rummage ships in the docks and bring me back stamps for my collection. The ones I liked best were the Belgian stamps. The picture of King Baudouin, the different colours. Pink, blue, green. Brown and grey. I liked the way the colours changed but the image remained the same. I wanted to own the whole set. I like having whole sets of things. Belgian stamps. Agatha Christie novels – Fontana paperbacks with the Tom Adams covers. No others.' I toyed with the sugar sachet and shrugged my shoulders. 'It's a man thing.'

I watched her check the digital voice recorder.

'When's your deadline?' I asked. 'Do you have to go away and write this up this morning?'

'I've got till tomorrow lunchtime,' she said.

'So what do you say we do this over lunch?'

I held my breath and caught her looking at my wedding ring. I said nothing. She smiled.

★

Rain falls without end from a sky made of lead. Your eyes are gritty. Your head lolls momentarily over the wheel.

Microsleep.

You exit the motorway. Pull over, rub your face. Get out, walk up and down. Fresh air, pouring rain. Get back in the car. Sit there looking out at the rain. You get your phone out of your pocket and stare at it. You check that you haven't missed any calls or texts. You haven't. You remember the time you spent ten minutes going all over the house looking for the phone, while talking on what you thought was the cordless landline. You even told the person you were talking to that you were looking for your mobile.

This wasn't so long ago.

You told your wife about it, hoping she would find it funny. She shook her head and said, 'It's a bit early even for you, isn't it?' You had had a drink, as it happened, but nothing more than that. You wondered if she had a point and you decided that she may well have done, but that it was disappointing all the same that she didn't just laugh about it and then perhaps everything would have been all right.

It's a long time since everything has been all right.

You go to the messages on your phone and reread the last text she sent. There's no real need, there are no fresh insights to be gained. You're just tormenting yourself.

You put the phone back into your pocket and turn the

key in the ignition.

More rain, more flat fields. Grey streets with occasional brick houses, shuttered, stark. More traffic cones, roadworks, another flash of fluorescent yellow. But the perspective's all wrong. It looks like he's lying down. You lean forward over the wheel, screwing up your eyes. He *is* lying down. Pull over, stop. Get out. Jacket over your head. Bend down. His hood over his face. Limbs at weird angles, as if he's been knocked down. Hit and run. You pull the hood back a little.

Jump.

The face isn't real. The rain doesn't roll off it in quite the right way. But the arms and legs look right; the torso is reassuringly bulky. You touch the leg. It's a real leg. You'd put money on it being a real leg. You haven't had a drink yet today. You squeeze harder. Maybe you're wrong. You look at the face again. Is it a mask? You remember the man on the tube, the blind man with the rubber eye mask. Two unblinking eyes painted on to a rubber mask held in place with elastic behind a pair of useless glasses. When you sat opposite, you stared at him so hard you ended up having to look away, because you became convinced he could see you doing it. Somehow.

When you took a photograph of him through a crowd on the platform and showed it to your wife, she called you a sick fuck, but only after making sure the children were not in the room.

You took your camera with you when you went to say goodnight to the children, because you wanted to show that picture to them. You thought they'd get it. But they were both already asleep, their hands clenched into tiny fists, mouths slightly open. The infinitesimal rise and fall of the chest. You bent right down over their beds until you could feel their breath on your cheek. The faintly sour smell. You would never stop loving them, you told yourself, no matter what they did. Yes, you'd lose your temper with them and yell at them, and afterwards you would feel bad because the anger melted away leaving only the love behind.

You couldn't imagine life without them.

Sometimes you'd sit and watch them breathe, sitting with one and then the other. Until your wife would call you. I thought you'd gone to the pub, she would say when you went downstairs. No, you'd say, and you'd look into her eyes and see if it was still there, the glimmer in her eyes that had drawn you to her, what, twelve years ago? Thirteen? It had lost some of its candlepower, perhaps, but it was still there, and so you'd hold her and you'd hug each other tightly and you'd say you loved her and you hoped she'd be patient with you and she'd say nothing, but nor would she let go of you.

You try to loosen the collar on the shirt, just in case. The neck looks no more realistic than the face close up. You look up, look around. There's no one. The nearest buildings are some distance away. There's no traffic. You gather the dummy's legs and thread your arm under his back, taking care to support the head with your upper arm. He's lighter than a fully grown man. Heavier than either of your children. You carry him the few yards back to the car and manage to open the passenger door. Your heart is beating fast and the blood vessels in your head are throbbing. You position his legs in the footwell and once you've got the seatbelt around him he sits up OK. His head hangs forward just a little.

You check your mirrors. There's a car in the wing mirror, far enough away for its driver not to have seen anything. In any case, your car would have acted as a shield. The other car now drives past without slowing down. You wait for the ringing in your head, from the hiss of the tyres on the wet road surface, to die down and then you pull out and drive on.

★

I took her to the Entrepôt du Congo for lunch and between us we got through so many Rodenbachs neither of us thought it was a bad idea when I suggested we carry on the interview back at my hotel. Of course when we got back there, the lobby area was busy and returning to the breakfast room didn't feel like an attractive option, so although I know I could have asked the concierge for conference facilities, it just seemed easier to head upstairs to my room.

We did finish the interview, but let's just say it took a while to get started on the afternoon session. Hilde said it was the first interview she'd conducted in which both parties were completely naked.

'Both parties?' I said.

She smiled.

We could have perhaps left it at that and not gone on and ruined everything. But during the time we spent in my room there were moments of tenderness, interludes when we lay side by side catching our breath gazing into each other's eyes like lovers. Most of the time, admittedly, it felt like a one-night stand, but there were moments when it didn't. And there was a mutual reluctance to part once we were dressed and Hilde said the batteries on her digital recorder were exhausted but that it didn't matter because she'd already got far more material than she could use. Somehow we ended up at a bar not far from the hotel drinking shots. I switched my phone back on to see that my wife had been trying to get hold of me. Instead of calling her back I ordered another round of drinks and heard myself answering Hilde's question about the origins of my love of Belgium in greater depth.

'It wasn't just the stamps,' I said. 'Well, it was, but it wasn't just the stamps *per se*. It was what they symbolised. They were like the equivalent British stamps. Different colours, monarch's head. We had a queen, you had a king. I couldn't get my head around how strange it must be to have a king rather than a queen.' I knocked back another shot and was about to order more, but checked myself and ordered two dark beers instead. 'We should drink them slowly,' I said. 'Here was this country,' I went on, 'just across the Channel from us. A small country, a monarchy. In a way it was a mirror image of Britain. As I grew up, I imagined that it was like a parallel world to the one in which I lived.'

Red light struck one side of her face, blue the other. I felt a compulsion to open up to her completely, to tell her everything about myself. In turn, I wanted to know everything there was to know about her. I took out my wallet and withdrew the battered picture of my kids that went everywhere with me.

'Jack and May,' I said.

She grinned and tossed her hair back and asked me how old they were. I told her eight and six, but that the photograph was a year old. She handed it back and as I slipped it into my wallet I fell into a sort of fugue. I couldn't work out why. Eventually I wondered if it was because she'd been happy to see a picture of my children. If she was happy that I had kids, did that mean she would also be happy when I went home to them, which I both did and didn't want to do.

★

You went home, of course. But it was clear – not to them, but to your wife – that something was up. You can't dissemble, can't hide the truth. You said nothing, but within a week you were back in Belgium. Another book to research, you said, next in the series. You stayed with Hilde. She was single even if you weren't.

You scrapped a planned De Groot novel and started a new one. He'd fallen in love, with a journalist. His job was on the line, his life falling apart. De Groot's wife was suspicious; yours too. It wasn't as if she read your work-in-progress, not normally, but accessing your back-ups remotely on your iDisk was beyond neither her imagination nor her technical know-how. Getting the password right was the easy part, since you had never had any secrets. The drink and drug habits had never been kept from her. How could they be? Their effects were written all over your face and bank statements.

When you got home, your wife confronted you and you broke down and confessed. You sat at the kitchen table and looked out of the window while she threw crockery – wedding presents – at the wall. In the garden, perched on the handrail that runs around the outside of the deck area, was a small green bird, a greenfinch, seemingly completely oblivious to the mayhem taking place only a few feet away. You watched that bird, its tiny head shifting position in jerky increments, and were filled with a vague longing. If you could have put your feelings into words you would perhaps have said that you wanted to swap places with the bird. That you wanted your spirit or your soul to escape from your own body like smoke and drift under the kitchen door and then enter the greenfinch, which you would henceforth, in some strange incomprehensible way, become.

Do you even believe in a spirit or a soul? Or is there nothing but a mind? A consciousness? A sense of identity?

You see a sign for Westvleteren and leave the main road. Some say Westvleteren 12 is the best beer in the world and you would not disagree. None of the three Westvleteren beers can be bought anywhere other than direct from the Westvleteren Abbey brewery. You've heard they even require you to have an appointment, but if you turn up and say give me an appointment in five minutes' time, what are they going to do? Turn you away? Or sell you some of the best beer in the world?

You see his yellow jacket out of the corner of your eye and it startles you. You'd forgotten he was there, sitting right next to you, steam rising off him. His raised hood conceals his profile. Didn't you lower his hood? You must have raised it again, either deliberately or accidentally, while getting him into the car.

You keep driving, although the signs to Westvleteren have disappeared. There was a village, or a hamlet. A settlement. Three or four buildings, all shuttered, no gardens. Brick fronts hard by the road. But no crossroads, no turnings, unless you missed one while sneaking a look at your passenger. Here's something on the left. You slow down. A walled enclosure. Carefully cut grass. Regular lines of white headstones. Identical black lettering on each.

You accelerate slowly as if out of respect. There is no let-up in the rain. At the next turning you go left. The windscreen wipers sound like a heartbeat. A Coca-Cola sign shimmers out of the gloom on the right-hand side of the road. You pull over and stop. Some kind of café. Step out of the car and lock it, then look back in and hesitate, the rain drumming on your shoulders and the back of your neck, before unlocking it and turning to walk towards the café.

★

I took the Eurostar back to Brussels and jumped in a cab. We spent the afternoon in Hilde's flat on avenue Emile Max. When I finally looked out of the window I saw a flash of green as a bird the size of a jackdaw, but much more streamlined with pointed wings and a long tail, swooped down into the garden and then climbed back up from its dive just as quickly, like a BMXer on a ramp. I knew instantly what bird it was.

'Look,' I said to Hilde, 'a ringed-neck parakeet. They've become common in London, apparently, though I've never seen one. I had to come to Brussels to see my first one. It's an omen.'

She asked me what had happened in London.

'She told me to fuck off,' I said. And straight away, as a shadow seemed to pass across her face, I knew it was a strategic error. You don't tell your lover that your wife has kicked you out. It doesn't matter that you may have talked about the possibility. When it happens, you say nothing, unless what you want to end up with is precisely that, nothing.

We went out to a bar in Schaerbeek where a friend of Hilde's was celebrating a birthday. I drank steadily as I watched Hilde drinking and sitting with her arms around a succession of people, male and female, all of them younger than me, as she was herself of course, and I started to feel obscurely sad. Self-pity pricked at my eyes as I turned to look out of the window and thought about Jack and May.

And Sara. My wife.

I left the bar and walked in a random direction. Before long I realised I had entered the red light district by the Gare du Nord and I went into the next bar I came to. Pinewood panelling covered the walls. I ordered an Orval because it appeared to be the only beer they had. I detest Orval, so I drank it quickly and ordered another. And then another. It was dark when I left the bar. Red, blue and ultraviolet lights slid past me in a sickening blur. When I somehow found my way back to avenue Emile Max, I waited outside Hilde's building until someone came out. The door to her flat gave easily enough without causing too much damage, but really I was past caring. While I was blundering around inside looking for her car keys, I felt my phone vibrating in my pocket. A text message.

★

You don't like Jupiler any more than Orval, but when it's all they've got, you'll swallow it. Three small bottles. Take the edge off. A fat man sits at a till. You give him a handful of coins and go on through into a long narrow room filled with dusty display cases containing scraps of battle dress, a scabbard, a German helmet. Strange wooden boxes squat on tables. You put your eye to the eyepiece and twist the knob to change the photograph being viewed. Some optical trickery inside the box creates a 3D effect. Pictures of terrible wounds and corpses alternate with photographs of advancing columns of soldiers. The atrocity exhibition with slot machines. Somehow, their being in black and white makes it worse, but after a while, the pictures no longer shock. You become inured to the horror. At the far end of the room a doorway leads outside.

You follow a path into a field dotted with trees and lined, you now see, with passageways dug into the earth.

Trenches.

You remember the cemetery filled with war dead. Are these real trenches or some sick replica, a theme park, dug by the fat man? Or that the fat man had dug for him? From what you know of Belgium, it would not surprise you at all to learn that these are the real thing. In another country this would be a monument. Here it's a disgrace. You'd almost rather it were the fat man's plaything, that just one man was to blame instead of a federal state for failing to honour the sacrifice of others.

You half-clamber, half-slip down into one of the trenches and it's all you can do to remain on your feet in the mud. You feel a damp sensation on the left side of your chest. Something trickling. Sweat from all the exertion. You feel like a ghoul. Time to leave.

You collapse in the driver's seat. Turn to look at your passenger.

'Weird place,' you say, and wait for a response. 'Suit yourself. Let's go.'

You realise you've not taken your coat off and Hilde's car will now be covered in mud.

'Too bad,' you say. 'She should have thought of that.' And you laugh.

You know you shouldn't be driving, but you don't care. You can feel that wet sensation on the left side of your chest again. Still sweating? You look down, tugging at your coat. There's blood. Quite a lot of blood. Stop the car. Pull at your T-shirt, covered in blood.

There's a big hole in your chest. Fist-sized. As if something has been torn out of you.

You bend over to look more closely. Tentatively insert the tips of your fingers. Your hand slowly falls away and you look up through the windscreen at the ever-falling rain. The only sound you can hear, apart from the rattling of the rain, to which you have become so accustomed you don't notice it any more, is the *ba-dum ba-dum ba-dum* of the wipers.

★

The text said she had taken the kids and gone. I could come back, she said, but they wouldn't be there. I'd be coming back to an empty house.

It wasn't like she was kidnapping them and I'd never see them again. They'd be going to school as normal and I could hang around the school gate. But I wouldn't get to be with them properly. I could fight it, but I knew I didn't have a hope.

It was a long text.

I got in Hilde's car and drove out of Brussels, heading north-west towards the coast. Not that I had any kind of plan. It was already late and dark, and the combination of alcohol, tiredness and the constant rain meant I had to stop. I found a DIY superstore with a large car park on the outskirts of Gent. I parked by the wall facing the exit and slept on the back seat. In the morning I went in search of food, then sat in the car while waiting for the DIY store to open. I went in, got what I wanted and returned to the car with it coiled in a plastic bag, which I put in the boot. I then drove on with no fixed destination in mind.

There was a pain in my chest. From having slept badly, I presumed.

★

You drive until you reach the coast. Still it rains. The first cheap hotel you see, you leave the car and carry the dummy in over your shoulder. The woman gives you a twin room. You lay him on one of the beds and you take the other, kicking off your shoes. You turn and turn but sleep won't come. You get up and gently move him along a little so that you can get on the same bed. Facing away from him. You lie absolutely still, listening, but all you can hear is the rain hitting the window.

You turn to face him. There are raindrops on his yellow jacket. You pull the jacket to one side and rest your head on his chest. After a few moments you realise you can hear a noise like the windscreen wipers and you wonder if it's a kind of hypnagogic auditory hallucination or if it's the pulse in your temple.

You wake up in the original position you had occupied on the shared bed, facing away from him. A thin grey light from the window reveals large brown flowers on the wallpaper. You turn over and look at him. His face looks the same, smooth, unlined, eyes open. On his chest a line of stitching provides a point of detail on the otherwise featureless dark fabric that covers his frame and padding. Remembering the last thing that happened before you fell asleep, you press your ear to his chest. It's faint, but still there, but again, it could be the blood in your own head. Or it could be auto-suggestion.

You go into the bathroom and run the shower. When you come out, I'm sitting up on the edge of the bed staring at the floor.

'Shall we go?'

You drive along the coast towards Zeebrugge.

'What did you buy from the DIY store?'

My voice is flat, affectless.

'I think you know.'

We take a ferry to England and are then faced with a long drive to London. By the time we reach the M25, it's late.

THE DUMMY

In Upper Holloway you park Hilde's car outside the kids' school. It's a very short walk to your house. I follow you up the path. The house is in darkness. The kids' rooms are empty, their cupboards and drawers bare. You offer me your bedroom and say you're going to sleep in your son's room.

In the morning, you look in on me, your face blank, and you say goodbye before going downstairs. I hear the chink of a glass as a drink is poured, then another, and finally the sound of the front door. I get up and watch from the window as you cross the street. You open the boot of the car and look inside. The plastic bag from the DIY store is still sitting there. You close the boot, then open the driver's door and get in.

I feel a tiny stabbing pain on the left side of my chest as I think about what might be in that bag and what it could be used for.

It's not long before the street becomes busy with parents dropping off their kids, some on foot, others by car. I watch you watching the street and the school gate. A large black car stops in the middle of the road and two children get out. A boy and a girl. The black car moves off and you get out of Hilde's car and call them. They stop and look at each other, then run towards you and I see you holding them close to you. A short conversation takes place and you open the rear door of the car and they look at each other again before getting in. You start the engine and pull out of the parking space. As you move off down the street I have a last glimpse of the children sitting in the back seat, their heads nodding with the movement of the car. When you reach the end of the street, you turn left.

How far will you go before you stop and open the boot? The outskirts of London? Somewhere more remote?

It's usually somewhere remote.

The Sorting Out

Christopher Priest

She walked home in the warm night air, feeling the wind from the sea, sensing rather than hearing the movement of trees and bushes. Melvina was tired from her day in town, from the slow train journey home afterwards, but it had been a successful trip. Two commissions received, and a medium-sized cheque, as well as a general feeling that her career was back on track after recent upheavals. The bag on her shoulder weighed her down, because she had celebrated in her own preferred way, in a bookshop close to the railway terminus. She thought about the weariness of her legs and back, and the prospect of a shower before falling into bed. She planned to sit up in bed browsing through her new books. Also, because thoughts are not linear or orderly, she was musing in disjointed fragments about an article she had just thought of writing, while she was on the train, inspired by watching some of the passengers as they dozed. Thoughts of Hike intruded as well at random moments, the familiar irritation.

Now she was walking alone, almost home. It was a clear summer's night, with the stars brilliant above. It was a pleasant time to walk, although she would have enjoyed it more if she had not felt so weary. She passed the small park and war memorial on her left, where some of the houses that overlooked the open space still showed lights in their windows. Then at the end of that street came the flight of steps up to the loneliest part of the walk, a short passage across an area of open land. This was in fact the mound of one of the clifftops, with the sea away to her right and just a well-worn but unpaved path between the large bushes of gorse and tamarisk. Night scents briefly wafted by on the wind. At the end of this path was the terrace where her house was situated. Soon she saw the shape of the tall houses in their long darkened row, the single streetlamp close to where she lived.

As she approached the short path that led through her overgrown front garden, she noticed there was something wrong. Her white-painted door was hanging ajar, an angle of the dark interior visible behind it. Suddenly alert to danger, she felt her breath tightening. left it open that morning? Was the door open all day? Had someone broken in? Had Hike called round again while she was out? She hurried anxiously up the path to the door, pushed through.

Light from the streetlamp fell in from behind, casting her shadow at a steep angle across the floor, a shape of unexpected dread. She put her hand to the light-switch, felt the sharp-edged plastic, the metal ring that held it in place, both so familiar to the touch. Her chest was heaving, her breath coming in uneven gasps. She felt as if she was suffocating. Terror of intrusion gripped her. The light came on: the familiar dim beginning, then the quick gain to full luminosity.

At first, nothing appeared to have been moved. Nothing she could see. The books on the shelf, the coats and scarves on the hooks, the two small paintings by the mirror. Hike's paintings.

Behind her, the door swung open with another gust of wind. Melvina went back and saw where some tool or heavy instrument had been bashed against the hasp, breaking it irretrievably, wrenching the lock out of the body of the door.

Frightened of the darkness outside, the darkness that so recently she had relished, Melvina pushed the door to. There was a pile of books on the door mat, apparently knocked to one side when the door opened. She had no memory of putting them there. She eased the door across them, then propped it closed by leaning her bag against the base of it.

She stacked the books neatly, out of the way.

Now. She took a deep, shuddering breath. The house.

There were two rooms off the entrance hall, both on her right. She pushed a hand through the crack of the door to her study, reached around the door jamb to find the light switch and clicked it on. Dreading what might be in there, she kneed the door open and peered into the room. Her computer was there, her printer, the scanner, her cluttered desk, the bookshelves, the filing cabinet. Nothing disarranged. A green LED flickered on her answering machine.

Familiar calm rested in the untidy room. There was no one in there, no one hiding. She walked across to the windows, feeling her knees tremble with the temporary relief. At least the intruder had not come in here, stolen or broken anything. She swayed, so she stepped back momentarily from the window and pressed down on the surface of the desk with a hand, steadying herself. She could see her own reflection in the rectangle of window and beyond it the light from the streetlamp.

She stepped back close to the window and peered out into the night. There was a car parked in the road not far from the entrance to her house. It was unusual to see any car here after dark. She swished the floor-length curtains closed.

A book fell off the windowsill, landed on the carpet by her feet. She picked it up, closed it, laid it on the cupboard.

She had lived alone in this house from the start, when she bought it after Pieter's sudden death. Then it had been an escape, a new challenge and a fresh start. She became an unwilling widow, a single woman again, a role she had not expected. Piet's death was something she had no control over, but she had felt that a change of scene afterwards was necessary. As the months and years went by, she grew comfortably into this place by the sea, always missing Piet, full of regrets about things they had never had the chance to do together, but getting by.

She had never felt threatened by her solitude, before this. There was no one to help her. The silence of the house surrounded her, enveloped her fears. Who had been in? Were they still there?

In the hallway again, she called, 'Hike? Is it you?'

So silent. She heard a familiar clicking sound from the kitchen, and the thump of the gas boiler igniting itself. Emboldened momentarily, she pushed open the second door, which led to the living room with the kitchen beyond, and stood in the doorway as she turned on the light.

For a moment she realized how exposed and vulnerable she was, should there in fact be anyone lurking in the darkness within, but the light came on and filled the room with comforting normality. Nothing appeared to have been disturbed. One of her books lay in the centre of the carpet, held open by one of her shoes. She walked past, went into the kitchen and turned on the light there. The fluorescent strip flashed noisily twice, then settled to its pink-white glare. In the corner was the boiler with its blue flame, visible through the inspection glass, the same as always. No one was there, no one concealed under the table, behind the open cupboard door. She looked everywhere. The door that led to the back of the house, the yard, the garden, finally to the open clifftop, was still securely locked and bolted.

She did not remember leaving the cupboard door open when she went out. It was normally kept closed, because it jutted into the room. She looked inside – everything seemed to be in place. She looked in the fridge: no food had been taken.

She knew she had to go upstairs, search the rooms there.

She returned to the hall, looked at her bag holding the door closed. The lock hung away from its fitting. Bright scratches of exposed metal flared around it, where the paint had been scraped away. There was a deep groove where whatever had been used had dug in.

Why should someone be so desperate to break in? It had to be Hike – he was furious when she made him give her key back. But would Hike, even Hike, attack the door so violently?

She stood still, holding her breath, trying to detect the slightest sound from the upper floors. Next, she had to search upstairs. She was shaking with fear. She had not known such a reaction was possible, but when she looked at her hands she could not keep them still. Both her kneecaps were twitching and aching. She wanted to sit down, lie down, stop all this, return to the fear-free sanity she had known until three or four minutes before.

At the bottom of the stairs she laid a hand on the bannisters, looked up at the familiar carpet, the old one that had been here when she bought the house and which she had been meaning to replace ever since. Every worn patch, every strand of exposed canvas, was reassuringly familiar. She took another breath, then changed her mind. She hurried into her office, leaving the door in the hallway wide open so that she could see into the hall, and pulled her mobile from her pocket. She pressed the numbers that unlocked the keypad, but she fumbled it. She could not make her fingers go where she wanted. She tried again, muffed it again. She remembered Hike had an instant-dial number. *Numero Uno,* he said, when he had set it up for her five weeks earlier, just before he drove away.

She pressed the speed-dial key, then the '1' on the keypad. The ringing tone sounded in her ear.

She moved the handset away briefly, to listen for sounds from upstairs. She went back to the door, peered out at the bottom of the stairs, the part of the wall where one of Hike's old paintings still hung. The ringing tone continued.

How late was it? She glanced at her wristwatch: it was just after midnight. Hike was sometimes asleep by this time.

She felt the back of the handset growing slippery, where she held it so anxiously. Then at last he answered.

'Hullo?' He sounded curt, muffled, annoyed at being woken.

She started to say, 'Hike...', but as she tried to speak the only noise she could make came out as a single gasping syllable. '*Ha-a-a-a!*' That uncontrollable sound amazed and appalled her. She sucked in air, tried again. This time she managed a high-pitched squeak:

'*Hi-i-i-i!*' Silence at the other end. Humiliated by her own terror, she tried to control herself.

Finally, she got his name out, nearly an octave too high: '*Hike?*'

'Yeah, it's me. Is that you, Mel?'

'*Hi −!*' She swallowed, took another shuddering intake of breath, concentrated on the words she had to say. 'Hike! Help me! *Please?*'

'It's the middle of the night. What's up?'

'Someone − there's someone in the *house!* Here, when I came in. I found the door −' Again she remembered what had happened at the start, just those few minutes earlier. That dread feeling when she found the door open in the night, the darkness within, the silence. She almost let go of the handset at the memory. She sat down, lowering her backside against the edge of her desk, but immediately stood up again. Trying to keep her voice low, but hearing the stress make it harsh, she added, 'I think someone's still here.'

'Have you looked?'

'Yes. No! I haven't been upstairs. I'm too frightened. They might still be *in the house!*'

'Is this what it takes to get you phone me?'

'Hike, please ...'

'How long has it been? Five or six weeks?' Melvina could not answer, cross-currents of Hike and the fear of an intruder flooding together. 'Is there anything missing?' he said.

'I don't know. I don't think so.' The cross-currents gave her thoughts sudden freedom. 'Was it you, Hike? Have you been over here while I was out?'

He said nothing.

'Maybe it was just local kids,' he said after a moment. 'Kicking the door in for fun.'

'No... it's been forced. A chisel, a hammer, something heavy.'

'Are you asking me to drive over?'

Hike lived more than an hour away, by car. He had always said he disliked driving at night. She had kept him away all this time.

'No, I'm OK,' Melvina said. 'I've just had a fright, that's all. I don't think there's anyone still here. I'll be all right.'

'Look, Mel – I think I'll drive over and see you anyway. You want me to pick up my stuff, and this might be an opportunity to do that.'

'No,' she said. 'I told you and you agreed, you bloody agreed, that you would send a *friend* to get the stuff. I want that room cleared out.'

'I know. But you need me, otherwise you wouldn't have called me in the middle of the night.'

'No,' she said. 'I'll call the police. That's what I ought to do.'

Suddenly the phone went dead at the other end. Hike had cut off the call.

She put down the phone, laid it on her desk next to her keyboard. A mistake! A mistake to call him... but there was no one else. The flashing LED on the answering machine radiated normality, and for a moment she reached over and rested her finger on the *play* button. Then she remembered what had happened to the house. Talking to Hike had changed nothing. Just delayed things, just as always.

In the hallway she returned to the front door, looked again at the broken lock. She tried pressing the door into its frame and discovered that if she let the hanging lock be pushed back she could hold the door closed long enough to shoot the bolt at the top. As soon as she had done this she felt safer.

She picked up the pile of books that had been on the doormat when she came in, and without examining them stacked them roughly on the end of the lowest bookshelf.

Looking anxiously ahead of her Melvina began to climb the stairs, pausing for a few seconds on each step. She was straining to hear any sound from above. The silence was absolute: no apparent movement, nothing being moved about, no footsteps. No one breathing.

The mobile handset suddenly rang, behind her in the study where she had put it down. She went rigid for a moment. Then, relieved, she ran down the four or five steps she had climbed and hurried back into her study.

'Mel, did you call me because you wanted me to drive over tonight?'

'No, I —'

No, I just wanted to be sure it wasn't you, Hike, she added silently, looking over her shoulder at the light coming in from the hall.

'I'm a bit more awake now,' he said. 'Have you noticed anything stolen? Has anything been moved? Is there any damage?'

'It's OK. I've searched the house. There's no one here and nothing's gone.'

'Couldn't you ask one of the neighbours if they saw anything?'

'Hike, you know I'm alone here. The other houses are still empty.'

Some of them were used as summer lets and would start taking visitors in the next few days, but because of the recession most of the houses in this terrace were permanently vacant. Hike knew this, he knew the collapse in property values was why she had been able to afford the house on her intermittent earnings.

'Where did you go today?' he said suddenly.

'*What?*'

'You've been out of the house all day, and I've been trying to call you. Are you seeing someone?'

'It's none of your damned business! Is that all you're thinking about? What I've been doing all day? Someone's broken into my house and for all I know is still in here somewhere.'

'I thought you said no one was there.'

'I was still looking when you called again.'

'Are seeing someone, Mel?'

She tried to think of some answer, but she was obsessed with thoughts of the house, the open door, that darkness and silence. She felt the paralysis of her throat again, the mysterious seizing up of breath and vocal chords, the dominance of fear, the dumbness it caused. She gasped involuntarily, then moved the phone away from her ear. No more Hike.

She pressed the main switch on the top of the handset, watched the logo spinning back into oblivion, then darkness.

There were fourteen messages waiting on the landline answering machine – most of them would be from Hike, just as they were every other day. She flicked it off. Her hands shook.

Something moved upstairs, scraping on the floorboards. Involuntarily, she glanced at the ceiling. The room above, the spare room, the one where Hike's stuff was still piled up awaiting the day when he or one of his friends would collect it. She strained to hear more, thinking, hoping, she had misheard some other sound, perhaps from outside. Then again: a muffled scraping noise, apparently on the bare boards above.

She emitted another involuntary, inarticulate noise: a sob, a croak, a cry of fear. Propelled by the fright that was coiled inside her, but at the same time managing to suppress it somehow, adrenaline-charged, she ran two steps at a time up the stairs. She went straight to the door of the spare room, threw it open and pressed her hand hard against the light-switch inside. She went in.

Familiar chaos filled the room, the remaining debris of Hike's departure. His uncollected stuff had been pushed against one of the walls: piles of paper, canvases, pots, boxes. His broken computer scanner and a tangle of cables. Three large crates of vinyl records and CDs. That bloody music he played so loud when she had been trying to work. Two suitcases she had never opened, but which she assumed contained some of his clothes. Shelves where he had stacked his stuff, but not books – these were the only shelves in the house that were not crammed with books. This was the only *room* without books. Hike was not a reader, and had never understood why she was.

There were other traces of him everywhere, reminders of him, his endless presence in the house, the upset he had caused her almost from the first week, later the resentment, finally the anger, the days and weeks of pointlessly wasted time, all the early curiosity about him lost, the endless regrets about letting him move in and set up a studio, the feeling of being invaded, of trying to make the relationship work, even at the end.

Nothing in the room had been moved or interfered with and nothing had apparently been taken. The window was wide open as she had left it that morning, but the wind was blowing in from the sea. She pushed it closed, and secured it. There was a cupboard door hanging open, a glimpse of the dim interior beyond. Still fired up by anger and fear, she strode across the room, stepped past Hike's cases and pulled the door fully open.

The cupboard was empty. The rack where his clothes had hung, the shelves where he had crammed his messy things, were all vacant. Nothing in there. Just a paperback book, tossed down so that its cover was curled beneath the weight of the pages.

She picked it up: it was Douglas Dunn's *Elegies*. It must be her copy – Hike had no interest in poetry. She straightened the cover and gently riffled the pages of the book, as if comforting a pet animal that had been hurt. Holding it in her hand she left the room, but deliberately did not switch off the light. She now had an aversion to unlighted rooms, dark corners.

The light on the landing had gone out while she was in Hike's room. She turned it on again, only half-remembering if she had switched it off herself as she dashed upstairs to this floor. Why should she have done that? It made no sense.

The room next to Hike's was her own sitting room, a room set aside for reading, with more books, hundreds more books. There were shelves on three of the walls, floor to ceiling, a large and comfy armchair which she had bought as a treat for herself after Piet died, a reading lamp, a footstool, a small side table. A desk with papers and a portable typewriter she sometimes used if she didn't want to break off and go downstairs to the computer. The room had a closed, concentrated, comfortable feeling. She remembered Hike's derision when he saw the room the day he moved in. He said it was middle-class, bourgeois. *No, it's just where I like to sit.* The room had become a sort of battleground after that, a minor but constant aggravation to Hike. After he left, she realized that she had frequently found herself making excuses to be in here, to explain that which could not be explained to someone who would never understand.

She was glad he was gone, glad a hundred times, now a hundred and one. She never wanted him back, no matter what.

She glanced around the room: it was lit only by her reading lamp, but everything seemed to be untouched. Just books everywhere, as she liked them to be, in their familiar but comprehensible jumbles. She pressed the Dunn into a space on a shelf beside the door, preoccupied still with her worries, not noticing or caring which books she placed it beside.

She went next to the bathroom. Three of her books lay on the floor beneath where the glass cubicle door overhung the rim of the shower cubicle. They were three recently published hardback novels she had reviewed for a magazine a month before, and which she expected would have a resale value to a dealer. How had they come into the bathroom, though? She never took books in there.

She picked them up, examined them for damage. As far as she could see no harm had been done by water dripping on them. She opened the top one, and immediately discovered that it was upside-down. The paper dust-wrapper had been removed and put back on the wrong way round.

The other two books were the same.

Melvina stood on the landing outside her reading room, replacing the dust-wrappers one by one. She felt her throat constricting again – her hands were shaking. She could not look around, fearful of everything now in the house.

She took a step into her reading room, and placed the books on the shelf near *Elegies*. She backed out of the room without looking around too closely, horribly aware that something in there had been changed and she did not like to think what, nor look too closely in case she found out.

Hairs on her arms were standing upright. She was sweating – her blouse was sticking to her body under her armpits, against her back. But she was now determined to finish this. She climbed the final flight of stairs to the top floor of the house. She went to her sewing room first, under the eaves, with a dormer window looking out towards the road. The bluewhite glare fell on the car parked close to her house. It looked like Hike's car, but then most cars did.

She checked the room for any sign of intrusion. It was here she kept her sewing table

with the machine, the needlepoint she been working on for a year or more, the various garments she had been meaning to get around to repairing. There was a wardrobe, and in that she kept the old clothes she was planning to take one day to a charity shop. Some of those clothes were Hike's.

The unshaded lightbulb threw its familiar light across everything – there was no one in the room, nowhere that anyone could be hiding.

Finally, quickly, she went to her bedroom. This was the room with the best view of the sea. She had originally planned it to be her office, but once she moved in she realized she would be distracted by staring out all day.

She turned on the central light, went straight in, saw her reflection in the largest pane of the window. She paused just inside the door, remembering. Hike had tried to change this room, said it was too feminine. He hated lace, frills, cushions, things he deemed to be womanly. He never found out that for the most part she did too, and that there was no trace of them, never had been. It had not stopped him criticizing. He did move the bed away from the wall where she had initially placed it, because, he said, he did not want to fall over her stuff if he had to get up in the night.

Melvina planned to move the bed back soon, but she wanted to put up more bookshelves before she did. Money was tight, so she had been delaying.

Everything she remembered of Hike was negative, unpleasant, rancorous. How had it happened? Since he left she had grown so accustomed to being weary of him that she had to make a conscious effort to remember that Hike Tommas had once been eagerly welcome in her life. The early days had been exciting, certainly because they brought an end to the long aftermath of Piet's death. Hike intrigued her. His wispy beard, his hard, slim body, and his abrasive sense of humour, all were so unlike genial Piet. Hike changed everything in her life, or tried to. His opinions – they soon became a regular feature, his attitude to life, his harsh judgments on others, a constant undercurrent of ill-feelings, but at first she found his reckless views on other artists and writers stimulating and entertaining. Hike did not care what he said or thought, which was refreshing at first but increasingly tiresome later. Then there were the paintings he executed, the photographs he took, the objects he made. He was good. He won awards, had held an exhibition at a leading contemporary art gallery, was discussed on the arts pages of broadsheet newspapers. And the physical thing of course, the need she had, the enjoyment of it. They had done that well together. They made it work, but the more it worked the more it came to define what it was she disliked about him. She hated the noises he made, the obscene words he uttered when he climaxed, the way he held her head to press her face against him. Once she gagged and nearly suffocated as he forced himself deep into her mouth, but it did not stop him doing it again the next time. Hike was always in a hurry about sex. Get it over with, he said, then do it again as soon as possible.

Well, now, it was no longer a problem.

There was a pile of her books balanced on the end of the bed, placed exactly at the corner, leaning slightly to one side. Ten books, a dozen? They were paperbacks. She recognized them all, but they belonged in her study or reading room. She could not remember bringing them up here. On the top was another by Douglas Dunn: *Europa's Lover*. Then Nell Dunn's *Poor Cow*, J. W. Dunne's *An Experiment with Time*, Dorothy Dunnet's *The Unicorn Hunt*, Gerald du Maurier's *The Martian*.

She never alphabetized her books by author. She either stacked her books by type, or more commonly left them in unsorted heaps that she would get around to tidying up one day. She always knew where her books were, or could find them quickly using the habitual reader's radar. The poetry came from her study, the other books from her reading room. She felt her fingernails biting into the palms of her hands, the cold press of her perspiration-soaked blouse against her back.

Trying to stay calm she went to the books but the slight

pressure and vibration of her feet on the floorboards was enough to cause the pile to topple. She lunged forward to catch them but they thudded down on the floor, some of them landing with pages open and the spines bent. She knelt to pick them up.

On that level, face close to the floor, she paused. She was next to the bed, close beside the dark area beneath the bed.

Melvina bit her lip, leaned forward and down, so that she could look under it.

No one there. As she straightened with some of the paperbacks in her hand she felt exposed and vulnerable, moving backwards and getting to her feet without looking, not being able to see behind her, or to turn quickly enough.

But she stood up, looked around the room, then placed the books on the floor so that they would not fall again. She headed for the stairs.

Still feeling her knees quivering as she walked, Melvina went through every room in the house one more time, feeling that perhaps the worst was over. Both doors to the outside were secure, and everything was as she expected it to be.

Just the books. Why had the intruder moved her books around?

She went to the kitchen, closed the Venetian blinds and made herself a cup of hot chocolate. It was already long past midnight, but she was wide awake and still jittery.

She returned to her study and switched on her computer. Her mailbox would be full of Hike but tonight she would just delete everything from him without reading. She stared at the monitor, sipping her chocolate drink, while the computer booted.

She browsed through her emails, skipping over Hike's or simply deleting them unread. For a while he had been sending his messages from an email address that did not contain his name, apparently trying to get under her guard, but he had quit doing that last week. She stared at the screen, only half-seeing, half-reading the other notes from her friends. None of them ever mentioned Hike; to all her friends, he was a figure of the past.

She knew Hike was stalking her, and that one of a stalker's intentions was to make the victim think constantly about him. She also knew Hike was succeeding. It must have been him who came to the house. Who else would it have been? But then why had he taken back none of his property, which he knew she repeatedly asked him to have moved, but which he constantly used as one of his excuses for keeping in close contact with her? Perhaps he had said something about coming to the house in one of the emails she had already deleted?

Changing her mind, she found the trash folder of previously deleted emails and opened every one of his messages from the last three days. She skimmed through them, deliberately not reacting to his familiar entreaties, threats, reminders of promises imaginary and real, his endless emotional blackmail about loneliness and abandonment, his pleas for forgiveness, etc. Nothing new, nothing that explained what had happened today.

All she had to do was wait him out. Give it time.

She clicked away the trash folder, but a new message had arrived in her in-box, from Hike. The date stamp showed it had been sent a few seconds before.

Melvina closed her eyes, wondering how much time it would really need. When would he leave her alone?

Behind her there was a sound, heavy fabric moving.

Immediately she stiffened, was braced against fear. She strained to hear. There was a slight sense of movement, then a quiet noise that sounded like a breath.

In the room with her. Someone was behind her, while she sat at her desk.

She froze, one hand still resting on the computer mouse, the other with her fingers beside the keyboard. The computer's cooling fan was making a noise that masked most of the quiet noises around her. Noises like the sound of someone breathing.

She waited, her own breath caught somewhere between her chest and her throat. She hardly dared move.

Her desk was about a metre away from the bay window, so there was space for someone to stand behind her. She turned in a hurry, accidentally knocking some pencils from her desk with her hand. As they clattered to the floor she looked behind her.

She stood.

Every light in the room was on. She could see plainly. There was a figure standing by the window, concealed by one of the full-length curtains.

She could make out the bulge, the approximate shape of the body hidden behind. She stepped back in alarm but her chair was there and she knocked against it. She stared in horror at the figure. The bulge in the curtains, the sound of breathing, the source of every dread.

Whoever was there had taken hold of another of her books, because she could see it, a black hardcover without a paper jacket, held at waist height in front of the curtain. It was the only clue to the actual presence of the person hidden there. She was so close she could reach out and touch the book. It was being held somehow at an angle, an irregular diamond halfway up the curtain, in front of the bulge, supported from behind... by someone breathing as they stood behind the curtain.

The curtain moved slightly, as if lifted by a breeze. A breath.

Another involuntary sound broke fearfully from her. She pushed back, shoving her chair to one side until she was pressing hard against the edge of her desk. She groped behind and her hand touched some pens, her notepad, the mouse, her mobile phone... and a ruler. A wooden ruler, a solid stick, the sort that could be rolled.

She grabbed it and without a thought of what she was

doing she struck with revulsion at the book, like someone trying to kill a snake or a rat. The wooden ruler thumped hard against the book, dashing it to the ground. It fell in a violent flurry of pages, spine upwards, pages curled beneath it.

The curtain shook, swung, fell back against the window. She had expected a cry of pain as the book was dashed away.

Using the ruler, she parted the curtain.

No one was there. Just the black oblong of night-darkened window. She saw her reflection dimly in the pane. Her hair was wild, disarrayed, as if in fright. She smoothed it down without thinking why. The half-light window at the top of the frame was open, admitting a breeze, a breath of night air. She felt the cooling flow, but now she wanted the house to be secure, sealed. She balanced herself precariously on her office chair and closed the window.

The solitary car was still parked outside, under the streetlamp. It looked like Hike's, but he was more than an hour away. It could not be him − although mobile phones, wireless broadband, could be accessed from a car. Because of the light shining down from above, the car's interior was shadowed and she could not make out details − was there someone inside?

She stared, but nothing moved.

Stepping down from her chair she picked up the book that had given her such a fright. It was John Donne's *Collected Poetry*, a hardback she had owned since she was at university. She clutched it with the relief of recognition, closed the pages, checked that none of them had been folded back when she knocked it to the floor. There was a dent at the top of the front cover where she had brought down the ruler. The spine, the rest of the binding, the pages, looked none the worse for the incident, but as she turned to put the book on the shelf where it belonged she discovered that there was a large patch of sticky stuff on the back board. She tapped her finger against it and was surprised at the strength of the glue that had been smeared there.

She sat at her desk, despairing, and holding the damaged book. Why this one? She dabbed at the sticky stuff with a paper tissue, but it only made a mess, made the problem worse.

She put the book aside and closed down the computer. She wanted no more incoming emails. At last the room was silent — no whirring sound of the cooling fan, or of the wind from outside, or of anyone or anything moving inside the house. No footsteps or moving objects, no one breathing around her, no suggestion there was anyone near her, or hidden somewhere in a corner she had forgotten to search.

Tiredness was finally sweeping over her, as the physical exertion of the day's travels and the trauma of arriving home combined against her. But still she could not end the day without being sure.

She moved swiftly from her study, walked straight to the front door, pulled back the bolt and went outside. At once she was in the wind, the sound of trees and foliage moving, the night-time cleansing of the air.

She headed directly for the car parked beneath the streetlamp.

No one was inside, or no one appeared to be inside. She went forward, suddenly alarmed that there might in fact be someone hiding, who had ducked down as she left her house. In her haste she had not thought to bring a torch. She reached the passenger door of the car, braced herself, leaned forward, looked in through the window.

A parallelogram of light fell in from the streetlamp. There was a laptop computer on the front passenger seat, its screen opened up, and lying next to it was a mobile phone. Both revealed by their tiny green LED signals that they were in use, or at least were on standby. There was no sign of anyone hiding in the car. She tried the door, but it was locked. She went to the other side, tried the door there too.

When she turned to go back to her house she realized she had made no attempt to close the front door behind her. In a disturbing reprise of the first sign she had seen of the intrusion, it was swinging to and fro in the wind, a seeming invitation. She hurried back, rushed inside, pushed the door into place and slid the bolt closed.

She stood at the bottom of the stairs, looking up, listening for sounds from any of the rooms downstairs. The books beside the door, which she had not examined closely before, were still on the shelf where she had thrust them in haste.

Melvina picked them up with a feeling of dread certainty, and looked at the authors' names: Disraeli, Dickinson, Dickens, Dick, DeLillo, De La Mare...

Once again, full of fear, she toured the house. She checked all the doors and windows, she looked in every room and made sure that no one could be in any conceivable place of concealment. Then, at last, she began to relax.

It was past one o'clock, and although she felt tired she was not yet sleepy. She went back to her cup of drinking chocolate, now lukewarm, and finished it. Then she climbed up the stairs to the bathroom, brushed her teeth and took a shower.

For the first time since she had bought the house, she found being inside the shower frightening: the closing of the cubicle door and the noise of the rushing water cut her off from the rest of the house and made her feel isolated and vulnerable. She wanted to extend sensors throughout the house, detect the first sign of intrusion at the earliest opportunity. She turned off the water almost as soon as she had started, even before it had become warm enough, and stepped out of the shower feeling wet but unwashed. She towelled herself down, still on edge, nervous again.

In the bedroom, she collected the books that had been stacked on the end of her bed, took them down to her reading room. Most of them belonged there, and she would put the others back in her study in the morning. She went downstairs, found the other books, all with authors whose names began with 'D'. Why?

She turned on the central light in her reading room, and once again she had the unmistakable feeling that something was different, something had changed.

The books on the shelves looked tidier than usual: no books rested face-up on the tops of others. No books leaned to one side. None stuck out.

She looked at the shelf nearest her. Rossetti, Rosenberg, Roberts, Reynolds, Remarque, Rand, Rabelais, Quiller-Couch, Pudney, Proust... All sorted into alphabetical order. By author. In reverse, Z to A.

She put down the pile of 'D' authors she was carrying, and turned to the shelves by the window. On the top shelf, to the left, were *Thérèse Raquin*, *Nana*, *Germinal*, *La Débâcle*, a volume of letters, all by Émile Zola. Next to him, Israel Zangwill's play *The Melting Pot* and his novel *Children of the Ghetto*. Next –

She went to the other end of the shelves, by the door. Here was the copy of Douglas Dunn's *Elegies*, where she had hurriedly stacked it with the three review copies, after she found it in the spare room cupboard. She now realized she had pressed it in beside Le Guin and Kundera.

She took it down, added it to the pile of 'D' authors.

One of the hardcovers close at hand was her treasured copy of Le Guin's *The Dispossessed*. She removed it from the shelf carefully, with her hand shaking again. When she opened the book she found that it was upside-down inside its paper dust-jacket.

Carrying the 'D' authors, Melvina went downstairs again to her study. The first book at the top left-hand end of the main shelf was Jerzy Kosinski's *The Painted Bird*, and several more of his novels. Next to those, Koestler. Next to him –

Immediately beside her desk was a long gap in the

sequence, which began after Dunstan and the sequence resumed with Defoe. The books she was carrying in both hands, a tall heap of mixed paperbacks and hardcovers, fitted loosely in the space.

She put them back, instinctively sorting them into the reverse sequence – she could not help it.

At the far end of her study, where there was another kind of gap, a space for new acquisitions, the last title was *Inter Ice Age IV*, by Kobo Abe.

Melvina went around the house one last time. She double-checked that every window was closed and curtained, that the front and back doors were securely closed, and that every light in the house was on. At last, she went to bed.

She read for a while, she listened to music on her MP3 player and she turned on the 2:00am BBC news. She lay in the half-dark, with a reading lamp on but turned away towards the wall, and with light spilling into the room from the hall. She turned, she fluffed pillows, she tried to cool down and then to warm up. Eventually she drifted into a state of half-sleep: lying still with her eyes closed, but with her thoughts circling and repeating. Time passed slowly.

She must eventually have fallen into a light sleep, because she was awakened suddenly by a blow to her face. Something hard and heavy, and with a sharp corner, landed painfully on her cheekbone and temple. It rested there inexplicably. Instantly she was awake, and moving. Whatever it was slid off her face, landed on the mattress beside her and fell to the floor.

She sat up, and swung her legs out of the bed so that she could sit upright. She swivelled her reading lamp around, and in its glare she picked up the book that had fallen on her. It was Charles Darwin's *The Origin of Species*. It was her old paperback annotated edition, purchased years before, one of those many titles she was intending to read all the way through. One of these days.

From outside the house she heard the starter-motor of

a car, followed by an engine being revved. Still naked from the bed she went quickly to her sewing room next door, pulled aside the curtain, and looked down at the street. The car that had been parked outside her house was accelerating away. She could not see who was driving.

Melvina waited at the window, resting her hands on the sill, leaning her forehead against the cool glass. She watched until the car had driven away, out of sight, and could no longer be heard.

Pre-dawn quietude began to spread around her – in the east there was a grey lightening of the sky, a mottled paleness, unspectacular but steady. The trees across the road from her house gradually took on clarity and shape. She returned briefly to her bedroom, pulled on her robe, then she went back to the window. Almost imperceptibly, the world was sliding into visibility and colour around her – the trees, the curving road, the closed sheds of the council cleaning depot at the end of her street, the roofs of her nearest neighbours' houses down the hill, the flowers in her overgrown garden. Melvina opened the window fully, leaned out into the air, relishing the cool atmosphere. She had not been awake at sunrise for many years. Now she could hear the sea, away behind her on the far side of the house, making a constant shushing on the shingle beach. Calmness spread through her. She waited until the sun had fully risen, but almost as soon as it became visible it disappeared behind a bank of grey cloud. A bird, hidden somewhere, began to sing. The daylight spread inexorably but gently.

Fully awake, Melvina returned to her bedroom and dressed in her oldest work clothes.

She went to the spare room and began to carry Hike's stuff downstairs. It took her an hour to collect up and move everything, and at the end of that time she was sweaty, tired and in need of a bath, but when she had finished Hike's belongings, all his photographs and paintings, including the two that had been hung in her entrance hall, all his art materials, his photo equipment, his papers, magazines, records, broken scanner, bags of cables and clothes in need of recycling lay in a heap outside. But not anywhere near her own house. Two of the houses a short way from hers were due to be let to visitors in two days' time, and she knew someone would clear away all the junk that had inexplicably appeared outside them.

It was going to be another warm day. Melvina opened every window, and settled down to work.

Ped-o-Matique

Jane Rogers

The boots tightened their clasp around Karen's ankles. They began to vibrate. Karen tensed for a moment against the unfamiliar sensation, finding it oddly intimate. She half-tried to remove her feet, but they were firmly clamped in position. Relax. She drew a deep breath and settled back into the squashy comfort of the leatherette chair. She had a full half hour before she needed to be at the Gate. *Spoil Yourself*, the instructions urged. *Enjoy Ped-o-Matique Free Foot Massage.* Time to relax.

She began to review her list. She had forgotten to change her dollars into euros, but there would be time for that in Paris. It was surprising how much there had been to do. At first, a six hour connection lag between flights had seemed intolerable, and she had scoured the net for something better. But direct out of Adelaide, Quantas and Malaysian Airlines were equally bad. Once the wait in Changi Airport had become inevitable, it began to acquire a dreamily elastic nature, in her mind. She might go for a swim in the airport pool, after visiting the fully-equipped gym. She might take the free bus tour of Singapore, laid on for transit passengers. She might take the opportunity to 'be enchanted by our themed gardens from the serene Bamboo Garden to the ancient Fern Garden.' Or even visit the cinema.

In the event, this yawning gulf of time had been all too easily filled. Leaning forward in her seat, she studied the buttons on the machine and switched VIBRATE to *Fast*. The

93

vibration sent tremors all the way up her legs to her thighs. Embarrassed, she glanced at the other passengers gliding past on the travellator, and at the group further down near the Palm Tree internet access site. It felt almost indecent, to be sitting here in public receiving such sensations.

Since landing she had phoned home to check that Zac was happily tucked up in bed; picked up her e mails and sent a message to all her students reminding them that she would be absent this week; found a chemist that sold melatonin, for the jet lag; found a quiet seat in a restaurant and spent two hours re-revising her paper for Monday afternoon; bought an irresistible shell mobile for Zac, a length of batik cloth for Faye, and a green silk blouse which she hoped would look smarter than her turquoise shirt. Finally she had selected a postcard of a smiling lion and posted it to Zac with lots of kisses. He was too young to understand, but Faye could tell him Mummy had sent it. And now she was treating herself to a foot massage, which, according to the notice, entailed the benefits not only of stress relief and improved circulation, but also reduced the likelihood of deep vein thrombosis on long haul flights.

Leaning forward again she switched off VIBRATE and selected MASSAGE. There commenced a slow rhythmic squeezing of her feet. She flicked the switch through *Low* and *Medium* to *High*. The squeezing intensified to an almost alarming level. It began by tightening over the toes, and moved swiftly upwards, tightening in turn over the arch of the foot, the heel, the ankle, the lower calf, clasping her so tightly it was almost painful, before repeating the sequence. She switched her choice back to *Medium*. It was almost like dancing, she thought. Passive dancing. The machine danced your feet for you. How did it know how much to tighten, considering the different shapes and sizes of everyone's feet? Hers were small: if someone with big fat feet were as tightly squeezed as this, bones would be broken. It would be like Chinese foot-binding.

Karen checked her watch. Fifteen minutes till she needed to be at the Gate. She had not really succeeded in relaxing yet. Her stomach was churning with anxiety, as it had been ever since she climbed into the taxi and waved goodbye to an oblivious Zac, wriggling in Faye's arms. But it was ridiculous. He was nearly 8 months old. If she could leave him to return to work, as she had done when her maternity leave ran out, then she could certainly leave him for five days to go to a conference. Everyone thought so. She was fortunate, her Head of Department was really behind her career. He had encouraged her to submit an abstract for Paris, he had been more thrilled than she was when her paper was accepted. And Zac couldn't be in safer hands. Faye was her favourite postgrad, quiet, responsible, thoughtful. Karen had it all. A baby and a career and no man to tell her what to do.

She was tired, that was all. She had forgotten how to relax. She tried to remember the meditation instruction from her old yoga class. 'Focus on the moment,' the teacher had said. 'Our minds are always running to the future or the past. Gently draw your attention back to this present moment in time. Try to live in this moment.' The kindly Ped-o-Matique squeezed and caressed her feet, and she laid her head back on the head rest and closed her eyes, and told herself 'I am living, I am living, I am living in this moment.' But what time was it now in Australia? Zac might be waking up and crying for her. He would be shocked when Faye picked him up. She hoped Faye would hear him from the next room. It had seemed rather much to ask her to sleep in Zac's room, as Karen herself did. But it would be terrible if Faye were a heavy sleeper. Karen imagined Zac screaming, red hot with distress.

Forcing her attention back to the machine, she glanced at the controls; she had not yet tried MASSAGE and VIBRATE together. Switching MASSAGE to *Low*, she pressed VIBRATE. Now that definitely was the best of all – the movements felt less mechanical and more random – she upped MASSAGE to *Medium*, oh yes, very nice. Her feet were tingling and fizzing with life; she imagined them sparkling with tiny champagne bubbles. The squeezing movement just below the ankle felt particularly good. There was something wonderfully soothing, almost caring, about it. She thought about P, whom she had loved and who was married, and the way he would clasp her ankles, gently and firmly, when she bent up her knees either side of his head. He used to hold her securely, manipulating her into another position when they were both ready, the movement continuous as a ballet. When things were good, they seemed effortless. She was dancing and being danced at the same time.

Karen's feet felt wonderful. She was already looking forward to using Ped-o-Matique on the way back. Briefly she allowed herself to imagine coming back. It was only five days. In five days time she would be coming back! It was no time at all to be away – Zac would probably hardly notice. She had agreed to go to Paris because they all said she must, and because it would have been childish and ungrateful not to. But it was a strange thing to have to do, to fly to the other side of the world to talk to people she didn't know, when they could just as easily read what she thought in a journal. Of course, she knew academic dialogue was important. Conference attendance was essential, if she wanted to further her career. Networking, her Head of Department told her; networking is vital. But that meant hanging around at coffee time or in the bar before dinner, striking up conversations, trying to ask intelligent questions. When all she would be able to think of was running back to her room and ringing Faye to check on Zac. She was already eight hours flying time away from him. And there were another fourteen to go. How could she bear to be on the other side of the world?

Karen tried to remember why she had agreed to go. When she said she didn't want to, people had been incredulous. It was an honour – an accolade! It showed she was a real high flyer. Ha ha. And why would anyone in their right mind *not* go to Paris? Lucky her! Even her mother said it would be good for her. 'You spend too much time in that flat. You need to get out and meet people.' Her mother wanted her to meet a man. But I've met the man, Karen said to herself. I've even had his baby.

How could she relax? How could she relax when she allowed everyone around her to push her into doing things she didn't even want to do, which were allegedly for her own good? 'It's a subtle straw that bends and doesn't break,' she recited to herself. It was an old saying of her grandmother's and it meant that you should bend to the prevailing wind. You should go with the flow. Or was it a '*supple* straw that bends'? That would really make more sense, because how could a straw be subtle? Was she subtle? Was she supple? Was she doing the right thing? They should have Ped-o-Matiques for every part of your body, she thought; hands, arms, shoulders, neck, head. A head massager was what was needed. Something to pummel and smooth all these anxious rebellious thoughts out of her head.

It was time to go to the Gate. Leaning forward, she switched MASSAGE to off. The machine seemed to hesitate, then continued its slow, rolling, juddering squeeze. She switched VIBRATE to off, and the juddering stopped. The squeezing continued. She stared at the controls. Both MASSAGE and VIBRATE were off. She switched MASSAGE to low and then off again, to be sure. The rhythmic squeezing continued without pause. Feeling a little foolish, Karen checked the sides of the machine for the on/off power switch which she had clearly forgotten. But there were no switches on the sides. Leaning right forward, she glanced under the chair. Nothing. She double-checked the machine again. MASSAGE: High, Medium, Low, Off. VIBRATE: Fast, Slow, Off. Vibrate was off. Massage was off. She switched them both on and off again, just to be certain. Ped-o-Matique continued imperturbably.

There must be something wrong with it. Karen stared at

her legs, which disappeared at mid calf into the black pulsing oversize boots. It should be possible to wriggle out between squeezes – the thing was only on *Low* after all. She tentatively flexed her right foot but the toe-squeeze tightened on it instantly. She concentrated on the movement of the squeeze. Squeeze toes, squeeze instep, squeeze heel, squeeze lower ankle, squeeze ankle, squeeze calf, squeeze toes. The movement was a rolling one, so as each portion of foot or leg was squeezed, the hold was already tightening on the next. The toes were being squeezed again before the calf was fully released. The instep was being squeezed before the toes were free. Given the crushing strength of the thing, attempting to jerk her legs out might result in serious injury. In fact it said as much on the warning plate, which she had not previously noticed. *Safety warning. Do not attempt to remove feet while Ped-O-Matique is in motion.* It was clearly powered by electricity, so there must be a switch. But where where where was the switch? She must keep a lookout for an airport employee who knew how the damn thing worked. Several had already walked past; another would come by any minute.

What on earth was it that made that rolling squeezing motion? Springs? Paddles? The image of a bread-making machine sprang to Karen's mind; its action whilst kneading dough. She remembered how she used to make bread, back when she was a student. She had enjoyed kneading and pummelling. When she had been working too long on an essay and her mind wouldn't stop racing, the feel of the soft elastic dough under her palms, and the pungent scent of yeast, grounded her. Once she began lecturing and doing her own research, of course, there was less time for bread-making. So her mother kindly bought her a Bread-Maker. The timer was a real boon, she pointed out: Karen could pour in the ingredients before she went to bed, programme it, and wake to delicious warm bread. But the machine took up an inordinate amount of space in Karen's small kitchen. When inactive, it reproached her; if she bought a sandwich she felt guilty. Its open maw devoured a torrent of ingredients, and she realised her housemates had eaten up the loaves she used to bake. Her freezer filled with quarter-eaten loaves. Karen came to understand that the machine had appropriated the only aspect of bread which she truly enjoyed; the yield and stretch of the dough under her fingers. Now it languished in the cupboard under the sink and she only got it out when her mother was round. Perhaps it would come into its own when Zac was old enough for solid food.

Karen glanced at her watch. The gate had been open for 10 minutes. She shifted the Massage switch through all four positions again, and rammed it to *Off*. No change. It was embarrassing but she couldn't wait any longer.

'Excuse me. Excuse me!' The Chinese couple walking past glanced at her and smiled without slowing their walk. At the Palm Tree internet station, everyone was engrossed in their screens. There were no more pedestrians at that moment; she would need to attract the attention of the people on the travellator. 'Excuse me! Hello! Hello there!' A few people turned to stare in her direction. They wore the tranced expressions of people riding a conveyor belt.

'Hello, excuse me!'

A plump grinning boy waved at her and shouted back, 'Hello!'

'Help, please! I'm stuck!'

The passengers on the travellator stared at her blankly while they were carried down towards their gates. There was no way off the moving walkway until the toilets, 200 yards or so down the corridor. Why would anyone take the trouble to get off and walk back to see what she wanted? There must be a power switch. She carefully checked the machine again then thumped it hard and hurt her hand.

'Hey! Help! I'm stuck!' she shouted loudly, but the emailers continued, slaves to their machines. 'Help! I can't get up!' One of them glanced up from his screen, then shook his head fractionally and continued tapping on his keyboard.

Maybe he didn't speak English.

Eventually someone who worked here must pass: security, cleaning staff, check-in girl. But eventually was no good. The gate had already been open twenty minutes. It would close in half an hour. At 23.50 the flight for Paris would depart. 'Help! Help! Help!' Now she was yelling and people glanced up then quickly away. For god's sake, what did it take? Must she drop down dead at their feet?

Karen realised how utterly stupid she had been to time going to the gate so finely. What had possessed her? Why had she not gone straight there? How could she be in the airport for six hours waiting for her connecting flight, and then miss it? Suddenly she remembered her mobile. Thankfully, she drew it from her bag. But who to ring? No one at home could help her. The relentless mechanical squeezing of her feet was making them ache. The machine was grabbing each foot in turn in one spot after another, tighter than handcuffs, holding her fast: it was beginning to make her feel giddy. For a moment of pure terror she imagined being trapped here forever, and never seeing Zac again. What was the international emergency number? 111? 999? She didn't even know. And was it an emergency? Did she require medical attention? No! She tore through her travel documents, willing a number for the airline. The only one was the Australian booking office. Well they could ring Singapore for her. She tapped in the number, feeling the sweat prickling in her armpits, and a niggling pressure in her bladder. The phone went straight to answer. Staring at it in rage she noticed the time. It was 00.18 in Australia.

Closing her eyes against the horror and the shame, Karen began to scream. When she looked again, two middle-aged women with rucksacks were hurrying towards her.

'What's the problem?'

Thank god, Americans. 'I'm sorry, but something ridiculous has happened.' After she had explained, the pair of them tried all the controls, crawled around the chair and neighbouring wall in search of a socket or an on/off switch, and suggested she try pulling her legs out between squeezes. A few other people drifted over from the internet station, and began to make helpful comments. Some who spoke English suggested finding the on/off switch, unplugging the machine, or quickly pulling her legs out. A man advanced offering to help her yank her legs free.

'Please,' she begged the American women, 'please run and find someone who works here, for me.' The American women had an anxious debate about the time of departure of their own flight, then one of them set off at a half-run in the direction of the shopping mall. A young Indian woman in the growing crowd said that there was a real massage place a little further down, and she would ask the man there. A kindly elderly couple said they had to get on to their gate, but what was her departure gate number? Because if they passed it they could tell the staff to hold the flight for her. 'Your baggage will already have been loaded,' they pointed out. 'And they won't fly with unaccompanied baggage. It would take them a lot longer to unload it all and find yours, than to switch off the foot massage.' Karen told them her gate number. It would be closing in four minutes. Her feet were hot and throbbing and she was beginning to feel sick. People were starting to pull up the carpet tiles behind the chair, looking for a switch.

She remembered how P had changed, early last year. He had started grabbing and shoving and making bruises on her arms. Shifting her about to suit himself. With hindsight, of course, she should have ended it straight away. Instead of anxiously wondering what was wrong, thinking she needed to be different, appeasing him. He was trying to end it, she understood that now, and two miserable months later he finally did finish with her. Because she had been too stupid and blind to take the hint, she had allowed him to use her, to the greater misery and self-disgust of the pair of them. If she had only come out cleanly and said *It's not working any more.*

Then he wouldn't have had to operate his scorched earth policy. He wouldn't have had to make himself hateful. But while they were in that downward spiral she had never seen it clearly.

Maybe she was still getting it wrong. Did he really start to hurt her because he knew he would go back to his wife, and he felt guilty? Or did he decide to go back to his wife because Karen herself was too passive? Didn't it take a victim, to make a bully? Where did the imbalance begin, and the effortlessness end? Maybe it had never even been effortless, only seemed so to her. Maybe for him it had all been effort. How could she trust her own judgement?

Time passed. Karen's confused brain began to sound other alarm bells. If the thing had gone completely haywire, maybe it would give her an electric shock. How many volts of electricity were behind that pulsing, squeezing, insanely repetitive movement? She jerked at her legs in terror and was rewarded by a savage clamping onto the wrong part of each foot and ankle – a jarring pain which winded her. It took all her concentration and a couple of rounds of the massage to force her feet down into their original positions again. People peeled away from the crowd to catch their flights, and new people joined. They made helpful suggestions like 'try switching it all on and off again,' and, 'try whipping your feet out of it.' The Indian girl came back with the man from the massage shop, who felt all round the chair for a power switch and shook his head in disbelief. 'Hang on,' he said. 'I will ring security.' He hurried back towards his shop. The American woman appeared at a run and nodded to her friend to set off for their gate. 'I've told them on the Info desk. They are trying to get hold of someone in maintenance. They are trying to get someone out to you.'

'Thank you, but did they say how long –?'

The breathless woman shook her head and began to trot after her friend. Karen glanced at her watch. The gate would have closed by now. The flight would be taking off in 10 minutes. If there was really no switch, they would need to turn off a whole circuit to stop the machine. It would disrupt lighting and flight departures boards. They wouldn't do that in a hurry. Maybe they would need to dismantle the machine around her feet — the bruising, crunching, pummelling machine. It wasn't massaging anymore, it was masticating. It was chewing up her feet and legs — she imagined them when they were finally extricated, limp and mangled, boneless, hanging uselessly from her knees. Maybe they would end up cutting her out. She had a sudden lurid vision of the girl in the old story of the Red Dancing Shoes. Those shoes would never stop dancing, and they danced the poor girl all the way to the executioner's house, where she had to ask him to chop off her feet with his axe. It was the only way she could be still.

A woman was kneeling beside her patting her hand and saying 'Never mind.' Karen realised she was crying. She also realised with acute embarrassment that the crying had set off another fluid release. If the seat was electric as well as the foot thing, she would certainly be electrocuted now. She found herself beginning to laugh.

The affair with P had ended so wretchedly, it had taken her a long time to become aware of the astounding symptoms of pregnancy. She was never going to see him again. But she was expecting his child. By the time other people started noticing, it was six months, and the fact of the child had become inevitable. It was what her body was doing, just as it had grown and shed milk teeth and replaced them with bigger ones, and even, in time, wisdom teeth. She had Zac, who was hers, and nothing to do with anybody else.

A small Singaporean man in blue overalls was coming towards her; the crowd parted to let him through. Karen started to explain but he shook his head, No English. The woman who was patting Karen's hand, and who seemed to have developed a proprietorial interest in her, began to ask the crowd to leave. 'Please, if you can't help, why don't you move on? Can't you see you're upsetting her?' The man in blue overalls took up more of the carpet tiles, then spoke at incomprehensible length into his mobile. When he was done he smiled and nodded at Karen and began to walk away. The sharp aches in her feet had now become duller and deeper, as if the bones themselves had started to hurt. Most probably her feet would be extremely bruised and swollen. When she finally got them out, she probably wouldn't be able to get her shoes on. How could she possibly go to Paris? In clothes she had peed on, with damaged feet that couldn't fit into shoes?

A young woman in smart Airport uniform was hurrying towards her now. 'Please Madam, very sorry. The boys from maintenance are here. This will be no problem. Please to relax.' She shooed away the remaining onlookers. Karen watched in a daze as the man in blue overalls directed two men in brown overalls to prise up a block of flooring in front of the Ped-o-Matique. They probed amongst a nest of wires. After some discussion one of them inserted a long thin pair of pliers into the tangle, and decisively snipped one wire. The Ped-o-Matique gave a convulsive shudder and fell still. It held Karen clamped tight at heel and ankle, but now it was still she managed to twist and wriggle and wrench her feet through the tight part, and haul them out to freedom. They felt ready to explode.

'Oh my god, my god!' she heard herself crying, and thought angrily that she sounded melodramatic, and she hoped none of them were religious. The man in blue overalls nodded and smiled. The girl from Information squeezed her arm. 'I am very sorry for this trouble and any inconvenience it may cause,' she assured Karen. 'If there is anything I can do to assist, not a problem. '

Her feet were free. She wasn't trapped. She was free!

'I think I've missed my flight,' said Karen, feeling her toes with one hand and assessing the size of the wet patch with the other.

'I can seat you on the next Paris flight. It is not a

problem.'

'It'll be too late. My reason for going to Paris is — is tomorrow.'

'Tomorrow?' echoed the girl.

'Yes. I think I should return to Adelaide.'

'No problem. Not a problem at all,' the girl smiled. 'I will check availability.' The men in brown overalls were replacing the floor block, and recovering it with carpet tiles. The man in blue overalls came up and spoke quietly to the girl, nodding at Karen as he did so.

'He says,' the girl translated, 'he is very sorry for this machine fault. He says, he will look into the problem deeply.'

'Thank you,' said Karen. 'I think I'll just sit here for a minute. I'll follow you to the desk.'

'Not a problem,' said the girl. 'I will be seeing you.' The girl and the man in blue overalls set off back to the concourse, followed by the two men in brown overalls, carrying their toolbox. Karen relaxed back into her wet seat. She felt almost happy enough to dance.

Dolls' Eyes

A. S. Byatt

Her name was Felicity; she had called herself Fliss as a small child, and it had stuck. The children in her reception class at Holly Grove School called her Miss Fliss, affectionately. She had been a pretty child and was a pretty woman, with tightly curling golden hair and pale blue eyes. Her classroom was full of invention, knitted dinosaurs, an embroidered snake coiling round three walls. She loved the children – almost all of them – and they loved her. They gave her things – a hedgehog, newts, tadpoles in a jar, bunches of daffodils. She did not love them as though they were her own children: she loved them because they were not. She taught bush-haired boys to do cross-stitch, and shy girls to splash out with big paintbrushes and tubs of vivid reds and blues and yellows.

She wondered often if she was odd, though she did not know what she meant by 'odd'. One thing that was odd, perhaps, was that she had reached the age of thirty without having loved, or felt close, to anyone in particular. She made friends carefully – people must have friends, she knew – and went to the cinema, or cooked suppers, and could hear them saying how nice she was. She knew she was nice, but she also knew she was pretending to be nice. She lived alone in a little red brick terraced house she had inherited from an aunt. She had two spare rooms, one of which she let out, from time to time, to new teachers who were looking for something more permanent, or to passing students. The house was not at all odd, except for the dolls.

She did not collect dolls. She had over a hundred, sitting in cosy groups on sofas, perching on shelves, stretched and sleeping on the chest of drawers in her bedroom. Rag dolls, china dolls, rubber dolls, celluloid dolls. Old dolls, new dolls, twin dolls (one pair conjoined). Black dolls, blond dolls, baby dolls, chubby little boys, ethereal fairy dolls. Dolls with painted surprised eyes, dolls with eyes that clicked open and closed, dolls with pretty china teeth, between pretty parted lips. Pouting dolls, grinning dolls. Even dolls with trembling tongues.

The nucleus of the group had been inherited from her mother and grandmother, both of whom had loved and cared for them. There were four: a tall ladylike doll in a magenta velvet cloak, a tiny china doll in a frilly dress with forgetmenot painted eyes, a realistic baby doll with a cream silk bonnet, closing eyes and articulated joints, and a stiff wooden doll, rigid and unsmiling in a black stuff gown.

Because she had those dolls – who sat in state in a basket chair – other dolls accumulated. People gave her their old dolls – 'we know you'll care for her'. Friends thinking of Christmas or birthday presents found unusual dolls in jumble sales or antique shops.

The lady-like doll was Miss Martha. The tiny china doll was Arabel. The baby doll was Polly. The rigid doll was Sarah Jane. She had an apron over her gown and might once have been a domestic servant doll.

Selected children, invited to tea and cake, asked if she played with the dolls. She did not, she replied, though she moved them round the house, giving them new seats and different company.

It would have been odd to have played with the dolls. She made them clothes, sometimes, or took one or two to school for the children to tell stories about.

She knew, but never said, that some of them were alive in some way, and some of them were only cloth and stuffing and moulded heads. You could even distinguish, two with identical heads under different wigs and bonnets, of whom one might be alive – Penelope with black pigtails – and one inert, though she had a name, Camilla, out of fairness.

There was a new teacher, that autumn, a late appointment because Miss Bury had had a leg amputated as a result of an infection caught on a boating holiday on an African river. The new teacher was Miss Coley. Carole Coley. The head teacher asked Fliss if she could put her up for a few weeks, and Fliss said she would gladly do so. They were introduced to each other at a teaparty for incoming teachers.

Carole Coley had strange eyes; this was the first thing Fliss noticed. They were large and rounded, dark and gleaming like black treacle. She had very black hair and very black eyelashes. She wore the hair, which was long, looped upwards in the nape of her neck, under a black hairslide. She wore lipstick and nail varnish in a rich plum colour. She had a trim but female body and wore a trouser suit, also plum. And glittering glass rings, quite large, on slender fingers. Fliss was intimidated, but also intrigued. She offered hospitality – the big attic bedroom, shared bath and kitchen. Carole Coley said she might prove to be an impossible guest. She had two things which always came with her:

'My own big bed with my support mattress. And Cross-Patch.'

Fliss considered. The bed would be a problem but one that could be solved. Who was Cross-Patch?

Cross-Patch turned out to be a young Border collie, with a rackety eye-patch in black on a white face. Fliss had no pets, though she occasionally housed the classroom mice and tortoises in the holidays. Carole Coley said in a take it or leave it voice, that Cross-Patch was very well trained.

'I'm sure she is' said Fliss, and so it was settled. She did not feel it necessary to warn Carole about the dolls. They were inanimate, if numerous.

Carole arrived with Cross-Patch, who was sleek and slinky. They stood with Fliss in the little sitting room whilst the removal men took Fliss's spare bed into storage, and mounted the stairs with Carole's much larger one. Carole was startled by the dolls. She went from cluster to cluster, picking them up, looking at their faces, putting them back precisely where they came from. Cross-Patch clung to her shapely calves and made a low throaty sound.

'I wouldn't have put you down as a collector.'

'I'm not. They just seem to find their way here. I haven't *bought* a single one. I get given them, and people see them, and give me more.'

'They're a bit alarming. So much staring. So still.'

'I know. I'm used to them. Sometimes I move them round.'

Cross-Patch made a growly attempt to advance on the sofa. Carole raised a firm finger. '*No,* Cross-Patch. *Sit. Stay.* These are not your toys.'

Cross-Patch, it turned out, had her own stuffed toys – a bunny rabbit, a hedgehog – with which she played snarly, shaking games in the evenings. Fliss was impressed by Carole's authority over the animal. She herself was afraid of it, and knew that it sensed her fear.

Carole was a good lodger. She was helpful and unobtrusive. Everything interested her – Fliss's embroidery silks, her saved children's books from when she was young, her mother's receipts, a bizarre Clarice Cliffe tea-set with a conical sugar-shaker. She made Fliss feel that she was *interesting* – a feeling Fliss almost never had, and would have said she didn't want to have. It was odd being looked at, appreciatively, for long moments. Carole asked her questions, but she could not think up any questions to ask in return. A few facts about Carole's life did come to light. She had travelled and worked in India. She had been very ill and nearly died. She went to evening classes on classical Greece and asked Fliss to come too, but Fliss said no. When Carole went out, Fliss sat and watched the television, and Cross-Patch lay watchfully in a corner, guarding her toys. When Carole returned, the dog leaped up to embrace her as though she was going for her throat. She slept upstairs with her owner in the big bed. Their six feet went past Fliss's bedroom door, pattering, dancing.

Carole said the dolls were beginning to fascinate her. So many different characters, so much love had gone into their making and clothing. 'Almost loved to bits, some of them,' said Carole, her treacle eyes glittering. Fliss heard herself offer to lend a few of them, and was immediately horrified. What on earth would Carole want to borrow dolls for? The offer was *odd*. But Carole smiled widely and said she would love to have one or two to sit on the end of her big bed, or on the chest of drawers. Fliss was overcome with nervous anxiety, then, in case Cross-Patch might take against the selected dolls, or think they were toys. She looked sidelong at Cross-Patch, and Cross-Patch looked sidelong at her, and wrinkled her lip in a collie grin. Carole said:

'You needn't worry about her, my dear. She is completely well-trained. She hasn't offered to touch any doll. Has she?'

'No,' said Fliss, still troubled by whether the dog would see matters differently in the bedroom.

When they went to bed they said good-night on the first floor landing and Carole went up to the next floor. She borrowed a big rag doll with long blond woollen plaits and a Swiss sort of apron. This doll was called Priddy, and was not, as far as Fliss knew, alive. She also borrowed − surprisingly − the rigid Sarah Jane, who certainly was alive. 'I love her disapproving expression,' said Carole. 'She's seen a thing or two, in her time. She had painted eyes, that didn't close.'

Other dolls took turns to go up the stairs. Fliss noticed, without formulating the idea, that they were always grown-up or big girl dolls, and they never had sleeping eyes.

Little noises came down the stairs. A cut-off laugh, an excited whisper, a creak of springs. Also a red light spread from the door over the sage-green staircarpet.

One night, when she couldn't sleep, Fliss went down to the kitchen and made Horlicks for herself. She then took it into her head to go up the stairs to the spare room; she saw the pool of red light and knew Carole was not asleep. She meant to offer her Horlicks.

The door was half open. 'Come in,' called Carole, before Fliss could tap. She had put squares of crimson silk, weighted down with china beads, over the bedside lamps. She sat on the middle of her big bed, in a pleated sea-green nightdress, with sleeves and a high neck. Her long hair was down, and brushed into a fan, prickling with an electric life of its own. Cross-Patch was curled at the foot of the bed.

'Come and sit down,' said Carole. Fliss was wearing a baby blue nightie in a fine jersey fabric, under a fawn woolly dressing-gown. 'Take that off, make yourself comfortable.'

'I was – I was going to – I couldn't sleep…'

'Come here,' said Carole. 'You're all tense. I'll massage your neck.'

They sat in the centre of the white quilt, made ruddy by light, and Carole pushed long fingers into all the sensitive bits of Fliss's neck and shoulders, and released the nerves and muscles. Fliss began to cry.

'Shall I stop?'

'Oh no, don't stop, don't stop. I –'

'This is terrible. Terrible. I love you.'

'And what's terrible about that?' asked Carole, and put her arms around Fliss, and kissed her on the mouth.

Fliss was about to explain that she had never felt love and didn't exactly like it, when they were distracted by fierce snarling from Cross-Patch.

'Now then, bitch,' said Carole. 'Get out. If you're going to be like that, get out.'

And Cross-Patch slid off the bed, and slunk out of the door. Carole kissed Fliss again, and pushed her gently down on the pillows and held her close. Fliss knew for the first time that terror that all lovers know, that the thing now begun must have an ending. Carole said 'My dear, my darling.' No one had said that to her.

They sat side by side at breakfast, touching hands, from time to time. Cross-Patch uttered petulant low growls and then padded away, her nails rattling on the lino. Carole said they would tell each other everything, they would *know* each other. Fliss said with a light little laugh that there was nothing to know about her. But nevertheless she did more of the talking, described her childhood in a village, her estranged sister, her dead mother, the grandmother who had given them the dolls.

Cross-Patch burst back into the room. She was carrying something, worrying it, shaking it from side to side, making a chuckling noise, tossing it, as she would have tossed a rabbit to break its neck. It was the baby doll, Polly, in her frilled silk bonnet and trailing embroidered gown. Her feet in their knitted bootees protruded at angles. She rattled.

Carole rose up in splendid wrath. In a rich firm voice she ordered the dog to put the doll down, and Cross-Patch spat out the silky creature, slimed with saliva, and cowered whimpering on the ground, her ears flat to her head. Masterfully Carole took her by the collar and hit her face, from side to side, with the flat of her hands. '*Bad* dog,' she said, '*bad* dog,' and beat her. And beat her.

The rattling noise was Polly's eyes, which had been shaken free of their weighted mechanism, and were rolling round inside her bisque skull. Where they had been were black holes. She had a rather severe little face, like some real babies. Eyeless it was ghastly.

'My darling, I am *so* sorry,' said Carole. 'Can I have a look?'

Fliss did not want to relinquish the doll. But did. Carole

113

shook her vigorously. The invisible eyes rolled.

'We could take her apart and try to fit them back.'

She began to pull at Polly's neck.

'No, don't, don't. We can take her to the dolls' hospital at the Ouse Bridge. There's a man in there – Mr Copple – who can mend almost anything.'

'Her pretty dress is torn. There's a toothmark on her face.'

'You'll be surprised what Mr Copple can fix,' said Fliss, without complete certainty. Carole kissed her and said she was a generous creature.

Mr Copple's shop was old and narrow-fronted, and its back jutted out over the river. It had old window-panes, with leaded lights, and was a tiny cavern inside, lit with strings of fairy-lights, all different colours. From the ceiling, like sausages in a butcher's shop, hung arms, legs, torsos, wigs, the cages of crinolines. On his glass counter were bowls of eyeballs, blue, black, brown, green, paperweight eyes, eyes without whites, all iris. And there were other bowls and boxes with all sorts of little wire joints and couplings, useful elastics and squeaking voice boxes.

Mr Copple had, of course, large tortoiseshell glasses, wispy white hair and a bad, greyish skin. His fingers were yellow with tobacco.

'Ah,' he said, 'Miss Weekes, always a pleasure. Who is it this time?'

Carole replied. 'It was my very bad dog. She shook her. She has never done anything like this before.'

The two teachers had tied Polly up into a brown paper parcel. They did not want to see her vacant stare. Fliss handed it over. Mr Copple cut the string.

'Ah,' he said again. 'Excuse me.'

He produced a kind of prodding screwdriver, skilfully decapitated Polly, and shook her eyes out into his hand.

'She needs a new juncture, a new balance. Not very difficult.'

'There's a bite mark,' said Carole gloomily.

'When you come back for her, you won't know where it was. And I'll put a stitch or two into these pretty clothes and wash them out in soapsuds. She's a Million Dollar Baby. A Bye-Lo baby. Designed by an American, made in Germany. In the 1920s.'

'Valuable?' asked Carole casually.

'Not so very. There were a large number of them. This one has the original clothes and real human hair. That puts her price up. She is meant to look like a real newborn baby.'

'You can see that,' said Carole.

He put the pieces of Polly into a silky blue bag and attached a label on a string. *Miss Weekes's Polly.*

They collected her the next week and Mr Copple had been as good as his word. Polly was Polly again, only fresher and smarter. She rolled her eyes at them again, and they laughed, and when they got her home, kissed her and each other.

Fliss thought day and night about what she would do when Carole left. How it would happen. How she would bear it. Although, perhaps because, she was a novice in love, she knew that the fiercer the passion, the swifter and the harsher the ending. There was no way they two would settle into elderly domestic comfort. She became jealous and made desperate attempts not to show it. It was horrible when Carole went out for the evening. It was despicable to think of listening in to Carole's private calls, though she thought Carole listened to her own, which were of no real interest. The school year went on, and Carole began to receive glossy brochures in the post, with pictures of golden sands and shining white temples. She sat looking at them in the evenings, across the hearth from Fliss, surrounded by dolls. Fliss wanted to say 'Shall we go together?' and was given no breath of space to do so. Fliss had always spent her holidays in Bath, making excursions into the countryside. She made no arrangements. Great rifts and gaps of silence spread into the texture of their lives together. Then Carole said:

'I am going away for a month or so. On Sunday. I'll arrange for the rent to be paid while I'm away.'

'Where,' said Fliss. 'Where are you going?'

'I'm not sure. I always do go away.'

Can I come? could not be said. So Fliss said:

'Will you come back?'

'Why shouldn't I? Everyone needs a bit of space and time to herself, now and then. I've always found that. I shall miss the dolls.'

'Would you like to take one?' Fliss heard herself say. 'I've never given one away, never. But you can take one –'

Carole kissed her and held her close.

'Then we shall both want to come back – to the charmed circle. Which doll are you letting me have?'

'*Any of them,*' cried Fliss, full of love and grief. 'Take anyone at all. I want you to have the one you want.'

She did not expect, she thought later, that Carole would take one of the original four. Still less, that of those four, she would choose Polly, the baby, since her taste had always been for grown girls. But Carole chose Polly, and watched Fliss try to put a brave face on it, with an enigmatic smile. Then she packed and left, without saying where she was going.

Before she left, in secret, Fliss kissed Polly and told her 'Come back. Bring her back.'

Cross-Patch went with them. The big empty bed remained, a hostage of a sort.

Fliss did not go to Bath. She sat at home, in what turned out to be a dismal summer, and watched the television. She watched the Antiques Roadshow, and its younger offshoot, Flogit, in which people brought things they did not want to be valued by experts and auctioned in front of the cameras. Fliss and Carole had watched it together. They both admitted to a secret love for the presenter, the beautiful Paul Martin, whose energy never flagged. Nor, Fliss thought, did his kindness and courtesy, no matter what human oddities presented themselves. She loved him because he was reliable, which beautiful people, usually, were not.

And so it came about that Fliss, looking up idly at the screen from the tray of soup and salad on her knee, saw Polly staring out at her in close-up, sitting on the Flogit valuing table. It must be a complete lookalike, Fliss thought. The bisque face, with its narrow eyes and tight mouth appeared to her to have a desperate or enraged expression. One of the most interesting things about Polly was that her look was sometimes composed and babylike, but, in some lights, from some angles, could appear angry.

The valuer, a woman in her forties, sweetly blond but sharp-eyed, picked up Polly and declared she was one of the most exciting finds she had met on Flogit. She was, said the purring lady, a real Bye-Lo Baby, and dressed in her original clothes. 'May I look?' she asked sweetly, and upended Polly, throwing her silk robe over her head, exposing her woollen bootees, her sweet silk panties, the German stamps on her chubby back, to millions of viewers. Her fingernails were pointed, and painted scarlet. She pulled down the panties and ran her nails round Polly's hip-joints. Bye-Lo Babies were rarer, and earlier, if they had jointed composition bodies than if they had cloth ones, with celluloid hands sewn on. She took off Polly's frilled ivory silk bonnet, and exclaimed over her hair – 'which, I must tell you, I am 90% sure is *real human hair* which adds to her value.' She pushed the hair over Polly's suspended head and said 'Ah, yes, as though we needed to see it.' The camera closed in on the nape of Polly's neck. 'Copr. By Grace S. Putnam// MADE IN GERMANY.'

'Do you know the story of Grace S Putnam and the baby doll?' scarlet-nails asked the hopeful seller and there was Carole, in a smart Art Deco summer shirt in black and white, smiling politely and following the movements of the scarlet nails with her own smooth mulberry ones.

'No,' said Carole into Fliss's sitting room, 'I don't know much about dolls.'

Her face was briefly screen-size. Her lipstick shone, her teeth glistened. Fliss's knees began to knock, and she put down her tray on the floor.

Grace Story Putnam, the valuing lady said, had wanted to make a *real* baby doll, a doll that looked like a real baby, perhaps three days old. Not like a Disney puppet. So this formidable person had haunted maternity wards, sketching, painting, analysing. And never could she find the perfect face with all the requisite qualities.

She leaned forwards, her blond hair brushing Carole's raven folds.

'I don't know if I should tell you this.'

'Well, now you've started, I think you should,' said Carole, always Carole.

'It is rumoured that in the end she saw the perfect child being carried past, wrapped in a shawl. And she said, wait, this is the one. But that baby had just died. Nevertheless, the story goes, the determined Mrs Putnam drew the little face, and this is what we have here.'

'Ghoulish,' said Carole, with gusto. The camera went back to Polly's face, which looked distinctly malevolent. Fliss knew her expression must be unchanging, but it did not seem like that. Her stare was fixed. Fliss said 'Oh, Polly –'

'And is this your own dolly?' asked the TV lady. 'Inherited perhaps from your mother or grandmother. Won't you find it very hard to part with her?'

'I didn't inherit her. She's nothing to do with me, personally. A friend gave her to me, a friend with a lot of dolls.'

'But maybe she didn't know how valuable this little gift was? The Bye-Los were made in great numbers – even millions – but early ones like this, and with all their clothes, and real human hair, can be expected to fetch anywhere between £800 and well over £1,000 – even *well over*, if two or more collectors are in the room. And of course she may have her photo in the catalogue or on the website...'

'That does surprise me,' said Carole, but not as though it really did.

'And do you think your friend will be happy for you to sell her doll?'

'I'm sure she would. She is very fond of me, and very generous-hearted.'

'And what will you do with the money if we sell Dolly, as I am sure we shall –'

'I have booked a holiday on a rather luxurious cruise in the Greek islands. I am interested in classical temples. This sort of money will really help.'

There is always a gap between the valuation of an item and the showing of its auction. Fliss stared unseeing at the valuation of a hideous green pottery dog, a group of World War I medals, an album of naughty seaside postcards. Then came Polly's moment. The auctioneer held her aloft, his gentlemanly hand tight round her pudgy waist, her woolly feet protruding. Briefly, briefly, Fliss looked for the last time at Polly's sweet face, now, she was quite sure, both baleful and miserable.

'Polly,' she said aloud. '*Get her. Get her.*'

She did not know what she wanted Polly to do. But she saw Polly as capable of doing something. And they were – as they had always been – on the same side, she and Polly.

She thought, as the bidding flew along, a numbered card flying up, a head nodding, a row of concentrated listeners with mobile phones, waiting, and then raising peremptory fingers, that she herself had betrayed Polly, but that she had done so out of love and goodwill. 'Oh, Polly,' she said, '*Get her,*' as Carole might have said to Cross-Patch.

Carole was standing, composed and beautiful, next to Paul Martin, as the tens turned into hundreds and the hundreds to thousands. He liked sellers to show excitement or amazement, and Carole – Fliss understood her – showed just enough of both to keep the cameras happy, but was actually rigid inside, like a stone pillar of willpower and certainty. Polly went for £2,000, but it was not customary to show the sold object again, only the happy face of the seller, so, for Fliss, there was no moment of good-bye. And you were not told where sold objects were going.

All the other dolls were staring, as usual. She turned them over, or laid them to sleep, murmuring madly, get her, get her.

She did not suppose Carole would come back, and wondered if she should get rid of the bed. The headmistress at the school was slightly surprised when Fliss asked her if Carole was coming back – 'Do you know something I don't?' Then she showed Fliss a postcard from Crete, and one from Lemnos. 'I go off on my own with my beach towel and a book and lie on the silver sand by the wine-dark sea, and feel perfectly happy.' Fliss asked the headmistress if she knew where Cross-Patch was, and the headmistress said she had assumed Fliss was in charge of her, but if not, presumably, she must be in kennels.

A week later, the head told Fliss that Carole was in hospital. She had had a kind of accident. She had been unconscious for some time, but it was clear, from the state of her nervous system, and from filaments and threads found on her swimsuit and in her hair, that she had swum, or floated, into a swarm of minute stinging jellyfish – there are *millions* out there, this summer, people are warned, but she liked to go off on her own.

Fliss didn't ask for more news, but got told anyway. Carole's eyes were permanently damaged. She would probably never see again; at best, vestigially.

She would not, naturally, be coming back.

The headmistress looked at Fliss, to see how she took this. Fliss contrived an expression of conventional, distant shock, and said several times, how awful, how very awful.

The headmistress said 'That dog of hers. Do you think anyone knows where it is? Do you think we should get it out of the kennels? Would you yourself like to have it, perhaps – you all became so close?'

'No,' said Fliss. 'I'm afraid I never liked it really. I did my best as I hope I always shall. I'm sure someone can be found. It has a very uncertain temper.'

She went home and told the dolls what had happened. She thought of Polly's closed, absent little face. The dolls made an inaudible rustling, like distant birds settling. They *knew*, Fliss thought, and then unthought that thought, which could be said to be odd.

Tamagotchi

Adam Marek

My son's Tamagotchi had AIDS. The virtual pet was rendered on the little LCD screen with no more than 30 pixels, but the sickness was obvious. It had that AIDS look, you know? It was thinner than it had been. Some of its pixels were faded, and the pupils of its huge eyes were smaller, giving it an empty stare.

I had bought the Tamagotchi, named Meemoo, for Luke just a couple of weeks ago. He had really wanted a kitten, but Gabby did not want a cat in the house. 'A cat will bring in dead birds and toxoplasmosis,' she said, her fingers spread protectively over her bulging stomach.

A Tamagotchi had seemed like the perfect compromise – something for Luke to empathise with and to care for, to teach him the rudiments of petcare for a time after the baby had been born. Empathy is one of the things that the book said Luke would struggle with. He would have difficulty reading facial expressions. The Tamagotchi had only three different faces, so it would be good practice for him.

Together, Luke and I watched Meemoo curled up in the corner of its screen. Sometimes, Meemoo would get up, limp to the opposite corner, and produce a pile of something. I don't know what this something was, or which orifice it came from – the resolution was not good enough to tell.

'You're feeding it too much,' I told Luke. He said that he wasn't, but he'd been sat on the sofa thumbing the buttons for hours at a time, so I'm sure he must have been. There's not much else to do with a Tamagotchi.

I read the instruction manual that came with Meemoo. Its needs were simple: food, water, sleep, play, much like Luke's. Meemoo was supposed to give signals when it required one of these things. Luke's job as Meemoo's carer was to press the appropriate button at the appropriate time. The manual said that overfeeding, underfeeding, lack of exercise and unhappiness could all make a Tamagotchi sick. A little black skull and crossbones should appear on the screen when this happens, and by pressing button A twice, then B, one could administer medicine. The instructions said that sometimes it might take two or three shots of medicine, depending on how sick your Tamagotchi is.

I checked Meemoo's screen again and there was no skull and crossbones.

The instructions said that if the Tamagotchi dies, you have to stick a pencil into the hole in its back to reset it. A new creature would then be born. They said you could reset at any time.

When Luke had finally gone to sleep and could not see me molesting his virtual pet, I found the hole on Meemoo's back and jabbed a sharpened pencil into it. But when I turned it back over, Meemoo was still there, as sick as ever. I jabbed a few more times and tried it with a pin too, in case I wasn't getting deep enough. But it wouldn't reset.

I wondered what happened if Meemoo died, knowing that the reset button didn't work. Was there a malfunction that had robbed Luke's Tamagotchi of its immortality? Did it have just one shot at life? I guess that made it a lot more special, and in a small way, it made me more determined to find a cure for Meemoo.

I plugged Meemoo into my PC – a new feature in this generation of Tamagotchis. I hoped that some kind of diagnostics wizard would pop up and sort it out.

A Tamagotchi screen blinked into life on my PC. There

were many big-eyed mutant creatures jiggling for attention, including another Meemoo, looking like its picture on the box, before it got sick. One of the options on the screen was 'synch your Tamagotchi'.

When I did this, Meemoo's limited world of square grey pixels was transformed into a full colour three-dimensional animation on my screen. The blank room in which it lived was revealed as a conservatory filled with impossible plants growing under the pale-pink Tamagotchi sun. And in the middle of this world, lying on the carpet, was Meemoo.

It looked awful. In this fully realised version of the Tamagotchi's room, Meemoo was a shrivelled thing. The skin on its feet was dry and peeling. Its eyes, once bright white with crisp highlights, were yellow and unreflective. There were scabs around the base of its nose. I wondered what kind of demented mind would create a child's toy that was capable of reaching such abject deterioration.

I clicked through every button available until I found the medical kit. From this you could drag and drop pills onto the Tamagotchi. I guess Meemoo was supposed to eat or absorb these, but they just hovered in front of it, as if Meemoo was refusing to take its medicine.

I tried the same trick with Meemoo that I do with Luke to get him to take his medicine. I mixed it with food. I dragged a chicken drumstick from the food store and put it on top of the medicine, hoping that Meemoo would get up and eat them both. But it just lay there, looking at me, its mouth slightly open. Its look of sickness was so convincing that I could practically smell its foul breath coming from the screen.

I sent Meemoo's makers a sarcastic e-mail describing his condition and asking what needed to be done to restore its health.

A week later, I had received no reply and Meemoo was getting even worse. There were pale grey dots appearing on it. When I synched Meemoo to my computer, these dots were revealed as deep red sores. And the way the light from the Tamagotchi sun reflected off them, you could tell they were wet.

I went to a toy shop and showed them the Tamagotchi. 'I've not seen one do that before.' The girl behind the counter said. 'Must be something the new ones do.'

I came home from work one day to find Luke had a friend over for a playdate. The friend was called Becky, and she had a Tamagotchi too. Gabby was trying to organise at least one playdate a week to help Luke socialise.

Becky's Tamagotchi gave me an idea.

This generation of Tamagotchis had the ability to connect to other Tamagotchis. By getting your Tamagotchi within a metre of a friend's Tamagotchi, your virtual pets could play games or dance together (because of their limited resolution, Tamagotchi dances are indistinguishable from their 'hungry' signal). Maybe if I connected the two Tamagotchis, the medicine button in Becky's would cure Meemoo.

At first, Luke violently resisted giving Meemoo to me, despite me saying I only wanted to help it. But when I bribed Luke and Becky with chocolate biscuits and a packet of crisps, they agreed to hand them over.

When Gabby came in from hanging up the washing, she was furious.

'Why did you give the kids crisps and chocolate?' She said, slamming the empty basket on the ground. 'I'm just about to give them dinner.'

'Leave me alone for a minute,' I said.

I didn't have time to explain. I had only a few minutes before the kids would demand their toys back, and I was having trouble getting the Tamagotchis to find each other – maybe Meemoo's bluetooth connection had been compromised by the virus.

Eventually though, when I put their connectors right next to each other, they made a synchronous pinging sound, and both characters appeared on both screens. It's amazing how satisfying that was.

Meemoo looked sick on Becky's screen too. I pressed A twice and then B to administer medicine.

Nothing happened.

I tried again. But the Tamagotchis just stood there. One healthy, one sick. Doing nothing.

Luke and Becky came back, their fingers oily and their faces brown with chocolate. I told them to wipe their hands on their trousers before they played with their Tamagotchis. I was about to disconnect them from each other, but when they saw that they had each other's characters on their screen, they got excited and sat at the kitchen table to play together.

I poured myself a beer and half a glass of wine for Gabby (her daily limit), then, seeing the crisps out on the side, helped myself to a bag. There was something so comforting about the taste of the cold beer and salted crisps.

Later, when my beer was gone and it was time for Becky's mum to pick her up, Becky handed me her Tamagotchi.

'Can you fix Weebee?' She asked. 'I don't think she's feeling well.'

Becky's pink Tamagotchi was already presenting the first symptoms of Meemoo's disease: the thinning and greying of features, the stoop, the lethargy.

I heard Becky's mum pull up in the car as I began to press the medicine buttons, knowing already that they would not work. 'There,' I said. 'It just needs some rest. Leave it alone until tomorrow, and it should be okay.'

Luke had been invited to a birthday party. Usually Gabby would take Luke to parties, but she was feeling rough – she was having a particularly unpleasant first trimester this time. So she persuaded me to go, even though I hate kids' parties.

I noticed that lots of other kids at the party had Tamagotchis. They were fastened to the belt loops of their skirts and trousers. The kids would stop every few minutes during their games to lift up their Tamagotchis and check they were okay, occasionally pressing a button to satisfy one of their needs.

'These Tamagotchis are insane, aren't they?' I remarked to another Dad who was standing at the edge of the garden with his arms folded across his chest.

'Yeah,' he smiled.

'Yeah,' I said. 'My kid's one got sick. One of its arms fell off this morning. Can you believe that?'

The dad turned to me, his face suddenly serious. 'You're not Luke's dad, are you?' he asked.

'Yes,' I said.

'I had to buy a new Tamagotchi thanks to you.'

I frowned and smirked, thinking that he couldn't be serious, but my expression seemed to piss him off.

'You had Becky Willis over at your house, didn't you?' he continued. 'Her pet got Matty's pet sick 'cause she sits next to him in class. My boy's pet died. I've half a mind to charge you for the new one.'

I stared right into his eyes, looking for an indication that he was joking, but there was none. 'I don't know what to say,' I said. And truly, I didn't. I thought he was crazy, especially the way he referred to the Tamagotchis as 'pets', like they were real pets, not just 30 pixels on an LCD screen with only a little more functionality than my alarm clock. 'Maybe there was something else wrong with yours. Luke's didn't die.'

The other dad shook his head and blew out, and then turned sideways to look at me, making a crease in his fat neck. 'You didn't bring it here, did you?' he said.

'Well, Luke takes it everywhere with him,' I said.

'Jesus,' he said, and then he literally ran across a game of

Twister that some of the kids were playing to grab his son's Tamagotchi and check that it was okay. He had an argument with his son as he detached it from the boy's belt loop, saying he was going to put it in the car for safety. They were making so much noise that the mother of the kid having the birthday came over to placate them. The dad leaned in close to her to whisper, and she looked at the ground while he spoke, then up at me, then at Luke.

And then she headed across the garden towards me.

'Hi there. We've not met before,' she said, offering her hand with a smile. 'I'm Lillian, Jake's mum.' We shook hands and I said that it was nice to meet her. The precision of her hair and the delicateness of her thin white cardigan made her seem fragile, but this was just a front. 'We're just about to play pass the parcel.'

'Oh right.'

'Yes, and I'm concerned about the other children catching...' She opened her mouth, showing that her teeth were clenched together, and she nodded, hoping that I understood, that she wouldn't need to suffer the embarrassment of spelling it out.

'It's just a toy,' I said.

'Still, I'd prefer...'

'You make it sound like...'

'If you wouldn't mind...'

I shook my head at the lunacy of the situation, but agreed to take care of it.

When I told Luke I had to take Meemoo away for a minute he went apeshit. He stamped and he made his hand into the shape of a claw and yelled, 'Sky badger!'

When Luke does sky badger, anyone in a two metre radius gets hurt. Sky badger is vicious. He rakes his long fingernails along forearms. He goes for the eyes.

'Okay okay,' I said, backing away and putting my hands up defensively. 'You can keep hold of Meemoo, but I'll have to take you home then.'

Luke screwed up his nose and frowned so deeply that I could barely see his dark eyes.

'You'll miss out on the birthday cake,' I added.

Luke relaxed his talons and handed Meemoo to me, making a growl as he did so. Meemoo was hot, and I wondered whether it was from Luke's sweaty hands or if the Tamagotchi had a fever.

I held Luke's hand and took him over to where the pass-the-parcel ring was being straightened out by some of the mums, stashing Meemoo out of sight in my pocket. I sat Luke down and explained to him what would happen and what he was expected to do. A skinny kid with two front teeth missing looked at me and Luke, wondering what our deal was.

When we got home, Gabby was pissed off. 'There's something wrong with the computer,' she said.

'Oh great,' I said. 'What were you doing when it broke?'

'I didn't do anything! I hate the way you always blame me!'

I showed her my palms, backing away. After the party, I didn't have the strength for an argument.

The computer was in the dining room and switched off. I made tea while it booted up and forked cold pesto penne into my mouth. After I'd tapped in my password, the computer got so far into its boot-up sequence, and then made a frightening buzz. The screen went black with a wordy error message that didn't stay up long enough for me to read it. With a final electronic pulse, and a wheeze as the cooling fan slowed, it died.

'That's what it keeps doing,' Gabby said.

'Were you on the internet when it happened?'

'For God's sake!' Gabby spat. 'It wasn't anything I did.'

In my frustration, I jabbed the forkful of penne into my lip, making a cut that by the following morning had turned into an ulcer.

I had to wait until Monday to check my e-mails at work. There was still nothing from the makers of Tamagotchi. At lunch, while I splashed bolognese sauce over my keyboard, I googled 'Tamagotchi' along with every synonym for 'virus'. I could find nothing other than the standard instructions to give it medicine when the skull and crossbones appeared.

Halfway through the afternoon, while I was in my penultimate meeting of the day, a tannoy announcement asked me to call reception. When a tannoy goes out, everyone knows it's an emergency, and because it was for me, everyone knew it was something to do with Luke. I stepped out of the meeting room and ran back to my desk, trying hard not to look at all the heads turning towards me.

Gabby was on hold. When reception put her through, she was crying. Luke had had one of his fits. A short one this time, just eight minutes, but since he'd come round, the right side of his body was paralysed. This happened the last time too, but it had got better after half an hour. I hated the thought that his fits were changing, that it seemed to be developing in some way. I told Gabby to stay calm and that I would leave right away.

When I got home, Luke's paralysis was over and he was moving normally again, except for a limpness at the edge of his mouth that made him slur his words. I hoped that this wrinkle would smooth out again soon, as it had last time.

I hugged Luke, burying my lips into his thick hair and kissing the side of his head, wishing that we lived in a world where kisses could fix brains. I stroked his back, and hoped that maybe I would find a little reset button there, sunk into a hole, something I could prod that would let us start over, that would wipe all the scribbles from the slate and leave it blank again.

Gabby was sitting on the edge of the armchair holding her stomach, like she was in pain.

'Are you okay?' I asked.

She wiped her nose with the back of her hand and nodded. Gabby's biggest fear was that Luke's problems weren't just part of her, but part of the factory that had made him – what if every kid we produced together had the same design fault?

The doctors had all said that the chances of it happening twice were tiny, but I don't think we'd ever be able to fully relax. I knew that long after our second kid was born, we'd both be looking out for the diagnostic signs that had seemed so innocuous at first with Luke.

This fit wasn't long enough to call out an ambulance, but because the paralysis was still new, our GP came round to the house to check Luke over. Luke hated the rubber hammer that the doc used to check his reflexes. The only way he would allow him to do it was if he could hit me with the hammer first.

'Daddy doesn't have reflexes in his head,' Gabby said as Luke whacked me.

'Not anymore I don't,' I laughed.

Luke has a firm swing. I wonder whether one day he'll be a golfer.

A letter came home from school banning Tamagotchis. I knew this was my fault. Another three kids' Tamagotchis had died and could not be resurrected.

'People are blanking me when I drop Luke off in the morning,' Gabby said. She was rubbing her fingers into her temples because she had a headache. It felt like everything in the house was breaking down.

'You're probably just being a bit sensitive,' I said.

'Don't you dare say it's my hormones.'

The situation had gone too far. Meemoo would have to

go.

I was surprised at how hard it was to tell Luke that he'd have to say goodbye to Meemoo. He was sitting on the edge of the sand pit jabbing a straw of grass into it, like a needle.

'No!' He barked at me, and made that deep frown-face of his. He gripped Meemoo hard and folded his arms across his chest.

'Help me out will you?' I asked Gabby when she came outside with her book.

'You can handle this for a change,' she said.

I tried bribing Luke, but he wouldn't fall for it, and just got angrier because I was denying him a biscuit now too. I tried lying to him, saying that I was going to take Meemoo to hospital to make him better, but I had already lost his trust. Eventually, I had only one option left. I told Luke that he had to tidy up his toys in the garden or I'd have to confiscate Meemoo for two whole days. I knew that Luke would never clean up his toys. The bit of his brain in charge of tidying up must have been within the damaged area. But I went through the drama of asking him a few times, and, as he got more irate, stamping and kicking things, I began to count.

'Don't count!' He said, knowing the finality of a countdown.

'Come on,' I said. 'You've got four seconds left. Just pick up your toys and you can keep Meemoo.'

If he'd actually picked up his toys then, it would have been such a miracle that I would have let him keep Meemoo, AIDS and all.

'Three... two...'

'Stop counting!' Luke screamed, and then the dreaded, 'Sky badger!'

Luke's fingers curled into that familiar and frightening shape and he came after me. I skipped away from him, tripping over a bucket.

'One and a half.... one... come on, you've only got half a second left.' A part of me must have been enjoying this, because I was giggling.

'Stop it,' Gabby said. 'You're being cruel.'

'He's got to learn,' I said. 'Come on Luke, you've only got a fraction of a second left. Start picking up your toys now and you can keep Meemoo.'

Luke roared and swung his sky badger at me, at my arms, at my face. I grabbed him round the waist and turned him so that his back was towards me. Sky badger sunk his claws into my knuckles while I wrestled Meemoo out of his other hand.

By the time I'd got Meemoo away, there were three crescent-shaped gouges out of my knuckles, and they were stinging like crazy.

'I HATE YOU!' Luke screamed, crying, and stormed inside, slamming the door behind him.

'You deserved that,' Gabby said, looking over the top of her sunglasses.

I couldn't just throw Meemoo away. Luke would never forgive me for that. It might be one of those formative moments that forever warped him and gave him all kinds of trust issues in later life. Instead, I planned to euthanize Meemoo.

If I locked Meemoo in a cupboard, taking away the things that were helping it survive: food, play, petting and the toilet, the AIDS would get stronger as it got weaker and surrounded by more of its own effluence. The AIDS would win. And when Meemoo was dead, it would either reset itself as a healthy Tamagotchi, or it would die. If it was healthy, Luke could have it back; if it died, then Luke would learn a valuable lesson about mortality and I would buy him a new one to cheer him up.

It was tempting while Meemoo was in the cupboard to sneak a peek, to watch for his final moments, but the Tamagotchi had sensors that picked up movement. It might interpret my attention as caring, and gain some extra power to resist the virus destroying him. No, I had to leave it alone, despite the temptation.

Meemoo's presence inside the cupboard seemed to transform its outward appearance. It went from being an ordinary medicine cabinet to being something else, something... other.

After two whole days, I could resist no longer. I was certain that Meemoo must have perished by now. I was so confident that I even let Luke come along when I went to the cupboard to retrieve it.

'Okay,' I said. 'So have you learned your lesson about tidying up?'

'Give it back,' Luke said, pouting.

'Good boy.' I patted him on the head, then opened the cupboard and took out the Tamagotchi.

Meemoo was alive.

It had now lost three of its limbs, having just one arm left, which was stretched out under its head. One of its eyes had closed up to a small unseeing dot. Its pixellated circumference was broken in places, wide open pores through which invisible things must surely be escaping and entering.

'This is ridiculous,' I said. 'Luke, I'm sorry. But we're going to have to throw him away.'

Luke snatched the Tamagotchi from me and ran to Gabby, screaming. He was actually shaking, his face red and sweaty.

'What have you done now?' Gabby scowled at me.

I held my forehead with both hands. I puffed out big lungfuls of air. My brain was itching inside my skull. 'I give up,' I said, and thumped up the stairs to the bedroom.

I tried to read, but I couldn't concentrate. I put on the TV and watched a cookery show, and there was something soothing in the way the chef was searing the tuna in the pan that let my heartbeats soften by degrees.

Gabby called me from downstairs. 'Can you come and get Luke in? Dinner's almost ready.'

I let my feet slip over the edge of each step, enjoying the pressure against the soles of my feet. I went outside in my socks. Luke was burying a football in the sandpit.

'Time to come in little man,' I said. 'Dinner's ready.'

'Come in Luke,' Gabby called through the open window, and at the sound of his mum's voice, Luke got up, brushed the sand from his jeans, and went inside, giving me a wide berth as he ran past.

A spot of rain hit the tip of my nose. The clouds above were low and heavy. The ragged kind that can take days to drain. As I turned to go inside, I noticed Meemoo on the edge of the sandpit. Luke had left it there. I started to reach down for it, but then stopped, stood up, and went inside, closing the door behind me.

After dinner, it was Gabby's turn to take Luke to bed. I made tea and leaned over the back of the sofa, resting my cup on the windowsill and inhaling the hot steam. Outside, the rain was pounding the grass, digging craters in the sandpit, and bouncing off of the Tamagotchi. I thought how ridiculous it was that I was feeling guilty, but out of some strange duty I continued to watch it, until the rain had washed all the light out of the sky.

Family Motel

Alison MacLeod

Route 6A was drenched in the green of high summer. Stands of oak and silver birch flickered past. Cat's-tails sprang from marshy ditches. As Dan accelerated out of a bend, a pair of wings, bright as blood, flashed across the windscreen. 'A cardinal!' said Mia, turning to the back. 'Felix, did you see the cardinal?'

He'd been looking in the wrong direction – and it didn't help that he didn't know what a cardinal was – but, propped high in his child's seat, he nodded and grinned for her.

Dan hunched forward in the driver's seat. The back of his T-shirt was marked by a line of sweat. She leaned across the seat and checked the needle on the gauge. It still wobbled too far to the right. 'Should we pull over?'

'We'll get there.' The joint of his jaw flexed.

Felix spotted a sign up ahead. 'Look! Pool! It says "Pool". But if you take the L off, it says poo!' Rosie started to wail in her baby-seat. Smoke or steam – Mia and Dan couldn't tell which – started to escape from the bonnet.

Felix covered his ears. 'Are we going to blow up?'

Dan swung into the wide drive, switched off the engine and slumped forward. Under the bonnet, the fans whirred like wind turbines.

'What does it say, Mum? On the grass. What does the sign say?'

'It says, "The Earl of Pembroke Family Motel. Refreshing Pool and Sundeck. Perfect relaxation morning, noon or night".'

'Yay!' he chimed, punching the air.

★

The motel was a sprawling one-storey building with a low sloping roof and a half-timbered facade. She glanced at the print-out: 'Constructed in the Olde English tradition, The Earl of Pembroke Motel features colourful garden beds and a tranquil duck pond.' She laughed at the Oldie Englishness, but the space at least was fantastic: wide lawns where the kids could run, picnic tables, a hammock, a barbeque pit, a wood-burning stove and, at the edge of the property, as advertised, a vast duck pond.

'But *where's* the pool?' Felix turned 360 degrees.

'We'll ask.'

After the dazzle of the late-afternoon light, the office was dark, cool. It smelled, oddly, of creosote. She could just see a check-in desk at chest height, the shape of a lamp, and a small window covered by a Venetian blind. The slats of the blind were shut.

'Yes?' A man's voice. Out of nowhere, it seemed. At the desk, Felix circled her leg with his arm.

'We have a reservation for three nights. The Hamlyns. Two adults, one child, one toddler. I phoned last week from England.'

'You wanted a playpen.' Their host reached across the registration book and pulled on the cord of the blind, opening it slowly.

'A crib or a playpen. Either's fine. Thanks.' The poor lighting wasn't helped by the fake wood-panelling and the clutter on the walls. Reproduction brass and copper lanterns gleamed dully.

'You'll need to sign.'

'Of course.'

'And you'll need to leave your passports.'

'Ah.'

'Law in the state of Massachusetts.' He passed her two keys on a ring. 'Room 6. I'll charge your card for the full tariff now.'

She looked up. 'Not when we leave?' But it was easy to imagine he'd had trouble over the years; smiling guests who'd done runners on check-out day.

'I'll bring your receipt to your room.'

'Where's the pool?' croaked Felix, inches below the desk.

He addressed a point beyond Mia's shoulder. 'In the wooden enclosure beyond Room 23. Sign here, please.' He switched on the anglepoise lamp, flipped open the registration book and pointed, with a blunt-tipped finger.

Mia took the pen, a ballpoint quill. She could see him better now: a man in his mid-fifties, not tall but broad; tense in his bearing. He had a crop of frizzy hair, iron-grey with touches of black – the kind of hair that doesn't move in a breeze. His face was tanned, clean-shaven, ordinary. Even so, Mia found it unnervingly neutral in its expression. His features – small grey eyes, grey eyelashes, thin lips, an almost delicate nose – seemed to disappear in the broad planes of his cheeks and forehead.

'We haven't been here in years,' Mia tried. 'Not since before the children were born. My husband and I love the Cape.'

As if suddenly required, a woman – the owner's wife, Mia presumed – appeared from the living quarters behind the office, where the light of a TV flickered. She looked tired, washed-out, in an oversized white blouse and faded cotton trousers. A tiny enamelled American flag was pinned to her collar. She smiled weakly at Mia and pushed a strand of brown hair out of her eyes. 'That's nice,' she offered, 'that you could come back.' She looked at the cleaning rag in her hand.

'Sadly, we're here for a funeral this time. On Saturday. My aunt's. She moved to the Cape from England in her twenties.'

Mia waited for a standard response: 'Well, we hope you enjoy your stay in spite of the sad circumstances,' or even, that peculiarly American form of sympathy, 'We're sorry for your loss.' But the owner simply closed the registration book, straightened the pen on the desk and switched off the lamp. He was like a man in a neck brace, minus the neck brace, and Mia felt a cold charge of resentment explode somewhere within her.

His wife forced another smile. Her teeth were yellowy, almost see-through, their enamel worn down. 'A take-out breakfast is available in the reception annex from 8 till 11.' Then she turned to polish a copper lantern.

Outside, Felix shook his arms and head, as if a current had passed through him. 'Was that The *Earl*?'

She grinned, ruffling his hair. 'You said it, bunny rabbit. That was The Earl.'

★

Dan was the first to find the words. 'Well, well, well.'

She warned him with her eyes not to laugh.

They were standing in the middle of a room into which was crammed two large four-posters, a nightstand, a playpen, a primitive air conditioner, two red leatherette armchairs, a desk and chair, a bar fridge, a bulky TV and two luggage rests.

'Spider-webs!' announced Felix, pointing to the crocheted canopies above the beds. Dust traps, thought Mia. On the wall by the apparently leaded window, a framed poster from *Shakespeare in Love* was in need of straightening. The window itself was covered by heavy burgundy curtains that matched the bedspreads.

Felix wrinkled his nose. 'It smells in here.'

Mia shifted Rosie to her other hip. 'It's just a little musty.' She switched off the air-conditioner and cranked open the window. But the curtains were on rigid hooks that wouldn't move more than a couple of inches along the rail. Dan dropped the two cases he was carrying. 'Not on the floor,' she said. 'The luggage-rests.' Bedbugs. She'd heard it was an excellent year for bedbugs.

Felix was unzipping his Thomas the Tank Engine suitcase and pulling out his trunks and towel. Dan bumped through the room with the last of the luggage. 'Good idea, squire.'

Felix tipped his head from side to side, baring his baby teeth. 'Perfect relaxation morning, noon or night. Perfect relaxation morning, noon or night. Perfect—'

'Okay, Felix.' Dan threw him his arm-bands. 'Thanks. We got it the first time.'

'Do me a favour?' she murmured. 'Pull the key out of his back,' and Dan smiled, the strains of the day draining from his face. Then he reached for his towel and snapped it across her bum. 'Last one in is a—'

'DEAD MAN!' roared Felix.

They looked at each other and rolled their eyes. Felix giggled.

★

He and Dan went on ahead with the sunscreen. Mia located Rosie's swimming cozzie and sun-hat, changed Rosie, then herself, mislaid her sunglasses, found them, forgot the key, then slipped it into the pocket of her camp-skirt. They'd get their swim. Then – the SUV being in the state it was – they'd order a take-away for supper. Later, with any luck, she and Dan would sit out under the stars with the duty-free and two Dixie paper-cups from the bathroom dispenser.

As she locked the door behind her, the golden light of early evening, the lush green lawns and the gaudy cheer of the azaleas dispelled the gloom of the room. Rosie tugged at her hair, twisting it impishly in her fingers. 'Hello, sweetness.

Are we going for a swim? Yes, we are!' and she bounced her in her arms.

An elderly couple, both in powder-blue shorts and white cotton T-shirts, smiled broadly as they passed in the car park. 'Can you wave, Rosie? Wave…' Mia held up her hand for her. 'Bye-Bye.'

'Bye-Bye!' sang the pair, their dentures gleaming.

The owner was out walking too, still wearing his invisible neck brace. From a distance, she watched him approach, his stride measured as he surveyed his earldom. He was something, she thought. While he gave the impression of looking into the middle distance, he was in fact sneaking sidelong glances at the cars in his car park; at the doors that opened and closed; at the extended family group that laughed by the barbeque pit. He wore a tan-coloured polo shirt buttoned up to his neck; khaki-coloured shorts, belted and crisply pressed; and brown sandals. Beside him, a lean black Doberman trotted without a lead.

She hoisted Rosie higher, nodding hello as they passed. He blinked in reply.

★

She could hear Felix – 'Watch me, Dad! Watch me!' – long before she saw him. The pool was surrounded on three sides by high pickets; the other side was bordered by a chain-link fence. A scattering of pink, white and purple sweat peas climbed up its iron links. She pressed Rosie's nose to a blossom while, on the other side, Felix surfaced in the shallow end, spluttering. 'Mum! Mum, watch me jump again!'

But Dan surprised him from the rear, scooping him up in his arms and hurling him into the air. Her son was a flash of orange arm-bands before he tumbled into the depths and bobbed up, grinning fiercely.

A plastic sign was nailed to the door of the enclosure. 'Open 6 a.m. to 10 p.m. No unaccompanied children below the age of 16.' The latch was high up, level with her eyes. Child-proof.

Inside, Felix thumped across the sundeck, streaming with water. His cheeks glowed. 'Mum, mum! I can hold my head under water for eighty-six seconds! I just counted!'

She loved the sight of his little breasts that shook as he ran. In another year or less, all his baby fat would be gone. 'You star! I'm really proud of you.'

'But I don't want to wear my arm bands any more.'

She peered out from under the brim of her hat. 'Too bad, so sad.'

'Are you coming in now?'

'In a minute.'

'I want you to pull me like you're my horse. Just you and me.'

'But sweetheart, Rosie wants to come in too.'

'Leave her on a chair.'

'No, Felix. Rosie is allowed to have fun too.'

'She can watch us *threeeee*,' he sang. He held his palms out for effect, as if he'd offered the obvious solution.

'Rosie and I will have a dip in the shallow end. Then Daddy will take Rosie, and I'll be your horse.' She was relieved they had the pool to themselves.

'Come on, Felix,' his father called. 'Show me how you do the Dog.'

But his face was clouding over. He kicked a stray pebble into the pool. 'Dad, pick up Mum. Pick up Mum and throw her in the water!'

★

She saw it right away. A white credit card slip on top of the desk.

'He was in our room.'

Dan looked up from the bag of wet towels. 'Who was?'

'The bloke.'

'The Earl?' asked Felix, his eyes wide.

She looked at Dan and nodded, sucking in her upper lip.

'Didn't he say he'd bring it to the room?'

'Yes, but I assumed he meant when we were in it. He knew we were at the pool. I passed him with Rosie on our way over.'

'Does it matter?'

'*Yes*. He has no right to walk into our room just because he has keys.' She looked beneath a curtain. 'He closed the window and turned on the air-conditioner again.'

'And what an air conditioner it is. The air it throws out must be twenty years old.'

'But Dan!' Her head felt tight; her eyes heavy. Now that they were back indoors, her damp swimsuit was cold. 'He can't come into our room and close our window just because he thinks the air conditioning should be on. Who knows what else he feels free to investigate?' She slumped on the bed. Felix stared at her over the Spiderman colouring book he'd pulled from his case.

'I'll have a word.' Dan kissed the top of the bridge of her nose. 'I'll take our passports over now and I'll have a word.'

★

The grass was cool between her toes. The air was balmy. And in the room behind them, the children were sleeping at last. She ran a finger across Dan's forearm, enjoying the solid construction of bone, muscle and tendon.

He slapped a mosquito on his ankle. 'I told his wife. She said she would pass on the message.'

'And you believed her?' But the whiskey was loosening her thoughts. She wanted to forget The Earl and Mrs Earl.

Dan stretched out in the canvas beach-chair and looked up. Overhead, the stars teemed. 'Do you know what the sky reminds me of tonight, out here?'

She tipped her head back, letting the whiskey burn her throat.

'That night years ago when we slept on the dunes, at the end of the boardwalk on – what's it called? – Town Neck Beach?'

She turned an ear to the open window behind them and listened for a whimper from Rosie, or a burst of sleep-talk from Felix. But all was quiet. 'Aunt Patricia was telling me the dunes lose a few feet every year.'

'That year, thanks in part to us.'

'We didn't know any better.'

'The fence was a bit of a clue.'

Her voice dropped to a whisper. 'I can't believe she's gone.'

Somewhere beyond the 6A, a train moaned in the night. She loved the trains in the States; the way they mouthed their loneliness to the land. But now, now the whistling cry seemed to cut through her head, through her chest, whittling her down.

He reached for her fingers. 'Seventy-nine ain't bad.'

'She wasn't ready. She might have been seventy-nine, but until three months ago, death seemed as impossible to her as it does to us right now.'

He nodded. 'I know.'

'I always assumed that, when a person lived their full span, death brought some kind of natural closure; that it was like… like a frame around a picture. You might not see it during the illness and through the chaos of hospitals and sickbeds, but I always thought the frame would be there, after.'

He squeezed her hand. 'She did well. All those talents. Her photography and the garden and her writing. God help the first dead person who tries to sell her on the idea of eternal rest.'

She swirled the whiskey in her paper cup. 'She was so down, at the end. When I phoned her each day at the hospice, she couldn't get her son out of her head. She'd never spoken of him to me in all my thirty-eight years, and suddenly she was telling me his name – Christopher – and his birthday, August the 5th, and how she'd tried to find him last year but there'd been no paper trail to follow.'

'I thought you said she'd had him adopted.'

'She did, but she's convinced the doctor who supervised the orphanage in Lexington simply took him on as his own son; that a doctor had that sort of authority in small towns in those days. He and his wife couldn't have children, and they liked Aunt Patricia. They got on. She even wondered afterwards if they were vetting her.'

'I suppose it's possible.'

'She told me she managed to track down the doctor's contact details a year ago; that she got up the nerve, phoned his house on August 5th and spoke to a man, the doctor's son apparently, who sounded as if he were in his mid-forties. The right age. She was sure she was talking to Christopher. Can you imagine what that must have been like? Talking to Felix on his birthday after a lifetime apart. But of course, what could she say?' Mia felt her tears coming. 'I mean, I know I panicked when I was pregnant with Felix – I know I was sick at the thought that I'd never sculpt properly again – and I know it took much longer for me to–'

'Sssh, Mia. Don't do this again.'

'But now, I couldn't imagine. Dan, I just couldn't imagine what it would be like, *having* to give him up in hospital. And you know, at the time – I never actually said this to you before – I wanted to.' She searched for the whites of his eyes in the darkness. 'Or a part of me did. I wanted to turn time back. I didn't want there to be a Felix. I actually felt dead when I looked at him the first time.' She blinked back the tears. 'I did, Dan. I swear I did.'

He drained his cup and stared into the night. 'You were post-natal. You were in a bad way.'

'If I'd been on my own, and if someone had assured me

it really was all for the best, I would have been relieved in that first fortnight to give him away. But there's Aunt Patricia, who had no one and no choice in the matter, and she's still pining for her baby boy every morning when she wakes up, even forty-five years later.'

'Look.' He pointed skyward. A star streaked above the treeline, its tail a surge of radiance.

She stared at the point where it burned itself out. 'And even though her talents could only ever be hobbies, and even though there wasn't a man who stayed, and even though she'd lost her son, she was still so... so...'

'Alive.'

'*Yes.*' She curled her feet beneath her in the chair. 'We're lucky.' She trembled and pulled her jacket over her knees. '*I'm* lucky.'

★

When she opened her eyes to the smothering night, her spine was rigid. Her pulse boomed between her ears. She was sticky with cold sweat. She tried to calm herself, to talk her heart off the ledge of panic.

The room was airless, that was all. Dan snored lightly beside her; Felix breathed, fast and shallow, in the next bed.

But her heart still thudded in her chest. A palpitation snaked in her leg. She'd never known a room so dark. No streetlight edged through the curtains. No haze of moonlight softened the darkness. It seemed palpable; a substance, not an absence, and slick as tar. Her chest, her lungs, were full of it.

She clambered to her feet and groped the distance to the playpen. Rosie lay half on her stomach, half propped up on her knees, her white nappied bottom a small, dear beacon in the darkness.

She crept to the door, eased it open, then pulled on the screen door, desperate for it not to creak, and slipped outside. In the car park, next to their broken-down car, she gulped the night air until her heart stopped banging.

The whiskey, she thought. It was only the whiskey.

★

They slept late. No morning light spilled into the room to wake them. Dan got the kids dressed and out. When she emerged at last in her kimono, they were seated at a picnic table on the front lawn feasting on yogurts, muffins and slices of bright watermelon.

Felix sat at the table, holding a wide arc of green rind to his mouth. 'Look, Dad! I'm happy. See? I'm happy.'

Dan rubbed her thigh as she sat down beside him. 'I phoned. The local garage is sending the break-down truck.'

She flashed him a covert smile and leaned toward his ear. 'Thank fuck for that.'

'Mum!' piped up Felix. 'I'm happy. See?'

'I'm glad, sweetheart.' She reached for a pulpy red slice, took Rosie from Dan's lap and nuzzled her neck. 'Did The Earl let you use the phone?'

'Mrs Earl did.'

'Ah.' She didn't know why she wanted to know. Then, 'Come on,' she said to Felix. 'Let's go feed those ducks while Dad waits for the man from the garage.' She turned. The Earl and his dog were striding past, on patrol again. His eyes darted their way.

She got to her feet and suddenly noticed Felix, suspended in mid-motion: his eyes were trained on The Earl's receding back; his mouth was a watermelon-frown. And as she wrapped two muffins in napkins, she took a small, ludicrous comfort in the knowledge that Felix hated The Earl too, for her.

★

At the far edge of the lawns, the pond glimmered. Three

ducks floated among the bright green algae, as still as decoys. A family of fat-bottomed geese waddled by on the muddy bank.

'They walk like Rosie in her nappy!' Felix declared, pleased by his powers of observation.

She lowered Rosie to the ground. The fence was as tall as Felix, but there were gaps, covered in chicken wire, between the wooden posts, where children could see through. On the opposite bank a bird-house squatted, the size of a garden shed. A path of duckboards ran from its door through the mud down to the water's edge.

'Here, Felix, throw them this bit of muffin. Throw it far.'

He drew his arm back and cast the cakey piece over the fence. It sailed high, then dropped down on the other side, only inches away. The geese padded over quickly, their orange beaks scissoring the air. Felix laughed, hugging his tummy. Rosie turned her face up and grinned, gap-toothed, at Mia.

'Watch me, Mum!' Felix flung the next piece into the middle of the gaggle. 'Bull's eye!'

The geese honked, and Mia turned at the rumbling of tires in the drive behind. The recovery-truck was pulling up behind their rental car. She lifted Rosie onto her shoulders and reached into her pocket for the other muffin. 'Here, Felix. You can feed the geese this one. I have to get dressed now and help Dad with the car.'

He nodded without looking up. 'Goosey goosey gander,' he sang to the geese, 'where do you wander?'

He hadn't learned the rest, as she recalled. His interest had always stopped at the lady's chamber.

★

The bloke from the garage was down on his hands and knees. 'See that?'

Dan got down and peered beneath the car. 'See what?'

'No water on the ground. I just poured in half a gallon, but I'm not seeing so much as a slow leak from the rad.'

The dentured couple, now sporting matching yellow shorts, walked by and waved. Mia and Rosie waved back.

'So there's no quick-fix, I'm afraid.' The garage man – Buck, according to his badge – wiped his hands on his overalls. 'I'll have to tow her to Friendly's.'

'The rental company will collect it. They're delivering our replacement tomorrow. It just leaves us rather stranded today.'

She shrugged. 'So no beach.'

Dan smiled apologetically. 'No beach.'

'I guess I could walk to that café back up the 6A and get food for the fridge.'

He brushed an eyelash from her cheek. 'I'll go.'

Felix came running, as the SUV was hooked and clamped. 'Where's our car going?'

'To the garage, squire. We'll get a new one tomorrow.'

'But you said we could play mini-golf.'

'If you're good for your mum while I'm out, we *might* spend the afternoon at the pool again.'

'Yay!' shouted Felix, punching the air. 'I want to go to the pool again. Definitely. Except first, I have to tell Mum something.' He crooked his finger.

She looked at Dan, a smile playing on her lips. Then she bent down.

'Guess what?' he whispered in her ear.

'What?'

He motioned her over to a picnic table. 'Go away, Rosie! Mum, Rosie can't listen.'

'Felix, calm down. She doesn't know what you're saying.'

'The Earl talked to me.'

She sat down on the bench. 'Where?'

'When I was feeding the geese. He sounded very cross.'

'What did he say?'

'He said' – Felix made his voice deep – '"Don't put your face so close to the fence or…"'

'Or what?'

'"Or the geese will PECK out your eyes!"'

'Felix, is that really what he said?'

He nodded slowly. 'Really. He scared me.'

'Well, he shouldn't have been cross and he shouldn't have scared you. But were you pressing your face to the chicken wire?'

'I can't remember. Do you know what else?' His hands waggled. 'I saw something.'

'What, Felix? Come on. Dad's waiting for us.'

'I saw The Earl has no eyes.'

'Felix.'

'The geese must have pecked them out.'

'Now you're being silly.'

He turned his palms out. 'Mum, I *saw* them. They're not alive eyes. And they don't have a real colour. Glass eyes are no-colour, and they make them in the same factories where they make marbles.'

She nodded, pretending to weigh up the information. 'Well I didn't know that.'

'I know. But now you do.'

★

She woke again that night, twisted in the sheet. She had a vague sense that she'd cried out – a warning or a threat – in her sleep. If she had, no one else had woken. She reached for Dan, for any bit of him that would orient her in the dark expanse of the bed. She needed water.

The flooring was cold beneath her feet, as cold as if it had been laid directly onto damp earth. She checked Felix, then Rosie, in their beds. Without turning on the bathroom light, she filled a paper cup. Then she slipped on her flip-flops, slid through the doors, and nearly cried at the relief of fresh

151

air.

The night was starlit. Not a breath of a breeze moved in the trees. To the east, the sky was beginning to glow wanly. A few lonely birds called. She guessed it had to be four, maybe five, in the morning. She pulled her kimono close. A short stroll and she'd feel better.

She turned left, starting off down the long drive towards the road, but a sudden image of The Earl and his wife, asleep in separate beds, their arms folded stiffly across their chests, made her turn back. She'd go the other way, as far as the pool.

On the front lawn, the rows of empty picnic tables looked strange, expectant, in the night. The hammock sagged between the two sumac trees. The stink of a skunk caught in her throat. As she passed a blue Chrysler in the car park, she smiled at its glow-in-the-dark bumper sticker. 'Make LOVE to Your Lawn. Trust Dave Vernon & Co For All Your Lawn Care Needs.' Outside Room 16, four shiny bikes stood propped against the wall – new arrivals, she guessed – while in Room 23, the last room in the strip, the blue light of a TV seeped through the curtains.

She raised her chin and closed her eyes to catch a scent. Sweet peas.

Suddenly she was sitting again with her aunt in her conservatory. She was admiring the profusion of sweet peas Patricia had cut for the table, and her aunt was saying, 'Here. Take them. Take them with you to the airport. You won't be so sad about leaving.' And she shuddered again at the thought of life with a Felix-shaped hole.

She squinted into the distance. There was something… She wasn't imagining it. A light was coming from the pool. Not the floodlight that shone until 10 p.m. A yellow glow.

At the corner of the chain-link fence, she stopped short. The Earl's dog was trotting restlessly back and forth along the pool's sundeck. Three brass lanterns shone at equal intervals along the edge of the deep end. For a moment, in the lantern-light, the pool looked like a deep, dark hole.

Then she saw him.

'Jesus.'

At the nearest edge, almost bumping the wall, The Earl floated lifelessly, his broad muscled back slack and white in the water; his face, immersed; his arms and legs, dangling from his torso.

Jesus Jesus Jesus.

She started to run – the door was propped open with a bucket – she'd have to haul him over to the stairs in the shallow end – and yell till someone, anyone, came. Could she still remember how to give the kiss of life? Then she was at Reception again, telling him about Aunt Patricia; he was looking away, closing the registration book and straightening his pen on the desk as a cold surge of emotion mainlined to her core. Her heart juddered, and she was running, running for the door to the pool – *oh God* – when she heard a loud splash. She pivoted on her heels and pressed her face to the fence.

The Earl had come to life. In one smooth motion, he'd flipped himself over onto his back and had pushed off from the side. He floated, spread-eagled and inert, at the centre of the pool.

★

The morning was humid again – eighty degrees by nine o'clock. The replacement car didn't arrive by ten, as promised. After the third call, Dan started shouting down the phone. 'Look, does a family funeral mean nothing to you people?'

The chamber-maid, a girl of about seventeen, knocked on the door. Dan asked if she would come back later. 'Better still, just give us a miss today. Our towels are fine.' The service started at one. It was nearly noon. Mia pulled her black skirt from her case, but her black ruffled blouse was nowhere. She ran the motel iron over Dan's trousers, noticing only too late the ugly yellow residue it spat over the pockets. 'You'll just have to keep your jacket closed all afternoon.'

'In this heat?'

She gave Rosie her bottle and asked Dan to take the kids outside so she could get their clothes together: Rosie's blue silk dress from Monsoon, Felix's jacket, shirt, belt and long shorts. But in a few minutes, he was back with their daughter in his arms. His jaw looked tight; his mouth was flat-lining. 'She dropped her bottle. It smashed in the car park.'

She sucked in her lip and continued to search for Felix's good shoes. Dan disappeared outside to ask the chamber-maid for a dustpan and brush. Car doors slammed in the car park. Felix came running in, shirtless, bare-footed and breathless. 'Mum, mum! Our car's here!'

She ran outside, holding one of the sought-after shoes. A canary-yellow saloon car waited by Reception. Perfect for a funeral cortege to a cemetery.

What next?

Dan signed the paperwork, then brushed past her, his head bowed, his thoughts in lock-down mode. He returned swinging a car-seat from either arm, and started strapping them into place.

'Damn it!'

'What?'

'Felix's won't lock on.'

She couldn't bear to know any more. 'I'll get Rosie dressed.'

Felix trailed after her. 'Mum, mum, I don't want to stay at The Earl's by myself!'

Her head started to throb. 'Felix, don't be silly. When have we ever left you somewhere by yourself? You're coming to Aunt Patricia's funeral.'

He punched the air. 'Yay!' But still, he trotted behind her, his tiny breasts shaking. 'Will the police arrest me if I'm not in my seat?'

'No,' she said, 'they will arrest Daddy.'

He started to howl.

'Felix! I was only–'

She turned. His eyes streamed. He was clutching his foot.

'Move your hand, sweetheart.'

Blood gushed from the sole.

His face was turning purply-red with the pain.

She scooped him up in her arms and started to run for the room. 'It's okay, bunny rabbit. Mummy's got you. It's okay.'

Glass from Rosie's bottle. Why hadn't she or Dan told him to put his shoes on?

'Oh, my poor love. Sssh now. Sssh... Mummy's here.' She was stumbling toward their room, struggling to carry him as he writhed.

'Mia!' Dan caught them up, put Rosie down and took Felix in his arms. 'Run to the office and get their First Aid kit.'

Felix screamed louder.

'What about Rosie?'

'Into the playpen.'

She looked into her son's swollen face and, for a breathless moment, was almost knocked back by its red-eyed fury. At moments like this, when he raged, the dread always came back: he knows, he remembers. *Somehow* he knows.

She sprinted, her blood-smeared kimono flapping behind her. At the reception desk, she shouted into the room behind. 'Hello...? Hello!' She would have pounded the bell on the desk if there'd been one.

The Earl appeared, his face wearing its trademark mask of neutrality. He laid his hands firmly on the desk. It was hard to believe that this was the same body she'd seen, slack and heavy, in the pool only hours ago. 'It's my son,' she breathed. 'He stepped on a piece of glass. He's bleeding quite badly. Do you have a First Aid kit?'

The Earl nodded, almost imperceptibly, and walked back into his living quarters.

She waited. She paced. Minutes passed. 'Hello!' she tried, bitterness getting the better of her voice. Had she been waiting here for a quarter of an hour or did it only feel that long? What if Felix needed stitches?

The Earl's wife appeared at the desk. The rims of her eyes were red. 'Here now,' she started. 'You're welcome to these.' She laid a small half-empty bottle of antiseptic on the desk, along with sterile wipes and two large plasters.

'Thanks.' Mia grabbed the meagre offerings and flew out the door.

★

In their room, Felix was curled, foetally, on his bed. In the absence of drugs, Dan had switched on the telly.

'Look, squire! Here's Mum.' But Felix only blinked at the television set. Dan turned to her, lowering his voice. 'Where *were* you?'

'They took forever to find this much.' She showed him the supplies.

'It's okay. I managed to get the glass out with the tweezers from your make-up bag. I sterilised them in whiskey. It was a big piece, but the bleeding's stopped.'

'Thank God.'

'He was very good. I told him how sorry I was about missing that piece of glass.'

She glanced at her son's pale face. 'You and Daddy make a good team, don't you, Felix?'

On the pillows, he nodded, without looking at her.

'You were very brave. I'm proud of you, bunny rabbit.'

Dan murmured in her ear. 'It's twenty to one.'

'Right.' She sucked in her lip. 'Let Mummy look at that poor old foot.'

Without taking his eyes away from Scooby Doo, Felix

stuck his leg in the air and rotated his ankle to display his wound. He was feeling better.

'Now, sweetheart. Do you want to stay here with Dad while Rosie and I go to Aunt Patricia's funeral? Or do you want to come with us too?' She could hear herself, subtly manipulating her wounded child, and she cringed inwardly.

Felix turned and grimaced at Rosie in her playpen. 'I'm going too.'

'Hooray! Mummy will put a plaster on your foot and get you dressed. Then we'll drive there in our new car.'

Dan muttered under his breath: 'Minus a car-seat.'

She looked at him and shrugged.

'You can sit on my lap just this once, okay, Felix? I, for one, would love a cuddle.'

'Yay,' he muttered. But he did not turn to her with his just-for-her smile. His small fist did not punch the air.

★

They arrived back late, after ten, each bearing a sleeping child. She held the screen door while Dan fumbled with the key. Inside, he smacked the switch for the overhead light.

She stopped, her back tensing. 'He was here again.'

He scanned the room. 'Who was? Oh God. Don't do this now, Mia. It's been a hell of a long day.' He lowered Felix onto his bed and started gently pulling off his clothes.

She paced from the door to the window, from the window to the bathroom, checking their things. 'I left the desk lamp on deliberately, Dan. I hate coming back into this room in the dark. And I left the window open a crack. He's closed it again.'

'So he's a control freak. It's not as if he's taken anything.'

She lay Rosie in the playpen and arranged her pillow and stuffed toys. 'It's *our* space, Dan. Who knows what he does when he's in here?'

'From what I understand, he turns off lamps and closes windows.' He struggled out of his jacket and tie.

'Or, he watches to see when people drive off, then rummages in their rooms.'

'I need to sleep, Mia. We're out of here first thing tomorrow anyway.' He cranked open the window. 'I'll leave the main door open tonight. Maybe we'll get a bit of a cross-breeze and you'll get a better kip.'

★

She'd forgotten to take off her watch before falling into bed. Twenty past five, it said. But no panic this time. No slamming of her heart in her chest. No cold sweat. Just restlessness. She couldn't wait to pack and be gone.

Dan was snoring lightly. Rosie gurgled in her sleep. She turned her head to listen for Felix's soft breathing.

She propped her head on her elbow and listened again.

She opened her eyes and studied the darkness for the glimmer of his face and hair. Then she was throwing back the covers and springing from bed.

Her hands groped his sheets.

'Dan. Get up!'

She turned, knocking over Felix's cup on the nightstand.

Dan's hand fumbled for the clock by their bed in London.

'Felix isn't in his bed!'

He rolled out from below the sheet before he could make sense of what she was saying. She flung back the curtains, half tearing them from the rail. Rosie started to whimper.

'What time is it?' He was zipping up his jeans.

'Twenty past five.' She pulled on a tank-top, her camp skirt and flip-flops. 'You left the main door open. There's no lock on the screen door.' She couldn't believe she was saying it, blaming him.

He was pulling on his trainers. 'I'll take Rosie and go right, towards the main road. You go left.'

She nodded and they ran into the morning.

★

She checked between parked cars and beneath picnic tables. She ran to the hammock. She called over the duck-pond fence, waking the geese. 'Felix! Felix!' She stared hard at the surface.

Something pale drifted near the far edge.

In the half light of day, she saw his forehead, smeared with green.

Oh God, oh God. She was over the fence and sliding down the bank before she realised.

It was a pale piece of wood. A half-submerged duckboard that had slid from the path. She bent double and was sick into the pond.

Then she clambered back over the fence and ran on, clenching her armpits. It felt as if the sobs she was forcing down would split her chest in two. 'Felix!'

At Room 17, a middle-aged couple appeared outside their door. 'Is anything the matter?' The woman's eyes were huge, kind.

'It's my son,' she started. The tears were coming. 'We can't find him.'

'We'll pull on our shoes,' said the man. 'What's his name?'

'Felix,' she mumbled through her sobs. 'It's Felix. Could you try the back lawn?'

She jogged past the barbecue pit, across flowerbeds, searching. Only the pool lay up ahead – she could see it now – mercifully fenced in. He *had* to have gone the other way, toward the road. The 6A. What was the speed limit? Sixty? Seventy?

'FELIX!'

Maybe Dan had him by now. Maybe in a few minutes she'd hear him calling: 'Mum! We're over here! You'll never guess what I did!'

She could hear the couple from Room 17 behind the motel. 'Felix...! Felix...!'

Lights were appearing behind closed curtains. If Dan didn't re-appear with him within minutes, she'd be on the phone to the police. She'd demand police dogs, a man-hunt. She'd show them hysterical.

She stopped. Up ahead, the door of the pool's enclosure was propped open with a cleaning trolley.

She slipped off her flip-flops and lurched into a run.

★

'Oh, my lovely boy,' she whispered hoarsely.

He was so still. So incredibly still.

He crouched at the edge of the sundeck.

'Felix, sweetheart?' she softly called. 'Daddy and I were so worried. We didn't know where you were.'

He was inches above the deep end.

'We woke up and thought, where's our Felix? Mummy was so sad.' She edged her way along the length of the sundeck.

He stretched his right arm above the water's surface, and uncurled his palm.

'But the only thing that matters now is that you're here and safe.'

She was close, almost close enough to touch him.

He shifted on the balls of his feet, then stretched his arm out further, so his weight rested only on his toes. Balance had never come easily to him. At home, on his bike, he found it hard not to wobble, even with the stabilisers.

'Felix?' She bent down over him.

His eyes were open but he was far away. He was lisping,

almost inaudibly. 'Goosey goosey gander where do you wander goosey goosey gander where do you...'

'Felix, love, can you hear me?'

He was feeding geese only he could see. His face was pressed to invisible chicken wire.

She reached for the hand that rested, limp, at his side and wrapped it in hers. 'It's Mummy, bunny rabbit. Mummy.' Then she hauled him into her arms.

★

As she bore Felix away, the Earl passed, laden with a mop and a hose on a reel. She stared, her eyes molten, but only the Doberman paused to observe them, its ears sharp and its nostrils flaring.

Dan came running, with Rosie pressed, pale-cheeked and tearful, to his chest.

'I've got him,' she breathed. 'It's okay. I've got him.' In the room, she collapsed on the bed under his weight.

They got him under the covers, then sat hunched, watching him sleep. Dan pressed his thumbs to his eyes. 'Maybe it was the funeral. The coffin being lowered...'

She could hardly speak. 'It's my fault.' She pulled the sheet over Felix's ankle. 'When I ran off to get the First Aid kit, I should have explained.'

'Explained what?'

'He was in my arms, and I was saying "Mummy's here". Then I was gone. I was running away. And afterwards, I knew he was upset about it, but I just papered over the cracks because we had to get to the funeral.'

'No. He was upset because he's never hurt himself that badly.'

'But what could he see? The back of me, leaving him.'

'Mia, if this is still about— You have to let it—'

'And when I found him just now, he was muttering about the geese.' She turned to her husband and winced.

161

'Yesterday, The Earl ticked him off over by the duck pond. He warned him not to go too close; Felix says he told him the geese would peck out his eyes. I didn't know if he was making it up or not. Maybe he was – to please me.'

'To please you? To please you how?'

She shook her head, cancelling the thought. 'Something did scare him, Dan, something that bloke did or said. Felix said his eyes weren't alive.'

'He's six, Mia.'

'I should have told you yesterday.'

'Why didn't you?'

'Because I thought you'd think I was making something of nothing. You know – over-egging The Earl. But it's my fault. I shouldn't have left Felix alone at the duck pond. I should have been with him.' She pushed her hand up his T-shirt and rubbed his lower back. 'I'm sorry.'

'You didn't let him down.' He reached behind and pressed his hand to hers. 'You have never let him down.'

★

She was at the office door as they opened for business. Dan waited in the car with Rosie. Felix had announced that he wanted to go to the office too. He wanted to see The Earl's glass eyes one more time. Mia breathed easier. He'd woken an hour before and bounded into their bed, himself again.

But it was Mrs Earl who looked up from the desk as he and Mia walked in. Felix sighed and kicked the floor softly. The Venetian blind was half open. He walked over to the window sill and made faces in the shiny lanterns on display.

'We're on our way,' she said, avoiding the woman's eyes. 'I'm just popping in for our passports.' She couldn't bear to speak of that morning. She had to believe what Dan had said. It was all just a horrible, sickening fluke.

Mrs Earl disappeared and returned with three passports.

Mia opened them. 'There should be four. The name on the other one is Felix Hamlyn.'

Mrs Earl crinkled her forehead and disappeared again.

Mia drummed her fingers. Outside, she heard Dan switch off the engine. Felix was trying to raise the blind.

When the woman re-appeared The Earl was behind her. He laid the missing passport on the desk. Felix turned to stare.

'I'm afraid it was in with Room 12's,' explained Mrs Earl. 'Sorry about that.' Her smile flickered. 'Safe journey.'

Mia watched her son. He didn't go shy this time. He didn't blink. He held The Earl's bland gaze, as if something was passing between them.

She felt her skin go cold.

Then Mrs Earl leaned across the desk. Her cheek twitched. 'Aren't you cute?' She looked at Mia. 'Six? Seven?'

Mia got hold of Felix's hand. 'Six.'

Mrs Earl looked from Felix to her husband and back again. She wiped her palm across her forehead. Then she leaned across the desk towards Felix, her smile straining. 'We're going to have to keep you!'

The Earl laid his hands on the desk and blinked.

The Un(heim)lich(e) Man(oeuvre)

Ian Duhig

Dad was choked.

It was the day I got the e-mail telling me I'd passed A-level Maths, Physics and Biology, all at grade A! Success beyond his wildest dreams! His dreams. Far from wild to me. He'd pushed me into the sciences, but only because he wanted me to have a safety net, he always said. He was keeping an eye out for me; it was the promise he'd made Mum. Well, over her grave anyway. I left her there, don't remember much of her, hardly saw her after I got the microwave, tv and computer with broadband in my bedroom, which then became my bedsitstudiocellspaceship. But Dad fixated on her once she was good and gone. A man is as good as his word, he'd say, and his word is his bond. And now I was the weakest link. He was letting me have it good style...

Sacrifice. I didn't know the meaning of it. Hard work. Alien to my nature. Shirking. All I'm good for. Appearance. A disgrace. Self, self, self. Mother. Grave. Turning. Duty. Indulgence. On his back. Shoulders of giants. Which led him to one of his heroes, Isaac Newton. Real geniuses worked hard, showed dedication, patience, attention to detail: can it be a coincidence so many were lens-grinders like Newton? Or Spinoza? Or Descartes? Or Hooke? He told me for the umpteenth time about Newton pushing needles into his eyesocket in the course of his experiments on optics. He knew this got me as I had a real thing about eyes – I'd been told at school about a kid in another class who was running with a newly-sharpened pencil...he'd have been safer with scissors. I never used a pencil again. It gave me nightmares for months. Some things are well beyond my ability to put into words (that's where the creative writing foundation course came in). I wanted to talk to Dad about images, about glass and mirrors, his world being the one, mine the other, that's all – in fact, as careers, they reflected each other... but I didn't have the bottle.

If I had said this, his eyes would have bulged out on their stalks like chapel hat-pegs, the veins on his face colour it to a road map, his loosened teeth in their retreating gums drop out and rattle into his glass of Sanatogen, then his whole head explode like in the film 'Scanners'. Scary but I'd like to have seen him explode. I'd keep that picture on my mobile so I could look at it and laugh to myself whenever the whim took me. Whim, not prescription. It would take more than a prescription to fix Lucy, another one I couldn't get out of my mind. St Lucy that is, not my Lucy. We saw a picture of her 'Exoculation' (good word, though) in an art gallery once; she's stood there with her eyes held out in front of her on a little silver dish as if they were a couple of oysters for the viewer to eat. The world is your. Choose. She didn't need them, saw better without them, like Oedipus.

11000100

I was born with a caul and espionage skills. Mum said she didn't even know she was pregnant until I was nearly due. I kept them guessing about when I'd arrive, was late, wrongfooting everybody. Eventually they resorted to a Caesarean, lancet not forceps. Blended into the background at school. Exams have always been easy for me: photographic memory and even speed-reading, a flypaper-mind for words, hoovering up millions from all kinds of books like a whale shark taking in plankton. Everything sticks, even much of what I wanted to get rid of – I envied Sherlock Holmes, who could do that easily. The Copernican theory? Do I look like I give a shit? I'm doing my best to forget lots. How do you do that? It's like trying to count up to ten without thinking of rabbits. The ties that bind. Even bondage freaks had their safe words. Dad wanted me to be safe in a way that he knew would work, because it had worked for him: to get married and give him grandchildren during the course of a successful career as an optician, like him. Ophthalmic, that was, not just Dispensing in a shop, a cut above: able to test and make out prescriptions. I'm sure Dad was on the square as well as square, though of course we couldn't talk about it. But he was always out for some 'meeting' or another, coming back half-cut with no explanation, strange creases in one trouserleg. But he wore the trousers in our house. I was a Lodge orphan, Mum a Lodge widow so he could play the Widow's Son. So the Widow's Son begat a widower's son, his mirror image, but unworshipful. Who said the only secret Masons possess is the secret of getting drunk? It's a secret.

My childhood was unspent in Harrogate. Har–Low–Gata: Anglo-Saxon name for an Anglo-Saxon town of Anglo-Saxon attitudes, but with a dark side. Biggest carbon footprint in God's Own County; Dickens' 'queerest place' (and he knew London), Agatha Christie's bolt-hole when she did her own disappearing trick. Dad liked it for different reasons. After Mum died he'd take me on walks around it. Bonding sessions. Making up for lost time. Like most healthy people my age, I travelled everywhere in my room, plugged in to the electronic, unsafety net of the world of unsafe words. But no – Dad thought he was passing something on to me, apart from blisters. So we'd stray on the Stray, me traipsing after him as he'd point out places associated with another of his heroes, Jack Metcalfe. Metcalfe had been a bit of a rogue (Dad would smile indulgently as he told this story) a quondam card-sharp, horse-dealer, smuggler and one of the original boys from the black stuff, laying most of the roads around here. But when his country needed him, he stood up to be counted, turning out for Bonnie Cumberland against the Jacobites and the Young Pretender. And Jack had been completely blind from the age of six. Wanker.

I'd call in to Dad's work on the way home from school sometimes to pick the keys up; I'd see a customer under that inverted pyramid of letters, wearing those iron-maiden metal goggles into which Dad slotted lenses like pennies. 'Better or worse?' But as I got older, all the customers began to look the same in them to me: they all began to look like James Joyce, one of my heroes, who had eyes only slightly better than Metcalfe's. But Jacobus Jocundus was more Jacobite than Jack. 'Non Serviam!' Even without the rebel yell, it's kind of goth, Catholicism: the guilt, the misery, the Latin, contemptus mundi − I loved the lushness of words like 'Papish' with its mammary etymological penumbrae. There were lots of anti-Catholic Gothic writers − 'Monk' Lewis, Maturin of Melmoth − but they were of the Devil's party without knowing it, tripping into Gil Martin's snares, the Devil Catholics prefer in literature. I wanted to be a writer even if that meant slighting my father's hopes of children, ending his line with his number one and only son, the withering of his family tree in me. I will make your name live on in my own way, I wished I'd told him. Better or worse?

If I tell you too any more about myself, I will have to kill you.

Wet joke.

Aqueous humour.

10110011

My new freedom made me kind of drunk all the time. Just not feeling like I was being watched was a fantastic sense of liberation. One of the things that made me realise that the idea of Heaven stunk was the notion that your parents would be there. Did you remember to tidy your room before you died? Free, not Freemason: free as a word. I wanted to forget about family and all that but Tyr agreed with Dad about following in his footsteps. Tyr has been my best friend in childhood; I hadn't seen him in a long time, but it was good to have him back. Tyr is short for something. Tyrone, like the character in 'Andromeda' on the TV? I asked once. Nearly right; from the Irish, he said, means 'Land of Owen'. Like in Tyrnanogue? Yes, he'd replied, the Land of the Young, a kind of heaven for heroes.

Now he was trying to make me feel guilty - Opththalmic opticians are respected professionals, just as good as, say, pharmacists, he declared. Hospital pharmacists, that is, not the high street kind just following prescriptions – a cut above. It's because I don't just want to follow prescriptions, I tell Tyr, that I want to become a writer. On the subject of writing, he added, who's going to be writing all the cheques for this? You won't get a grant for a foundation course. Where there's a will there's a way, I countered, and I don't just mean my Dad's will. I'm going to write stuff that sells, exciting stuff like spy novels or horror, under a pen-name, and the good stuff in the evenings. I went on, as if to demonstrate my research, Did you know that in World War II, Ian Fleming was in the secret services and he ran Aleister 'the Beast' Crowley? And that de Pessoa used to correspond with Crowley, de Pessoa who was an expert on Freemasonry and wrote an essay about it? He really was a master of disguise. In fact, de Pessoa was several masters of disguise.

Don't change the subject, snapped Tyr, you're in denial, as usual. Even if this ludicrous plan works out, what are you going to do for money until then? I proudly unveiled my secret plan: I was going to be a spy myself for MI5 into on-campus terrorist activity. They'd just opened a regional office in Leeds: the fact that this city's name is a pun, and the fact that it sells more surveillance equipment than anywhere else in the country must be good omens. It would be both research and grant aid. The universities are full of terrorists nowadays. Bradford is perfect – even their Chancellor got arrested under terrorism legislation in Pakistan. For now, my controller tells me, he just wants me to keep an eye out; the security services only know the tip of the iceberg of terrorist activities in our region. How come I didn't see this controller, Tyr wondered rhetorically, when I'm with you virtually 24/7? Because he's a professional, I countered triumphantly. You need to keep an eye out too. Tyr winked.

01100110

I'd only been to Bradford once before the course started, and then by night on my own, in a car and a rush. But if you train it to Forster Square from Leeds, as I was now having to do regular, it's like entering a parallel universe, trundling down the Aire valley past the ruins of Kirkstall Abbey – if there's been another theft of copper signal wire, you'll have plenty of time to contemplate the ironies of the once-Catholic heritage of God's Own County while sidelined in a sideline of a sideline, going nowhere on a train to a place going nowhere, cursing your Chinese watch, which is one of the things the stolen copper is eventually going to make more of, while our Western industries go down the pan. Cistercians, from 'cisterna' meaning cistern. Dry stone walls are a Cistercian signature in Yorkshire, they told us at school. Sometimes dry stone walls weren't built to keep animals in, but just to use stones cleared out of those fields, so you could plough them, or more likely nowadays drive your 4x4 around them without knackering its axles. They're thrown over the Dales like a huge net, but when you drive through, the fields enclosed by the dry stone walls are almost always completely deserted, the hefted sheep elsewhere, the goats invisible. I repaired some for a while as a conservation volunteer, for compulsory work experience at school (it was either that or an office). Gap-walling, it was called, which sounded ontologically interesting. Smoots, throughs, footings, heartings, vocabularies changing in every village, like codes. I found out too that the Mason's word for a spy, who Entered Apprentices were continually keeping an eye out for, was 'cowan', which means 'dry-stone-diker' in the OED. A different kind of apprentice now, I've got to practice a different kind of stonewalling. That's rather good, isn't it?

But these delays gave me a chance to get stuck into the anthology on the reading list. The size and weight of a footing for a Cyclopean wall, it soon became the foundation-stone of my reading. Reading it added to my sense of drunken freedom. Didn't Kipling say words were the most powerful drugs known to humanity? The right words are, in the right order. That's what literature is. A distillation: once for prose, twice for poetry. Like a wall, I was getting plastered. There's a Simic poem about being a wall, isn't there? As the train's engine ticked over, I read Martha Moulsworth's 'Memorandum' ('My muse is a tell clock'); goth ur-texts from Browne and Burton; Langland on how Plague can be a good and Godly thing; Gawain's Beheading Game and off-his-head Smart's Masonic imagery-poems; Marlowe ('One is no number'), also an intelligence agent, who got a spike in his eye for his trouble; Newton on light and Locke's 'association of ideas' (I'd say 'train of..' if that wasn't a bad joke in a stalled train) which prefigures the stream of consciousness; all the way back to Caedmon (England's first poet and another good thing about Whitby apart from Dracula and goth weekends) feeling too rude for 'his The Dream of the Rood' then writing his dream, a dream of a vision. There were letters between Ignatius Sancho and Sterne the unLocker, master of straying and digressions; but I digress...

11100101

Brat. It's written 'Bradford', but locals pronounce it 'Bratford'.

Formerly proverbial for millionaires (well, in Eliot anyway) it's now Leeds' runt kid brother, disinherited, impoverished. That Tory think tank wanker was right: this place will never recover, its decline is terminal. It should just be bulldozed, concreted over and turned into a car park for Leeds, as Sunderland for Newcastle - though some Mackem called that an Alice-in-Sunderland idea. In Leeds, so much new building goes on because the Council rubber-stamps planning applications to no overall plan, blind. Cranes on towers everywhere, rising like piles of coins on a counting house table. Bratford's got no towers with cranes on at all, just a bloody great hole down from the station, first place I came to, which I still wait impatiently for them to fill. But it does have the plan, Alsop's vision; they showed us a promotional video in Fresher's Week – 'Bradford Squared' it was called. In it, a road-sweeper wakes the sleeping city: Town Hall windows become brilliantly-coloured squares, exploding like a Mondrian with the city's wonderland future, illuminating water features and post-modernist architecture, flying around and eventually reforming as the letter B, for Bradford. Or Bullshit. Or Big Brother. Better or worse?

The National Media Museum was a bit disappointing, though it was interesting to find out that Michael Rennie, the alien disgusted with the human race in 'The Day The Earth Stood Still', was a local. Bradford would give you insight into worlds standing still. But Imax is fantastic. I watched a balloon ride and my stomach turned over when it crossed the Grand Canyon. The screen takes up your whole field of vision. I'm glad I had my curry after - good for curries, Bradford. I'd liked to have seen where they burned 'The Satanic Verses', but it's still a touchy subject, judging from the reaction of the waiters I asked.

Tyr came with me to Bradford when I started my foundation course. He even read all the same books as me so we'd have things to talk about. A real pal. Good thing as well, since the natives weren't too friendly, even in the halls of residence. Also, problems with sleep meant I had long hours to talk through. I sat for weeks of days in the Atrium – 'the Hub' they call it, of their 'e-campus', suggesting the hub of a wheel, a web, or of activity. Activity? Students? Here, they tended to group around their separate tables in little archipelagoes of people they already knew, some risking a paddle between islands from time to time to laugh and flirt in a strangely modest, ritualised manner. Who described social interaction as ping-pong in masks? Mostly though, they just looked at each other in shy and meaningful ways. They began looking at me too after a while. The whole campus was paranoid after the arrests of their fellow students and their big sentences, like those given out to the rioters after the Battle of White Abbey Road and the other parts of the City. They wrecked the BMW garage, which could have been a message to the rich, or drug-dealers, or both. You'll hear now round here that BMW stands for Break My Windows.

E stands for eye-campus: security cameras, scanners, informants, computer monitoring programmes, the government telling lecturers to spy on their students. Lecturers couldn't be relied on to do that. None of them could run a bath, never mind a surveillance operation. That's why they need me. I spy. Stand up and be counted. I to the Max.

01010110

Before too long, I had to give up this keeping an eye out due to the attention it was attracting, hollow-eyed and slurring my words with tiredness. Everywhere there are invisible walls, but the fact that you can see through them doesn't mean it's OK to look. I'd research in the Library then, whole museums and art galleries of words. I found out a high proportion of the student body were local, had been with the same friends from primary school, through middle and high into University. Still lived with their parents, dropped off at 9 picked up at 5. Close families. I thought the whole point of University was to get away from family, but it still seemed important to them. The family shop. How was I ever going to get to shop them? My controller suggested that if I continued to be isolated for a long time, I might consider making the first move – agent provocateur. I resented this slight on my dedication. I told him my eyes were now open nearly 24/7; in fact I was spending a fortune on over-the-counter preparations so I could get a bit of shut-eye just once in a while. And, if no one will talk with me how will I get them to plan bombings with me? He asked me if I really was creative. He liked to answer questions with more questions. Ping pong. Perhaps I should volunteer to be decapitated on the internet, I wondered aloud. I could tell from his silence he felt that this was another idea with more pong than ping.

The terrorist and the policeman, Tyr quoted Conrad, come out of the same basket. He speculated as to whether, if my controller was the Ian Fleming figure, did that make me the Beast? Then he laughed and mimicked the Lone Gunmen in the 'X-Files': 'We're going through the lookingglass here guys!' Strolling through the University winter wonderland, where even the lifts are glass, I checked out a few departments: Pharmacy was on the top floor of the tall block by the Atrium. Lucy in the Sky with Diamonds. LSD. Joyce's Lucy, Dracula's Lucy. My Lucy. The Exoculation of St Lucy. Sacrifice. All these boys and girls sacrificing their youths for careers. Dad would have loved them. But words were my drug of choice. The weirdest Department I investigated was Peace Studies – as obsessed with war as Uncle Toby. In Archaeology, I saw photographs of a local urn burial, reminding me of Browne: 'Circles and right lines limit and enclose all bodies', 1s and 0s of internet signals, Disjecta membra on the Circle Line, the ends of all those lines. Jacobus Heaney translates Horace in 'District and Circle': 'Anything can happen, the tallest towers//Be overturned, those in high places daunted,/Those overlooked regarded...

Through the overlookingglass: if the idea of calling Catholics 'left-footers' is to suggest something literally sinister in the way they dig, has it never occurred to these Prods that all right-footed people dig with the left foot so you can balance on your right? I've got the blisters on my instep to prove it. Tenderfoot. Catholics say haitch and Protestants say aitch. Over here it's the haves who say aitch. In the Key of H, as the German intelligence agent mentioned, to snare plucky Brit spies, who have no such key in their country.

Codes. We English love them. Even 'The Dream of the Rood' was influenced by the Anglo-Saxon 'Enigma' traditions. I read somewhere that the most requested poem at the Poetry Library in London was Leo Marks' WWII code-poem from 'Carve Her Name With Pride', 'The life that I have...' If it's not really a poem, it's OK for Brits to like it. I and love, where love stands for nothing, like in tennis: l'oeuf, egg. I'd even loved Dad sometimes, sometimes showed it in that man-code, hedged-around, bushido-ritualised way - i.e. totally wordless, a punch on the shoulder for a hug, walking together like chimpanzee males patrolling their territory. Secret, non-verbal communication. Circles and lines. Dots and dashes. Morse. If Inspector Morse is so anti-Mason, why is he father-figure to someone called Lewis, a Mason's name for his uninitiated son, like me? Was his author playing a double game? Was Colin Dexter really Colin Sinister?

00111001

The time passed for me in lengthening rhythms as I lost those of home and school. I could pursue an idea for days, nights, weeks, without another one coming along to displace it. My controller encouraged me to think in these ways now, take the long view. He hinted the security situation was changing, and I enjoyed the magisterial overlooking of history. Were the results of the Battle of Hastings bad? Too early to say. Horizons and timescales rolled back, disappeared. But the less I slept, the more I understood Joyce's line about history being nightmare and our struggle to wake from it. It applied even more to English history than Irish history. I felt terrible, but comforted by how deep I was becoming.

The time passed for other students as it does for students: tick = apathy/tock = hysteria, with no intervening period of normal organised behaviour; ping – this essay is due at some distant point in the future/pong – yesterdayomigod. Seminars were a waste of time attended by a waste of skin. The pooled stupidity of people who're here precisely because we don't know what we're doing. But even so, their egos! All oeuf and no oeuvre. One dumb bint announced, I don't like to read other authors in case it influences my style or makes me self-conscious about how I write. I asked her if she'd go to a doctor after s/he told her s/he didn't like to read medical textbooks in case it made him/her self-conscious about their bedside manner. I'd rather spend a whole winter bog-snorkelling around Vladivostok than another hour with my 'fellow writers' agonizing about the anxiety of influence. Ugh! I'm even getting the quotation marks habit, those snottily-raised eyebrows of punctuation. It's like saying, this is crap but because I'm being ironic it's alchemically transformed into the pure gold of kitsch, or satire, or something good that you just aren't cool enough to see. Silence is also golden, but nobody believes that. I obviously don't, do I?

It also became obvious that for nearly everybody there Englit was really Amlit. While I was getting higher and higher on the time-honoured historical concoctions of these islands, everybody around me was swapping intellectual Buckfast Abbey fortified wine for Duff Lite. Easy to see why, especially in poetry, which in the U.S.A. is predominantly college-boy stuff, campus poetry, I came to understand, as nobody else publishes the stuff. What would novels be like if they were only written by university lecturers, I wondered? Tilll now, I'd always thought Dad's anti-Americanism was well OTT – he'd characterised American military strategy in the last World War as waiting till it was nearly over, then moving in to bayonet the wounded and loot their corpses. Now, children of the corpses ape the bayoneters, dress like them, read their books, use their slang. Uncle Sam grinds his organ and English corpse-children dance. I remember the line from the Sisters of Mercy in 'Vision Thing': 'It's a small world and it smells bad.' It certainly does. And the smell was getting worse. I began avoiding people rather than risk being diminished by them.

I'm not a misanthrope, I told Tyr, I'm an apanthrope. I prefer solitude. Eagles don't flock. The writer should be a little apart always, the splinter of ice in the old heart, tip of the iceberg and all that. Your splinter could have sunk the Titanic, he replied. I pretended to look hurt, but I rather liked that. I'd use the line when I got the chance. Mature writers steal. Like then.

11001101

My tutor was crap too. We discussed the portfolio I'd submitted in early sessions, although I could hardly keep awake; the exquisite torture of the situation heightened by the fact that I knew I would only truly be able to sleep in Bradford while listening to him. He conceded that I was obviously well-read (he made that sound like something verging on the reprehensible, like putting weapons in the hands of children), but that my writing lacked heart and insight into human beings. I know, I smiled: the splinter of ice in my heart I've been told could have sunk the Titanic. He didn't laugh. Maybe he'd never heard of Graham Greene. 'The Third Man', greatest English film ever. Cuckoo clocks, Viennese sewers, jangly music. Here's lime in your eye.

Remember Klee, my tutor had interrupted: One eye

sees, the other feels. I liked that, but he went on. And on. My writing seemed strangely reluctant to give physical descriptions of people. Hello? Who cares what the robots look like? I should explore my childhood: As a writer, your childhood is your capital. What did he know about capital, dressed like he hadn't two pennies to put over his eyes, bits of tofu in his tobacco-y beard. And insight's something he could do with. Agenbite of inwit. He'd recommended I read Raymond Carver!

I raged about this to myself all night. I should read Carver? Why? To develop some sub-American, mid-Atlantic style? A cracked lookingglass of a Brit servant to yanks. Yankers. I like the way Joyce writes 'lookingglass' as one word; it seems to goggle back at you, reflecting itself and on itself. Light takes time to travel, reflected de Selby (his name has something to do with the German 'selbst', meaning 'self'), so when you look at a mirror, you're actually seeing yourself ever-so-slightly younger. In a pleasingly painless unNewtonian experiment, he then set two big mirrors opposite each other, to get that old infinity ping-pong going, and using a powerful magnifying glass, claimed to be able to see himself in his childhood. With modern magnifying technology, I'd see right through myself, Dad, back up the family line to, who? Adam?

I read this in an old local litmag, a piece called 'The Apple of My Eye/I' : 'I understand the impossibility of saying 'I', using the term only from a position of Irigarayan mimicry, which resists even as it seems to accept p(h)allo(go)centric norms. That's why I/eye can wryte 'I' now and you/ewe/u will know exactly what I mean, Ryght?' Sub-Joycean, joyless theorrhoeia. I wanted to tell the author a joke: What do you call a fish with no eye? A fsh. I needed this like a fsh needs a bicycle, if this was the sort of stuff tutors wanted to see, so it was agreed I'd just email stuff in rather than going to every single seminar, after I told them I had this masterwork I really wanted to get on with, shamelessly comparing myself with Joyce, whose 'Ulysses' started life as a short story, then just growed like Topsy – i.e. hinting that was what might be happening with me. I struggled to represent myself as a figure of monastic dedication, a hermetic hermit guarding the Arcanum of my art, a Sebastian Melmoth with nothing to declare but, in time, my genius. Nobody noticed. Wankers.

00111001

You need to get out more, said Tyr one day, scratching a crescent of light in the dirt on my window with his fingernail. I'm into De Maistrean room-travel, I replied. De Selbian you mean, he quibbled, accurately. When do you next meet your controller? When I've something to report, I hissed back. Till then, I'm a sleeper. If I could sleep, bloody kids. What kids? he asked.

So we went to a Geoffrey Hill reading in Leeds, where he was Professor once before he took up arms to fight the invading sea of theorrhoea from the incontinent Continent at Cambridge. He's the most goth poet I know. The great man said in an American annotated edition of his poems, they glossed 'Overlord of the M5' as 'Head of the British Secret Service'. Donnish sniggers from the university audience, which sounded as if they had all simultaneously inhaled their glasses cloths. But talking about it all later, Tyr seemed to think that Hill had sold out by going to America - 'the Belly of the Beast', he called it. He had been getting more anti-American as the term wore on. I noticed him referring to the American War of Independence as the 'American Mutiny', and our 'American Yoke', like the 'Saxon Yoke' to Fenians, or the 'Norman Yoke' to Levellers.

Round here they call the Beast Dajjal, said Tyr on the way back. Google it, he challenged. And I did, for hour after hour, I Googled and goggled, goggled and Googled - I couldn't sleep, anyway. Don't brats go to school in Bratford? Dajjal is an Antichrist, not exactly a mirror-image of the Christian version but with key features in common, such as seductive eloquence. The Christian version would also be distinguished by this eloquence, which would enable him to bring peace to the Middle East. I suddenly thought: maybe Bush isn't as stupid as he looks. Maybe it's all an act so he can't be accused of being the Antichrist: he's the opposite of eloquent and brought more war to the Middle East. Maybe he took fright after some elements of the US Christian right identified Ronald Reagan as Antichrist, because of the six letters in each of the three parts of his name, and decided to convince them that Antichrist was to be found in the United Nations rather than the White House. One World Government – or, in the USA, ZOG: Zionist-Owned Government. Even Islamists could agree with that.

Hadiths suggest the End of Days will be marked by, among other signs, the end of the use of horses in war. The US Cavalry nowadays rode almost anything except horses – think about 'Apocalypse Now'. Music everywhere is another sign, and I only had to think about the pervasiveness of American music to see how that fitted. Most interesting was the Lodge connection to Dajjal, his one eye and the Masons' symbol of an eye on top of a pyramid, as seen on the US dollar, an inversion of my Dad's optical test (maybe he was passing secret messages to his customers while he did this). I also hadn't appreciated the historical change from Operative to Speculative Masonry, the former being actual workers in stone, the latter taking over their lodges and turning them into secret societies. Speculative Masons... 'The forerunners to the Dajjal are none other than the Freemasons,' he read on another site, which went on to describe just how widespread references to their influence were in American culture: 'the Freemasonic eye has also been featured on the video for one of Madonna's songs where Madonna actually appears with the One Eye coming out from her forehead,' I'd read there. I couldn't remember which of Madge's songs that referred to, but it might have something to do with Kabbalah.

It went on to describe the Simpsons' Stonecutters' episode, the Stonecutters obviously being the Masons, then traces a vast conspiracy back to the Templars, who infiltrated the Masons on their own suppression (these still use Templar names and terminology), and how they dominated the USA through its Presidents from Brother George Washington onwards. One section listed famous Masons like Lewis Carroll (though I wasn't sure that was true), dwelling particularly on the royal arch-imperialist Rudyard Kipling, and the role of the Brotherhood in his 'The Man Who Would be King', made into a Hollywood film starring Harry Palmer and James Bond. My head spun on. The man who would be king in the land of the blind should put out the eye that offends him.

Then Tyr told me that on the Bradford University website there was mountains of Masonic material which Humanities staff claimed to know nothing about. And he was right! A local solicitor called Wilmhurst had amassed it (I could imagine solicitors and opticians doing this sort of weird shit together), and the archive was put online by a famous Masonic author who had worked in Business Studies. Surfing the web and the energy from insomnia, I dug out just how deep the Masonic conspiracy went: left trouserlegs around Buckingham Palace/the Pentagon/Kremlin/Vatican roll up on their own constantly. Nobody will admit it, of course. The Mason's Word. Wankers.

10101011

Some memories I was not so desperate to suppress. On one of my pilgrimages of ill grace with Dad on the Stray, when he was laying down the moral law like Polonius, I'd decided to take him on and his homespun philosophy. I'd said, Hypothetically, aren't secret societies pledged to privilege their members' interests over other people's manifestly unfair? He twitched as if I'd suggested he was a paid-up member of

Spearmint Rhino. I mean, I went on, Doesn't that sort of, you know, ghettoize the comfortable just at the time our Government is calling on everybody to be more integrated?

As he wriggled on my line, I moved in: I'm sure everybody would like to integrate more with the well-off, but that isn't made too easy for them, especially when you think about organisations like, O, I don't know, the Masons. Isn't that a bit like those American country clubs barring Jews or Blacks? Now he was spluttering like an old tap. I knew the implied slighting of his sense of English fair play, that scandalous comparison with American practices, not to mention to equation with Romish or Muslim religious intolerance would have him on his back foot. In truth, as usual I didn't listen closely to what he was saying because I knew what that would be; I had driven him onto the killing-ground of the argument he would advance. In 'Sun and Steel', Mishima describes the blow, how you manoeuvre your foe into your chosen space for him in the air, the space you want him to occupy because that is where you have prepared yourself to strike. While Dad wittered on, I was oiling my blade, son and steel, eyeing up the hole he had no choice but to get himself into, and as I tuned in again to his hackneyed, predictable defence at the point where he was indignantly declaring that Masonic 'Volume of the Sacred Law' could equally be a Qur'an or Torah or an Adi Granth as a Bible, and how Masons could believe in their individual ideas of a God, and how all were welcome on this basis blah blah. I paused, a little theatrically. It was the first time my silence silenced him, wasn't just talked over by him. Then I asked gently, And atheists? Can they become Masons though they don't believe in any God?

It was a rhetorical question. Of course they couldn't. It wasn't an Oedipal moment: I was more like the Sphinx, foxing the ignorant, protecting the Plague that fed on them. Why does Plague get such a bad press? Aren't they just a life form like any other? If we release kites or beavers or wolves back into the British countryside, shouldn't we release some Black Death too? In that lousy Costner film where he's the first white man among these misfortunate Native Americans, isn't he a harbinger of Plague? Hard to imagine a film with Typhoid Mary or Bubo Baggins as the star, though I'd go to see it. Anyway, Dad was speechless, choked. 'Sphinx' means 'strangler', after all.

NOTE TO SELF: Avoid cliches like the Plague...

er...

00111001

By now I was getting to suspect the extent to which I, too, was under surveillance. Not just the sluggish net connections working through their security programmes but the sluggish locals, the other students and tutors, looking at me sideways, even canteen staff, porters, car park security staff on my way to the Priestley Library. Sometimes, as I passed, I'm sure I heard a scrabble of whispered acronyms: CID ('El Cid' to locals), CPS, CIA, FBI, KFR. I was getting messages from everywhere – my tutor said I was 'semiotically aroused' in his last e-mail. Wanker.

Later I noticed that in our anthology, the translator of 'Brut' rendered its author 'Layamon', but in her own separate American edition, he becomes 'Lawman'. It seemed to suggest Rome tolerating regional variations under its Law. How could you fight it? Take up arms against a sea and all that, as goth Hamlet said. Which side was black and which white? I asked myself the question over and over again, day after day. Fight or flight? With us or against us? Halal or haram? A Turing Machine would have succeeded where I was failing, going around in circles, Turing and Turing in a widening gyre. The Turing of the key. Unlike Turing, I was straight but couldn't act it, drinking Night Nurse by the pint, Covonia cocoa, Benilyn and Buckie cocktails. Insomniac goths count black sheep, but they're hard to see in the dark, so it doesn't work. I wasn't working, either.

01011001

You could write 'Layabout's Brut', sneered Tyr when I shared my discoveries about the Brut's translator. Traduttore tradittore, he went on, 'the translator is a traitor'. It goes with the turf. Better than silence and doing nothing. Better or worse? I was as yellow as my wallpaper, not facing up to the necessity for sacrifice. All he had done for me. In this world, look round, sacrifice the only option. Now, he looked like my father, like Gil Martin. Then he chanted a poem, appropriately for our new lookingglass world, by Kipling:

Tyr thought hard till he hammered out a plan,
For he knew it was not right
(And it is not right) that the Beast should master Man;
So he went to the Children of the Night.
He begged a Magic Knife of their make for our sake,
When he begged for the Knife they said:
'The price of the Knife you would buy is an eye!'
And that was the price he paid!

A scanner, though scanning a bit wobbly, but I knew he was trying to freak me out with this exoculation song. Thank God I don't need pencils to write anymore. He looked me in the eye with his one eye and said, You will never see me again. Fantastic, I laughed, I'll have no reflection. Like a vampire. How goth is that?

10010110

I think I'm turning into Dad. I've started taking walks, partly to spread the circuit of chemists I hit for Night Nurse, I must admit. Only in Bradford is this a way of avoiding people. Recently, I went to Little Germany because I'd heard that some TV programme about Kafka had been filmed there. It would certainly have been appropriate. Kafka is more in tune with the City than Alsop. I feel like telling the asylum seekers selling the Big Issue they're looking for it in the wrong kind of asylum. Bradford in metamorphosis, says the T & A newsstand. So why doesn't it get on with it then, for a start filling in that bloody great hole which was the first thing here that caught my eye? On an etymological level, why bugs? I mean, I know now they are trying to implant brain-control devices into cockroaches, but that couldn't have been the reason they started using the word for a concealed mic. A bug in a computer system. Maybe from bug-eyed? Or bugaboo? It bugs me.

There's a big wheel (the Bradford Bug Eye?) in front of the Town Hall which looks like something out of Renaissance Florence. Town Hall and big wheel make me think of Harry Lime, when he talks about how little these insect-lives mean. I'm with him there; eggs, omelettes etc. And if you're an insect, who would not prefer to be a bug in the machine, bug up the clockwork of the state, to just being crushed in this shit-hole? Yet, when I shared this insight with my controller, he didn't want to know. The first real insight I'd had into all this and nobody wanted to know.

01011001

On my way to the chemists yesterday, I met this woman from the course. She said hello to me, last of them still doing that. I pretended to be nice and talked about my projects, plots and plans, all the while secretly raising my Teflon shielding, sacrificial armour I could abandon without exposing too much. Wrong-footing me, she seemed interested. She said she used to be a nurse and that the way I'm so obsessively interested in words and etymology, was something (she paused) autistic people demonstrate. I said that didn't sound like me as I couldn't even draw. She laughed and I burst into tears. I'd made a spectacle of myself or rather, half-following in Dad's footsteps, I should say I made a monocle of myself.

I surprised even myself by letting her take me for a coffee. She talked about her past, working in the NHS and I let her drone on, resisting the temptation to ask her if she'd been a night nurse. Pong. Ping. After a while I realised she was asking me about my family. From someone I had found reassuring and attractive, the mask slipped. Her eyes froze over like winter ponds and the words I thought I understood I saw were just a trick, a magician pulling endless vowel-bubbles of ping pong balls from some volunteer from the audience's mouth. But it was a good trick and I laughed and clapped my hands till she got startled, made her excuses and left. The full Monty. A pair of spectacles.

10110011

Last night, the children were even louder than usual, like they had concealed mics with reverb set to 11. I would have liked to hand out scissors and sharpened pencils to them, encouraging them to run around faster and faster. Something about their music reminded me of the children in 'Lost Hearts'. Tell-tale hearts. It wasn't innocent-sounding, though: loud feral games, rhymes, chants, Just-Another-Brick-in-the-Wall-type dirges – I found out a local word for them is 'nominies'. I think this is cod-Latin, taking the piss out of Catholics. I've read that Bradford used to have lots of Orange lodges. Catholics were not supposed to be keen on Masons, till P2 anyway, though both have resurrection rituals. Quite a trick, resurrection. A magician, 'the world's finest escapologist,' comes from Bradford, I saw in the Atrium exhibition – Shahid Malik, I think he was called. And Fr John O' Connor, who was the model for Chesterton's Father Brown. And Onions, the horror writer. City skins, wheels within wheels, mouths within mouths
ooooo0000OOOO...

Time for more Night Nurse and Buckie.

THE UN(HEIM)LICH(E) MAN(OEUVRE)

00101001

I got a letter from the Dean this morning, a warning about downloading material from the net that might be of use to terrorists, bearing in mind what happened to the five students. Thanks, wanker. Almost anything could be useful to terrorists, when you think enough about it. Dad told me in the last World War they took down country signposts in case the Germans invaded – I've got an A-Z of Leeds, a place with more terrorists per square foot than Bradford. And good ones, not just those useless Londoners who couldn't blow up a balloon. If I could be bothered to panic more I would.

If they've got a file on me, they'll know I used to go to Leeds all the time before Mum died, back when I was still a goth on top (pre-mufti). I'd go with Lucy on the 36, past Harewood House, down the Chapeltown Road into Leeds that Metcalfe laid, passing the Lithuanian sex-slave traders then into the bus station with a plaque up to Tom Maguire, great socialist political organiser, writer of terrible poems, though he had a jokey one about typhoid called 'The Song of the Microbe' which was truly goth. I'd try it to different tunes for Lucy while we hung about outside the Corn Exchange with the rest of our brethren. That's where I was introduced to Buckfast Abbey – 'Killfast' was the nickname for it I heard then. Certainly beat the usual goth cocktail of cider 'n' blackcurrant. We got our old black clothes from the Oxfam across the street, and Lucy's make-up style was also part of the Look – insomniac-panda eyes countersunk into plaster of Paris Noh mask. Black on white, writers' colours, melancholy goth livery. The spectrum is for squares. She was my one and only – my none and only, to be honest: I struck out, 0-0. I wanted 'The Story of O' but the story I got was No. Eye oh. Maybe I'm destined to die a virgin like Isaac Newton. Tyr didn't like her anyway. She was a looker but she just wanted to be looked at. I used to read her Poe. Nevermore.

Anyway, it was goth to be miserable, to have 'the monk on', in a local expression I liked. Ours was the most despised youth culture in history. We were like Dirty, Dirty Leeds United FC – no one loves us we don't care; hated nearly as much as the English abroad. Although I no longer wear the livery, my veins still run black with goth blood, my paperwhite skin is still undimmed by overexposure to vulgar sunlight. Black and white, them and uz, saints and sinners. We had goth martyrs too, that woman beaten to death for just looking goth; this boy with his ear cut off for the same reason. I was terrified I'd get caught and my eye put out. I didn't want to be an exoculated martyr. That's when I started going under cover. Mufti = plain clothes and a Muslim legal expert. How did they get connected?

01100111

A bombshell! Apocalyptic disappointment! The Bradford Five have their sentences quashed! Only guilty of thought-crime! Prosecution too creative with the evidence. I was gobsmacked. Where did that leave me?

'All my walls are lost in mirrors, whereupon I trace/ Self to right hand, self to left hand, self in every place,/ Self-same solitary figure, self-same seeking face.'

I'd try and walk off the nightmare, a Monk's Trod. Posters everywhere on campus: a genuflecting African in chains, Am I not a man and brother? Wilberforce anniversary. Apparently now there are still 27,000,000 slaves left in the world. Somebody's taken their eye off the ball since Abolition. Eye-service, a good expression that: only working when the boss comes into eyeshot. I found it in Berkeley's sermon to the American colonists, explaining why the slaves should be Christianised. Then they'd work all the time because God would be watching them. I see therefore I am, said Berkeley, see?

THE UN(HEIM)LICH(E) MAN(OEUVRE)

Once, testing an invisibility spell, Crowley walked naked through a roomful of the breakfasting clientele at the French hotel where he was staying. Broad-minded, indulgent of the eccentric Englishman, they ignored him, whereupon the Beast rushed off to tell his acolytes of his success. By now I had achieved a kind of invisibility in the Atrium, no longer attracting suspicious glances as I sat with my strange flask and smell. In fact, I'd got a wide berth everywhere, more or less, since I began forgetting to eat, wash, shave or change. Yet, I became more aware of other people, even felt affection for them, in a distant way. People even smiled at me, sometimes. All kinds of people. I thought, maybe I could do this. The human thing. Love even, perhaps. I emailed my controller and said I was resigning. I didn't want to keep an eye out on these people anymore and be on Big Brother's side, but on the side of brothers' keepers. He asked if a fsh could resign from water. Fsh! He monitored my thoughts!

10011101

I meditated on the number five instead of writing now, or even reading. Five months without decent sleep, no dreams at all never mind my dream. Five months of milk of amnesia that didn't work. Five senses addled, five wits astray, fish alive, beans, a bunch of, the locked-up students, the Virgin's Joys, Soviet economic plans. The Five Points of Calvinism for old Calvinist Bradford, Gil Martin's new home. Five is the number on which the square stands up to be counted, rising to get a point like a pyramid, then unfolding into a cube like the Ka'aba, its stone white until blackened by the sinful breath of men, words of confession. The Arabic sin is called 'shirk', and I have shirked my duty, sacrifice. I have witnessed, but not as a martyr. I have not risen like the Northern rebels whose banner was The Five Wounds of Christ. Gawain's pentagram glossed by Stone: 'It is worth emphasising the 'fiveness' of the multiple concept of "truth"...'

Truth. Confession. Maybe it would help. Absolution. Sacrifice.
I had lost my grip, needed to take the situation and myself in
hand, in all five fingers of my hand. IOU an I for an I. OK.
Shake on it. I shook, went home and prepared for midnight.

01100110

I'm back to help you see this through, said Tyr; I can't just sit
back and watch any more. A tear came to my eye, and not just
because of Tyr's return: in honour of my father, who I choked,
croaked with his own tie, tied and buried deep in a hole
for a new building in Bradford city centre to stall over, a
foundation sacrifice for my foundation course; whose writing
I had forged on cheques so I could forge my writing and
uncreated conscience; to wake him who gave me the chance
for my dream, I return to his science of the eye, his Newton
the Masonic alchemist, whose experiment I will take even
further. For the Joycean lancet of my art, I use a rusty old
pen knife, for true pen knives only have one blade. And this
is about one, symbol and sign. Capital I for its blade? No,
more a 1 with the pointy bit on top, like a weak fishhook
straightened by taking on something too big. Like a monk's
knife cut errors from a page of vellum, so will mine: si f/(ph)
allor sum. I will keep an eye out for my brother. I will be my
brother's keeper. I will learn to write for other people.
Serviam.

   Time for one last big push, a surge, squeaky bum time.
I wonder if 'sphinx' is related to 'sphincter'? What was it that
Oedipus' dad did to bring on the Plague? In denial, I digress.
The more I get to the point on either side, the closer I get
to a real breakthrough, the more the pen knife runs with
blood, oyster-water and aqueous humour dribbling down
onto its handle and under my fingers. I thought this
would make it sticky, help my grip, but it's slippery like ice
melting or a poem. Just do it. A Swiss army knife would
have an attachment for this. How come a neutral country

ended up making the world's most famous army knife? Get on with it. Should I name my pen knife something magnificent, like Excalibur? Swords have great names – but Arthur's spear was called 'Ron' in Geoffrey of Monmouth, a name so working class it was instantly erased from the legend. Get back to the point. I name the knife Tyr. Tyr smiles his fatherly smile, his controller smile, his Gil Martin smile.

Lining up my broken mirror for this operation is a performance in its own right, never mind this late. But this is what it's all about, guts not sex. Sometimes a knife is only a knife. Better or worse? This is about the meaning of sacrifice, the mechanics of the dream, the vision. No one said becoming a writer would be easy. Time for the last big push to come to shove and open up that inkwell in my left socket and get right to the point. My right socket, left point. The one that feels or the one that sees? The clock strikes one. Which one?

Long Ago, Yesterday

Hanif Kureishi

One evening just after my fiftieth birthday, I pushed against the door of a pub not far from my childhood home. My father, on the way back from his office in London, was inside, standing at the bar. He didn't recognize me but I was delighted, almost ecstatic, to see the old man again, particularly as he'd been dead for ten years, and my mother for five.

'Good evening,' I said, standing next to him. 'Nice to see you.'

'Good evening,' he replied.

'This place never changes,' I said.

'We like it this way,' he said.

I ordered a drink; I needed one.

I noticed the date on the newspaper he'd been reading and calculated that Dad was just a little older than me, nearly fifty-one. We were as close to equals – or contemporaries – as we'd ever be.

He was talking to a man sitting on a stool next to him, and the barmaid was laughing extravagantly with them both. I knew Dad better than anyone, or thought I did, and I was tempted to embrace him or at least kiss his hands, as I used to. I refrained, but watched him looking comfortable at the bar beside the man I now realized was the father of a school friend of mine. Neither of them seemed to mind when I joined in.

Like a lot of people, I have some of my best friendships with the dead. I dream frequently about both of my parents and the house where I grew up, undistinguished though it was. Of course, I never imagined that Dad and I might meet up like this, for a conversation.

Lately I had been feeling unusually foreign to myself. My fiftieth hit me like a tragedy, with a sense of wasted purpose and many wrong moves made. I could hardly complain: I was a theatre and film producer, with houses in London, New York, and Brazil. But complain I did. I had become keenly aware of various mental problems that enervated but did not ruin me.

I ran into Dad on a Monday. Over the weekend I'd been staying with some friends in the country who had a fine house and pretty acquaintances, good paintings to look at, and an excellent cook. The Iraq war, which had just started, had been on TV continuously. About twenty of us, old and young men, lay on deep sofas drinking champagne and giggling until the prospect of thousands of bombs smashing into donkey carts, human flesh, and primitive shacks had depressed everyone in the house. We were aware that disgust was general in the country and that Tony Blair, once our hope after years in opposition, had become the most tarnished and loathed leader since Anthony Eden. We were living in a time of lies, deceit, and alienation. This was heavy, and our lives seemed uncomfortably trivial in comparison.

Just after lunch, I had left my friend's house, and the taxi had got me as far as the railway station when I realized I'd left behind a bent paper clip I'd been fiddling with. It was in my friend's library, where I'd been reading about mesmerism in the work of Maupassant, as well as Dickens's experiments with hypnotism, which had got him into a lot of trouble with the wife of a friend. The taxi took me back, and I hurried into the room to retrieve the paper clip, but the cleaner had just finished. Did I want to examine the contents of the vacuum? my hosts asked. They were making faces at one another. Yet I had begun to see myself as heroic in terms of what I'd achieved in spite of my obsessions. This was a line my therapist used. Luckily, I would be seeing the good doctor the next day.

Despite my devastation over the paper clip, I returned to the station and got on the train. I had come down by car, so it was only now I realized that the route of the train meant we would stop at the suburban railway station nearest to my childhood home. As we drew into the platform I found myself straining to see things I recognized, even familiar faces, though I had left the area some thirty years before. But it was raining hard and almost impossible to make anything out. Then, just as the train was about to pull away, I grabbed my bag and got off, walking out into the street with no idea what I would do.

Near the station there had been a small record shop, a bookshop, and a place to buy jeans, along with several pubs that I'd been taken to as a young man by a local bed-sit aesthete, the first person I came out to. Of course, he knew straight away. His hero was Jean Cocteau. We'd discuss French literature and Wilde and pop, before taking our speed pills and applying our makeup in the station toilet, and getting the train into the city. Along with another white friend who dressed as Jimi Hendrix, we saw all the plays and shows. Eventually I got a job in a West End box office. This led to work as a stagehand, usher, dresser – even a director – before I found my 'vocation' as a producer.

Now I asked my father his name and what he did. I knew how to work Dad, of course. Soon he was more interested in me than in the other man. Yet my fear didn't diminish: didn't we look similar? I wasn't sure. My clothes, as well as my sparkly new teeth, were more expensive than his, and I was heavier and taller, about a third bigger all over – I have always worked out. But my hair was going gray; I don't dye it. Dad's hair was still mostly black.

An accountant all his life, my father had worked in the

same office for fifteen years. He was telling me that he had two sons: Dennis, who was in the Air Force, and me – Billy. A few months ago I'd gone away to university, where, apparently, I was doing well. My all – female production of 'Waiting for Godot' – 'a bloody depressing play,' according to Dad – had been admired. I wanted to say, 'But I didn't direct it, Dad, I only produced it.'

I had introduced myself to Dad as Peter, the name I sometimes adopted, along with quite a developed alternative character, during anonymous sexual encounters. Not that I needed a persona: Father would ask me where I was from and what I did, but whenever I began to answer he'd interrupt with a stream of advice and opinions.

My father said he wanted to sit down because his sciatica was playing up, and I joined him at a table. Eying the barmaid, Dad said, 'She's lovely, isn't she?'

'Lovely hair,' I said. 'Unfortunately, none of her clothes fit.'

'Who's interested in her clothes?'

This was an aspect of my father I'd never seen; perhaps it was a departure for him. I'd never known him to go to the pub after work; he came straight home. And once Dennis had left I was able to secure Father's evenings for myself. Every day I'd wait for him at the bus stop, ready to take his briefcase. In the house I'd make him a cup of tea while he changed.

Now the barmaid came over to remove our glasses and empty the ashtrays. As she leaned across the table, Dad put his hand behind her knee and slid it all the way up her skirt to her arse, which he caressed, squeezed, and held until she reeled away and stared at him in disbelief, shouting that she hated the pub and the men in it, and would he get out before she called the landlord and he flung him out personally?

The landlord did indeed rush over. He snatched away Dad's glass, raising his fist as Dad hurried to the door, forgetting his briefcase. I'd never known Dad to go to work without his briefcase, and I'd never known him to leave it anywhere. As my brother and I used to say, his attaché case was always attachéd to him.

Outside, where Dad was brushing himself down, I handed it back to him.

'Thank you,' he said. 'Shouldn't have done that. But once, just once, I had to. Suppose it's the last time I touch anyone!' He asked, 'Which way are you going?'

'I'll walk with you a bit,' I said. 'My bag isn't heavy. I'm passing through. I need to get a train into London but there's no hurry.'

He said, 'Why don't you come and have a drink at my house?'

My parents lived according to a strict regime, mathematical in its exactitude. Why, now, was he inviting a stranger to his house? I had always been his only friend; our involvement had kept us both busy.

'Are you sure?'

'Yes,' he said. 'Come.'

Noise and night and rain streaming everywhere: you couldn't see farther than your hand. But we both knew the way, Dad moving slowly, his mouth hanging open to catch more air. He seemed happy enough, perhaps with what he'd done in the pub, or maybe my company cheered him up.

Yet when we turned the corner into the neat familiar road, a road that had, to my surprise, remained exactly where it was all the time I hadn't been there, I felt wrapped in coldness. In my recent dreams – fading as they were like frescoes in the light – the suburban street had been darkly dismal under the yellow shadows of the streetlights, and filled with white flowers and a suffocating, deathly odor, like being buried in roses. But how could I falter now? Once inside the house, Dad threw open the door to the living room. I blinked; there she was, Mother, knitting in her huge chair with her feet up, an open box of chocolates on the small table beside her, her fingers rustling for treasure in the crinkly paper.

Dad left me while he changed into his pajamas and dressing gown. The fact that he had a visitor, a stranger, didn't deter him from his routine, outside of which there were no maps.

I stood in my usual position, just behind Mother's chair. Here, where I wouldn't impede her enjoyment with noise, complaints, or the sight of my face, I explained that Dad and I had met in the pub and he'd invited me back for a drink.

Mother said, 'I don't think we've got any drink, unless there's something left over from last Christmas. Drink doesn't go bad, does it?'

'It doesn't go bad.'

'Now shut up,' she said. 'I'm watching this. D'you watch the soaps?'

'Not much.'

Maybe the ominous whiteness of my dreams had been stimulated by the whiteness of the things Mother had been knitting and crocheting – headrests, gloves, cushion covers; there wasn't a piece of furniture in the house without a knitted thing on it. Even as a grown man, I couldn't buy a pair of gloves without thinking I should be wearing Mother's.

In the kitchen, I made a cup of tea for myself and Dad. Mum had left my father's dinner in the oven: sausages, mash, and peas, all dry as lime by now, and presented on a large cracked plate, with space between each item. Mum had asked me if I wanted anything, but how would I have been able to eat anything here?

As I waited for the kettle to boil, I washed up the dishes at the sink overlooking the garden. Then I carried Father's tea and dinner into his study, formerly the family dining room. With one hand I made a gap for the plate at the table, which was piled high with library books.

After I'd finished my homework, Dad would always like me to go through the radio schedules, marking programs I might record for him. If I was lucky, he would read to me, or talk about the lives of the artists he was absorbed with – these were his companions. Their lives were exemplary, but only a fool would try to emulate them. Meanwhile I would slip my hand inside his pajama top and tickle his back, or I'd scratch his head or rub his arms until his eyes rolled in appreciation.

Now in his bedwear, sitting down to eat, Dad told me he was embarked on a 'five-year reading plan.' He was working on 'War and Peace.' Next it would be 'Remembrance of Things Past,' then 'Middlemarch,' all of Dickens, Homer, Chaucer, and so on. He kept a separate notebook for each author he read.

'This methodical way,' he pointed out, 'you get to know everything in literature. You will never run out of interest, of course, because then there is music, painting, in fact the whole of human history...'

His talk reminded me of the time I won the school essay prize for a tract on time-wasting. The piece was not about how to fritter away one's time profitlessly, which might have made it a useful and lively work, but about how much can be achieved by filling every moment with activity! Dad was my ideal. He would read even in the bath, and as he reclined there my job was to wash his feet, back, and hair with soap and a flannel. When he was done, I'd be waiting with a warm, open towel.

I interrupted him, 'You certainly wanted to know that woman this evening.'

'What? How quiet it is! Shall we hear some music?'

He was right. Neither the city nor the country was quiet like the suburbs, the silence of people holding their breath.

Dad was holding up a record he had borrowed from the library. 'You will know this, but not well enough, I guarantee you.'

Beethoven's Fifth was an odd choice of background music, but how could I sneer? Without his enthusiasm, my life would never have been filled with music. Mother had been a church pianist, and she'd taken us to the ballet, usually 'The Nutcracker,' or the Bolshoi when they visited London. Mum and Dad sometimes went ballroom dancing; I loved it when they dressed up. Out of such minute inspirations I have found meaning sufficient for a life.

Dad said, 'Do you think I'll be able to go in that pub again?'

'If you apologize.'

'Better leave it a few weeks. I don't know what overcame me. That woman's not a Jewess, is she?'

'I don't know.'

'Usually she's happy to hear about my aches and pains, and who else is, at our age?'

'Where d'you ache?'

'It's the walk to and from the station – sometimes I just can't make it. I have to stop and lean against something.'

I said, 'I've been learning massage.'

'Ah.' He put his feet in my lap. I squeezed his feet, ankles, and calves; he wasn't looking at me now. He said, 'Your hands are strong. You're not a plumber, are you?'

'I've told you what I do. I have the theatre, and now I'm helping to set up a teaching foundation, a studio for the young.'

He whispered, 'Are you homosexual?'

'I am, yes. Never seen a cock I didn't like. You?'

'Queer? It would have shown up by now, wouldn't it? But I've never done much about my female interests.'

'You've never been unfaithful?'

'I've always liked women.'

I asked, 'Do they like you?'

'The local secretaries are friendly. Not that you can do anything. I can't afford a "professional".'

'How often do you go to the pub?'

'I've started popping in after work. My Billy has gone.'

'For good?'

'After university he'll come running back to me, I can assure you of that. Around this time of night I'd always be talking to him. There's a lot you can put in a kid, without his knowing it. My wife doesn't have a word to say to me. She doesn't like to do anything for me, either.'

'Sexually?'

'She might look large to you, but in the flesh she is even larger, and she crushes me like a gnat in bed. I can honestly say we haven't had it off for eighteen years.'

'Since Billy was born?'

He said, letting me caress him, 'She never had much enthusiasm for it. Now she is indifferent... frozen... almost dead.'

I said, 'People are more scared of their own passion than of anything else. But it's a grim deprivation she's made you endure.'

He nodded. 'You dirty homos have a good time, I bet, looking at one another in toilets and that...'

'People like to think so. But I've lived alone for five years.'

He said, 'I am hoping she will die before me, then I might have a chance... We ordinary types carry on in these hateful situations for the single reason of the children and you'll never have that.'

'You're right.'

He indicated photographs of me and my brother. 'Without those babies, there is nothing for me. It is ridiculous to try to live for yourself alone.'

'Don't I know it? Unless one can find others to live for.'

'I hope you do!' he said. 'But it can never be the same as your own.'

If the mortification of fidelity imperils love, there's always the consolation of children. I had been Dad's girl, his servant, his worshipper; my faith had kept him alive. It was a cult of personality he had set up, with my brother and me as his mirrors.

Now Mother opened the door – not so wide that she could see us, or us her – and announced that she was going to bed.

'Good night,' I called.

Dad was right about kids. But what could I do about it? I had bought an old factory at my own expense and had converted it into a theatre studio, a place where young people could work with established artists. I spent so much time in this building that I had moved my office there. It was where I would head when I left here, to sit in the café, seeing who would turn up and what they wanted from me, if anything. I was gradually divesting myself, as I aged, of all I'd accumulated. One of Father's favorite works was Tolstoy's 'How Much Land Does a Man Need?'

I said, 'With or without children, you are still a man. There are things you want that children cannot provide.'

He said, 'We all, in this street, are devoted to hobbies.'

'The women, too?'

'They sew, or whatever. There's never an idle moment. My son has written a beautiful essay on the use of time.'

He sipped his tea; the Beethoven, which was on repeat, boomed away. He seemed content to let me work on his legs. Since he didn't want me to stop, I asked him to lie on the floor. With characteristic eagerness, he removed his dressing gown and then his pajama top; I massaged every part of him, murmuring 'Dad, Dad' under my breath. When at last he stood up, I was ready with his warm dressing gown, which I had placed on the radiator.

It was late, but not too late to leave. It was never too late to leave the suburbs, but Dad invited me to stay. I agreed, though it hadn't occurred to me that he would suggest I sleep in my old room, in my bed.

He accompanied me upstairs and in I went, stepping

over record sleeves, magazines, clothes, books. My piano I was most glad to see. I can still play a little, but my passion was writing the songs that were scrawled in notebooks on top of the piano. Not that I would be able to look at them. When I began to work in the theatre, I didn't show my songs to anyone, and eventually I came to believe they were a waste of time.

Standing there shivering, I had to tell myself the truth: my secret wasn't that I hadn't propagated but that I'd wanted to be an artist, not just a producer. If I chose, I could blame my parents for this: they had seen themselves as spectators, in the background of life. But I was the one who'd lacked the guts – to fail, to succeed, to engage with the whole undignified, insane attempt at originality. I had only ever been a handmaiden, first to Dad and then to others – the artists I'd supported – and how could I have imagined that that would be sufficient?

My bed was narrow. Through the thin ceiling, I could hear my father snoring; I knew whenever he turned over in bed. It was true that I had never heard them making love. Somehow, between them, they had transformed the notion of physical love into a ridiculous idea. Why would people want to do something so awkward with their limbs?

I couldn't hear Mother. She didn't snore, but she could sigh for England. I got up and went to the top of the stairs. By the kitchen light I could see her in her dressing gown, stockings around her ankles, trudging along the hall and into each room, wringing her hands as she went, muttering back to the ghosts clamoring within her skull.

She stood still to scratch and tear at her exploded arms. During the day, she kept them covered because of her 'eczema.' Now I watched while flakes of skin fell onto the carpet, as though she were converting herself into dust. She dispersed the shreds of her body with her delicately pointed dancer's foot.

As a child – even as a young man – I would never have

approached Mother in this state. She had always made it clear that the uproar and demands of two boys were too much for her. Naturally, she couldn't wish for us to die, so she died herself, inside.

One time, my therapist asked whether Dad and I were able to be silent together. More relevant, I should have said, was whether Mother and I could be together without my chattering on about whatever occurred to me, in order to distract her from herself. Now I made up my mind and walked down the stairs, watching her all the while. She was like difficult music, and you wouldn't want to get too close. But, as with such music, I wouldn't advise trying to make it out – you have to sit with it, wait for it to address you.

I was standing beside her, and with her head down she looked at me sideways.

'I'll make you some tea,' I said, and she even nodded.

Before, during one of her late-night wanderings, she had found me masturbating in front of some late-night TV program. It must have been some boy group, or Bowie. 'I know what you are,' she said. She was not disapproving. She was just a lost ally.

I made a cup of lemon tea and gave it to her. As she stood sipping it, I took up a position beside her, my head bent also, attempting to see – as she appeared to vibrate with inner electricity – what she saw and felt. It was clear that there was no chance of my ever being able to cure her. I could only become less afraid of her madness.

In his bed, Father was still snoring. He wouldn't have liked me to be with her. He had taken her sons for himself, charmed them away, and he wasn't a sharer.

She was almost through with the tea and getting impatient. Wandering, muttering, scratching: she had important work to do and time was passing. I couldn't detain her anymore.

I slept in her chair in the front room.

When I got up, my parents were having breakfast. My

father was back in his suit and my mother was in the uniform she wore to work in the supermarket. I dressed rapidly in order to join Dad as he walked to the station. It had stopped raining.

I asked him about his day, but couldn't stop thinking about mine. I was living, as my therapist enjoyed reminding me, under the aegis of the clock. I wanted to go to the studio and talk; I wanted to eat well and make love well, go to a show and then dance, and make love again. I could not be the same as them.

At the station in London, Father and I parted. I said I'd always look out for him when I was in the area, but couldn't be sure when I'd be coming his way again.

Continuous Manipulation

Frank Cottrell Boyce

It must have been Spring 2005. Which means we'd only been going out for a few weeks. The relationship was definitely still in its Frequently Asked Questions phase – the sitting up late, swapping childhood stories bit. Adé had a big advantage there. He was brought up in Ghana. Everything about his past was new to me. The names of streets, soft drinks, TV favourites, top ten tunes – they were all delicious and fresh. I had to spice up my own past just to justify opening my mouth. There was a story my mother used to tell about the four year old me, how I'd tried to cure a headache by pressing a Junior Aspirin to my temple, instead of swallowing it. I never believed it. Whenever she told it, I winced. But I told that story now, along with half a dozen others, as though I really remembered them, as though I'd never told them to anyone else. I turned myself into a fictional character, just to keep the conversation going. Cousins, aunts, teachers became cartoon franchises. My first real boyfriend, Peter Dillon – the one whose parents got divorced and then married each other again – I made it sound like they did that every week.

Then we got to the 'I'd really like to meet your family, Sue' phase. What do you do then? You either say, 'Look I've exaggerated. My mother is not, in fact, some sort of obsessive compulsive hygiene terrorist. She's just a bit fussy.' Or it's goodbye. I booked a pair of Awayday Weekend Saver Firsts and took him to Carlisle. From the minute we arrived, I was apologising for the place. Carlisle has a rich, dramatic history but let's be honest, it's over. If you wanted to see Carlisle at its best you had to be here during the Roman occupation.

'Stop it,' said Adé. 'To me this town is the Theme Park of Sue. I want to see it all.'

He really did talk like that. My mother fell for him obviously. And my sisters. The four of them sat, wrapt, as he told them the name of his street, favourite soft drink, and TV programme. He sang them his top ten tunes. In the end I had to borrow a car and drive him to Silloth just to get a word in.

'Silloth? What d'you want to take him to Silloth for?'

'He's never seen the English seaside.'

'Silloth's not a seaside. Silloth's mud flats.'

'It has an Edwardian promenade, and is home to breathtaking flocks of wader birds.'

'He's seen birds. They have birds in Africa.'

'Different birds.'

'Better ones. Why would he want to see barnacle geese when he's got flamingos at home.'

'Mother, just give me the car keys.'

Silloth of course is where Peter Dillon used to live. Everyone fantasises about bumping into their ex in the company of a fabulous new partner. But that really, really is not why we went to Silloth. Or why we walked up all the way to the far end of the promenade where his house stood, staring out across the mud.

As we passed I said, 'If you wanted to see Silloth when it was buzzing, you really had to be here before the ice age.'

'Sue, stop it.'

'See that house there? See the porch? That's where I had my first proper snog.'

'Can we go and take a closer look?'

'No we can't. His Mum and Dad are probably home.'

'Probably in the middle of a divorce.'

'Or a wedding.'

But we did go into that porch. And we did ring that

doorbell. There was no reply at first. I peeped in at the window, shading my eyes with my hand. And there they were, Peter's parents, sitting at opposite ends of the couch, as still and vacant as Playmobil. Mortified, I tried to duck down out of sight, but his mother got up in one single sudden movement, stood for a second as if deciding what to do, then swiveled towards me and smiled.

'I'm sorry,' I said when she answered the door, 'I couldn't just pass the house without saying hello.'

'Hello,' she echoed. 'Come in.'

Her tone was welcoming but impersonal, like a supermarket greeter. Did that bother me? Did I even notice? Not then. I had my own agenda. I was there to show them how well I'd done without their precious Peter. I was there to get Adé to eclipse my past. We went in. I wish we hadn't.

Peter was there. In the garden playing penalties with a little red headed girl. When he heard we were there, he came straight in, all smiles. His parents were all smiles. They asked all the polite questions. Adé gave new and fascinating answers. I said that Peter hadn't changed. Which he hadn't. And nor had the house. There was the cupboard with the board games in, the bookshelf full of carefully chronological photo albums. There was even still a shelf of films on VHS. The little girl in the garden reminded me of his little sister, Ruthie – the same brass coloured hair. I was beginning to feel warm and nostalgic, which wasn't in the plan, which wasn't comfortable. Anyway, I'd made my point the moment Adé walked through the door. Hanging around would just be rubbing it in. So I said no thanks to tea and headed for the door.

Peter, his Mum and his Dad, all followed us to the door. A bit too closely to be honest, crowding us the way kittens crowd you when you're opening the Whiskas. 'You must stay to tea,' smiled his Mum.

And I thought, yes, of course we must. Adé has never had a full-on Cumbrian spread. Of course we must stay to tea. Peter leaned forward, like he was going to whisper something, or kiss me on the cheek. But before he got close enough, he pulled back suddenly. He turned − almost span − on his heel and stepped away from me. It was the suddenness of it really. A mechanical, almost involuntary suddenness. I'd seen that movement once before. Ten years before. Seeing it again, here, I remembered. The two instances connected, they made a story. But not one I could share with Adé.

We didn't stay to tea.

'I would've liked to stay,' said Adé as we walked into the wind along the promenade. 'They seemed so happy. The happiest family I've ever seen. Peter seems like a good guy, too. I love the way he plays with that little girl. Is that his daughter?'

All his questions seemed like moves in a game I didn't want to play any more. I drove home in silence. I haven't really seen him since. I don't see anyone much anymore.

I started going out with Peter in Year Eleven. I suppose he was upset when his mum walked out but we were going off to university so what did it matter. We went to Manchester, both of us, together. New street names, new music, new food, new conversations, Manchester was as fresh as Ghana to us back then. We neither of us gave a thought to home till that first Christmas on the train home. As soon as we got north of Preston, Peter started fidgeting and staring pointedly out of the window when I was talking to him. It didn't phase me. I said, 'I'll come to yours if you don't mind. Before I go home. I fancy a stroll along the prom.'

You could tell he was pleased with the idea from the way he said, 'Whatever.'

When we got there, Andrea was there. His dad's new bit. Tanned, toned, and twitchy. She kissed Peter with her glossed lips and smiled all over him with her whitened teeth. I think about her now, the way she'd altered her appearance to please Peter's dad. Just as I altered my past to impress Adé. How we girls do chip away at our own reality.

She was thrilled to meet me at last, by the way, she'd heard so much about me. She even took my bag upstairs for me. She put it in Peter's room, at the foot of his bed and winked, 'You two will be nice and cosy in here, I suppose.'

I must have blushed or something because she said, 'Oh. If you don't then...'

'No, no. We do,' I said. 'Thanks.'

Peter and I laughed about it afterwards. 'I can't believe I told her we were having sex.'

'I can't believe she got that out of you.'

'I thanked her. I thanked her for providing sex facilities.'

Peter's dad breezed by, wrapped in a towel and smelling of aftershave. 'Hi there,' he said, as opposed to 'No visitors in the bedrooms,' which was what he used to say.

'This place has changed a bit since Mum was here.'

When we looked up little Ruthie was in the doorway, staring at us. I can still remember the way the light fell on those thick brass curls. She would have been eight.

'Hey Ruthie,' I said. And held out my arms to her. She didn't budge.

'I didn't know you were home,' said Peter. 'Why didn't you come down and say hello?'

'I prefer it upstairs now. Are you going away again?'

'Not till after Christmas. It's Christmas holidays.'

'So you're going away again.'

'After Christmas. Have to go back to uni.'

'Can I come?'

'You're not old enough. Plus you don't have any A-levels.'

She went back to her room.

Peter shrugged. 'What d'you want me to do?'

I followed Ruthie to her room. Ruthie's room had

changed. The Angelina Ballerina wallpaper was still there but the shelves were groaning with personal electronics – a TV, a PlayStation, a phone, a PC, a DVD player, even a popcorn machine. It was like a girly branch of Comet. 'Woah,' I said.

'Dad took me out and bought all this,' she said. 'Then two days later she moved in.'

'Right. Well... she seems nice enough.'

'I can't even play these games. I don't understand the instructions.'

'What have we got?'

We had pretty much everything to be honest. It was me who chose Sims. That's the one where you have a family to look after. The Sims. You have to satisfy their needs – nutrition, exercise, hygiene – nurture their development – reading, hobbies, conversation and help them fulfill their aspirations. Stuff keeps happening that you've got no control over – they get visitors, they get flooded. Sims get hungry and bored so you have to keep ahead of the game, keep them fed and entertained. Sometimes it seems like they have a will of their own. The trick is to master that will and get them to do what you want.

'How do you win?'

'You don't win. You just keep it going. Some people keep their Sim families going for years.'

'Do they die?'

'They can die. They can walk out on you. You have to keep them healthy and keep home interesting.'

'How d'you do that?'

'Just make sure the Aspiration Meter is filling up.'

You can design your own family but that first night we played with the default family. Are they called the Newbies? Ruthie found it all a bit emotionally draining at first. When Mr. Newbie started hitting his own thighs in fury, she almost burst into tears. 'I've given him a good job and a lovely supper. Why is he so ungrateful?'

'He needs the toilet.'

'Oh.'

But mum was hitting her thighs too by then. 'Lack of appreciation. You need to give her a hug.' I showed her how. 'It's non-stop Ruthie. It's called "Continuous Manipulation".'

Once she'd calmed them down, she was thrilled by her own power and their pliability. She hugged, cooked, tickled, bought presents. In the end I fell asleep in her bed. The idea of an Andrea-sanctioned sex session had lost its appeal by then in any case.

When I woke up the next morning, she was still playing.

'Have you been at it all night?'

'You can design your own family, look. Did you know that? Look you can make their eyes bigger, give them muscles, whatever.'

'I know.'

'If you make the eyes big, that looks good because they look like babies. Babies have big eyes. But if you make them too big, that's horrible. Because that's like insects pretending to be babies. When they look weird, that's called the Uncanny Valley. It's all in the manual. And d'you know what? If you don't want them to, they won't get any older.'

'That sounds good.'

'Doesn't that sound good?'

She came downstairs with me for breakfast. I could see why she'd mostly stayed upstairs. Andrea had redecorated. The place looked like the reception area of a graphics company – simple lines, everything white, with aggressive splashes of colour. When Ruthie walked in with me, Andrea purred with pleasure.

'Terry looks who's here for breakfast.'

'Hello, Ruthie.'

'Look, look what we got for you yesterday.' There was a big shopping bag over by the Aga. Andrea reached in and pulled out a white shift dress. Beautiful, simple lines, with a bold splash of blue across the shoulder. A dress that coordinated perfectly with the kitchen. A dress that would turn Ruth into fixtures and fittings.

'Thanks,' said Ruth.

'We can go again today and get you something for Christmas morning, what d'you say?'

Ruthie didn't say anything. What she did was hug her dad. He looked astonished. 'What's brought this on?' he said, flushed with pleasure.

She didn't answer. She said, 'Dad, what's the offside rule?'

'What?'

'In football, what's the offside rule. I asked Sue but she didn't know.'

'Why would you want to know that?' asked Andrea.

Ruth didn't reply and by then her dad was already building a three-dimensional diagram of the offside trap out of Weetabix and milk cartons.

'Yeah,' said Peter, 'Why would you want to know all that?'

'It's all in the manual,' I whispered.

When I went up to collect my bags, Sims was still running on the screen. It was the smoothest running game I'd ever seen. The little figures were reading, exercising, cooking. Improving themselves, enjoying each other. And the family was all her own design. There was a mother, a father, a teenage son and an eight year old girl. All rubbing along happily in the same house. They were called Mum, Dad, Peter, and Ruthie Dillon.

Video games don't normally make me cry. But the next few days I thought a lot about the tiny pixilated family inside the computer monitor, living the life that Ruth wished she was living. I thought at the time it was her version of the way things used to be, before Andrea.

I didn't go back over to the house on the prom till Christmas day. The plan was midnight mass with my family, open presents with my sisters, then over to the Dillons' for Christmas lunch. The Dillons' plan was Christmas lunch all together, then Ruthie's mum would come and collect her and take her over to her grandmother's. Peter and I might go too.

We sat in the immaculate dining room while Andrea served hors d'oeuvres. I asked Ruth what she got for Christmas, 'I...' she struggled to remember.

'She got a Carlisle United away strip,' beamed her Dad. 'And... a season ticket.'

'Wow, Ruthie.'

Andrea's muscley arms were tensed. 'She also got a pony. Which is what she's always wanted.'

'Oh. Yeah. Forgot about that.'

Ruthie leaned into me. 'Want to see what my family got each other? Shall I show you.'

'Not now, Ruthie,' smiled Andrea. 'We're about to eat.'

All through the meal, Ruthie said nothing out loud. But I could see that the unsatisfactory people round the table were less real to her than the family upstairs. She was talking to them in her head. When Andrea went into the kitchen to sort out the Christmas pudding, Ruthie dragged me upstairs.

There was the other Dillon family, gathered around a poorly animated Christmas tree. 'It doesn't seem right to leave them on their own while we're down there eating,' said Ruthie. She must have got some kind of expansion pack because the tiny dad was doing magic tricks for his children. When each trick finished they would throw their heads back to an angle of ninety degrees and applaud – their hands a hummingbird blur of appreciation.

'Look. Look what the dad got the mum.'

She must have bought some sort of expansion pack. I'd never seen branded products in Sims before. Dad had bought Mum a bottle of perfume. Charly.

'You know that's a really cheap perfume.'

'I know but it's what she was wearing the day he met her.'

'They don't even make it any more.'

'I know. That's why she's so surprised, look.'

Tiny Mum really was very surprised. She had her arms in the air and was more or less spinning with pleasure.

Tiny Peter by the way got all kinds of stuff for his bedroom – a multigym, a double bed, coffee making facilities. 'It's like a flat. So he can be happy,' said Ruthie. 'And look how happy he is.' His Aspiration Meter was twitching away at the top of the dial.

Real Mum came half an hour later. I hadn't seen her since the split up. She gave me a hug and asked about uni. I got my coat and said we'd all come with her and Ruthie. But in the kitchen, Ruthie was slumped across the table, groaning about having a temperature.

'What's wrong with her?' asked her mum.

'Nothing. She's fine. She's been having a great time.'

'Having a great time? She looks half dead.'

Peter tried to put her coat on her. 'Come on, Ruthie, we're going to Grandma's,' he said.

'Too hot,' said Ruthie.

There was a massive row about how Ruthie had got so ill without anyone noticing. It was obvious that she wasn't going anywhere but new arrangements could only be made after grudges and resentments had been aired at high volume. In fact things were only really settled when Andrea walked out, slamming the door behind her.

I watched her go from the window. I said, 'Temperature. She really did read that manual, didn't she?' At the time it seemed funny that Andrea stood in the drive and beat her thighs in fury, for all the world like a Sim that'd wet itself.

And later when I sat around the tree with Ruth and Peter and their mum and dad, I thought it was sweet that her game had come true for a moment.

Mum opened her present, almost dropped it in surprise, then threw her hands up in the air. 'Charly!' she gasped. 'How did you remember?'

'You know I'm not sure.'

'They don't even make it any more. Where did you get it?'

'The internet.'

'But why?'

'You know, I can't remember.'

She kissed him. She kissed him on the lips. Ruthie was watching them, as intently as a child playing a computer game.

Two days before the start of term, I went round to sort out the travel arrangements. 'Big news,' said Peter. 'Andrea has gone.'

'What?'

'Completely gone away and never coming back.'

'How's your dad?'

'Fine I think. He just keeps smiling.'

Peter just kept smiling too. He carried on smiling as he told me he wasn't going back to university.

'You're not what?'

'I'm not going back to university.'

'What are you talking about? Why aren't you going back?'

'Why would I want to leave here? Look.'

He gestured towards the endless winter mud flats. I remember a scribble of geese drawn on the sky.

'It's mud,' I said. 'And geese. Even the geese can't stick it all year.'

'It's home,' he said.

'OK so you're not coming back. OK. Fine. Thanks for telling me. You could at least try and not smile about it.'

Because he was smiling. A wide, blank smile.

'Why are you smiling?'

'I don't know,' he said.

So Peter's mum and dad got married again that Easter. I came home for the wedding. I was happy for them. Really I was. I got changed in Ruthie's room. When I came in, she paused her Sims game. I watched them on the monitor as they subsided into their chairs, all smiles. The mother was in a wedding dress.

During the afternoon, I tried to talk to Peter about uni. 'Come back,' I said. 'Everything's worked out here. They won't miss you. You could start again in September.'

At first he seemed to struggle to know what I was talking about.

'Manchester. Come on. Come back with me. It's good.'

Then his eyes brightened, as though he'd remembered something good.

'Manchester!' he said, and he sounded just like his mum had sounded when she said, 'Charly'! Like he'd recovered some forgotten treasure. I really thought he was going to say yes, but then he span on his heel very suddenly, almost involuntarily, and walked away into the party, passing his blandly smiling parents. Passing Ruthie, who was frowning until she caught my eye. Then she smiled too.

The sudden spin on the heel; the sentence bitten off in the middle; the involuntary quickness of it all made it seem less than human. It troubled me then. And it troubled me afresh when I saw it again ten years later.

The thing is, it wasn't the only time I saw it that day. Later in the afternoon, I was walking back along the prom. Cars from the party were parked all the way back to the town. A figure came jerkily up the steps from the shore, pausing on each step as if each step was an effort of will. An angular restless figure. Only when it turned to face me, did I recognise Andrea. It wasn't that her face had changed, but her deportment had. She moved like something mechanical and remote controlled.

'Sue...' she hissed. Her eyes were wide and urgent. She grabbed my forearm. 'Listen to me.'

'I'm listening.'

'I...' Her eyes I remember were staring and wide, like terrified eyes, but oddly expressionless. 'I... please...'

'I'm listening.'

Then she turned, just as Peter had turned, spinning on her heel and walking rapidly away. As suddenly as if a switch had been thrown. I looked up and saw Ruthie on the prom. She waved to me, a big, enthusiastic wave. She ran up and hugged me and thanked me for being her friend and told me she was sad that it was all over between me and Peter. She tickled me under my arms. I think it was this scene that made me forget that moment with Andrea. That made me forget looking over the handrail later and seeing her beating her thighs in that jerky, Sims-like way.

I only remembered that moment when I went back to Silloth with Adé. When Peter leaned in to whisper something, then turned suddenly away. When I saw for a second a look of horror and pleading flicker across his eyes, before the bland smile resettled itself. As though someone was trying to escape from that body. That body which had not changed. But which now subsided into a chair as though its power source had been cut off, as though it was on pause.

'Bye then,' said Adé. 'Lovely to meet you. I've heard so much about you.'

It was only when we opened the door to go that the little girl came running in from the garden.

'Are they going?' she cried. 'Oh. Don't go. Don't go...' and she hugged me round the waist and tickled my ribs a little.

'Who's this?' smiled Adé, rubbing the child's lovely, twisted red hair. 'You must be Peter's little girl. What's your name?'

'Ruthie,' said the girl, looking up at me and smiling. 'Stay,' she said. 'Stay and play.'

And I saw that she wasn't Peter's little girl at all. She was Ruthie, the same Ruthie, ten years on but still eight years old.

Anette and I Are Fucking in Hell

Etgar Keret

She was sweating, I was sweating, the ground was sweating. We could feel the rumbling in her bowels, sense that in another minute, she'd open her mouth to vomit. 'Tell them to stop,' she pleaded, her hand stroking my damp, greasy hair, 'please, make them stop.' The imps capered around us, screeching in their shrill voices, making obscene gestures. Every once in a while, they ran a long, filthy fingernail over my ass or hers, giggling annoyingly each time. And we fucked. When my tongue caressed her nipple, the acrid taste of the sulphur got into my mouth too. I felt her hand slide down my wet back, or maybe it was one of the imps. I forced myself to stick my tongue out again and trailed it slowly down her body, trying to ignore the taste, the smells, the sounds. I reached her crotch. The imps clapped and whistled in ecstasy, but I tried to ignore them, focused on my moving tongue. She started to moan, but didn't close her eyes for a minute. Her gaze was fixed somewhere on the ceiling and she must have seen the giant blind bats hanging upside down over our heads, or the ones that were flying around the room, dropping their shit pellets. You can't ever close your eyes here, not when you're asleep, not when you pass out, not when you're making it with a woman. And there's another special thing about this terrible place – you have a constant hard-on, if you're a man, and if you're a woman, you're always wet, and the whole sex thing turns into an almost involuntary act, like breathing, like breathing moldy air that makes your lungs convulse as if you're about to puke.

One of the imps jumps right over us, scoops up a little bit of the vomit on her stomach with its finger and leaps around in the air waving it to the others. My tongue is still going at it, and she keeps moaning. As I raise my body to penetrate her, my erect penis disturbs a dozing rat. The imps are in a frenzy now. They bombard us with gobs of phlegm and pellets of bat shit. Our shame and suffering delight them, and we can't stop. If only I'd listened to the preacher when I was a kid, if only I'd stopped when I still could.

Translated from the Hebrew by Sondra Silverstone

Contributors

A. S. Byatt was born in Sheffied, South Yorkshire, and educated at Newnham College, Cambridge, and Somerville College, Oxford, She is the author of eight novels to date: *Shadow of a Sun* (1964), *The Game* (1967), *The Virgin in the Garden* (1978) *Still Life* (1985) which won the PEN/ Macmillan Silver Pen Award, *Babel Tower* (1996), *A Whistling Woman* (2002), *Possession: A Romance* (1990), won the Booker Prize for Fiction and the *Irish Times* International Fiction Prize, and *The Biographer's Tale* (2000). She has also written two novellas, published together as *Angels and Insects,* several works of non-fiction, and five collections of short stories: *Sugar and Other Stories* (1987); *The Matisse Stories* (1993), *The Djinn in the Nightingale's Eye* (1994), and *Elementals: Stories of Fire and Ice* (1998). She was made a dame in 1999 and currently lives in London.

Ramsey Campbell Ramsey Campbell is described by the Oxford Companion to English Literature as 'Britain's most respected living horror writer', and in 1991 was voted the Horror Writer's Horror Writer in the Observer Magazine. His many award-winning novels include *The Face That Must Die, Incarnate, The Overnight,* and *The Grin of the Dark.* He has also published thirteen collections of short stories to date, most recently *Told by the Dead* (2003).

Frank Cottrell Boyce is a novelist and screenwriter. His film credits include *Welcome to Sarajevo, Hilary and Jackie, Code*

46, 24 Hour Party People and *A Cock and Bull Story*. In 2004, his debut novel *Millions* won the Carnegie Medal and was shortlisted for The Guardian Children's Fiction Award. His second novel, *Framed*, was published by Macmillan in 2005. He also writes for the theatre and was the author of the highly acclaimed BBC film *God on Trial*. He has previously contributed stories to Comma's anthologies *Phobic* and *The Book of Liverpool*.

Ian Duhig has published four poetry collections, including *Nominies* (1998) which was named as one of the 1998 Sunday Times Poetry Books of the Year and received a Poetry Book Society Special Commendation; and most recently, *Lammas Hireling* (2003) which was a Poetry Book Society Choice. His first short story was published in *The Book of Leeds* (Comma, 2007).

Matthew Holness won the Perrier Comedy Award in 2001 for *Garth Marenghi's Netherhead*, and has since appeared in *The Office*, *Casanova*, and his own Channel 4 television series *Garth Marenghi's Darkplace* and *Man to Man With Dean Learner*. His first short story was published in *Phobic* (Comma, 2007).

Etgar Keret is an Israeli writer whose award-winning short story collections include *Pipelines, Gaza Blues* (with Samir El Youssef), *The Bus Driver Who Thought He Was God, The Nimrod Flip-Out*, and *Missing Kissinger*. He is the author of three graphic novels, several award winning scripts for TV, and the novella *Kneller's Happy Campers*, which was adapted by director Goran Dukic into a feature-length film *Wristcutters: A Love Story* starring Patrick Fugit and Tom Waits. His fiction has been translated into sixteen languages and has been the basis for more than 40 short films.

CONTRIBUTORS

Hanif Kureishi's first play, *Soaking the Heat*, was performed at the Royal Court Theatre in London in 1976. Since then he has enjoyed success as a playwright, screenwriter, novelist and short story writer. His first novel, *The Buddha of Suburbia*, was published in 1990 to widespread acclaim, and won the Whitbread First Novel Award. He has published also three collections of short stories: *Love in a Blue Time, Midnight All Day* and *The Body and Other Stories*.

Alison MacLeod is the author of two novels, *The Changeling* and *The Wave Theory of Angels*. Her first collection of short stories, *Fifteen Modern Tales of Attraction*, was published in 2007. She lives in Brighton and teaches creative writing at the University of Chichester.

Sara Maitland grew up in Galloway and studied at Oxford University. Her first novel, *Daughters of Jerusalem*, was published in 1978 and won the Somerset Maugham Award. Novels since have included *Three Times Table* (1990), *Home Truths* (1993) and *Brittle Joys* (1999), and one co-written with Michelene Wandor – *Arky Types* (1987). Her short story collections include *Telling Tales* (1983), *A Book of Spells* (1987) and most recently, *On Becoming a Fairy Godmother* (2003).

Adam Marek's stories first appeared in *Parenthesis (Comma 2006)*, and *New Writing 15*, edited by Maggie Gee and Bernardine Evaristo. His debut collection *Instruction Manual for Swallowing* was published by Comma Press in 2007.

Christopher Priest is the author of ten novels and two collections of short stories. *The Glamour* won the 1988 Kurd Lasswitz Best Novel award and *The Prestige* won the 1995 World Fantasy Award, the 1995 James Tait Award for best novel and was shortlisted for the Arthur C. Clarke Award. In 2006 it was adapted into a feature film by Christopher Nolan.

Jane Rogers was born in London in 1952 and lived in Birmingham, New York State (Grand Island) and Oxford, before doing an English degree at Cambridge University. She has written seven novels, including *Separate Tracks, Mr Wroe's Virgins, Island* and *Voyage Home,* as well as original television and radio drama. Her short stories were collected in *Ellipsis 2* (Comma 2007).

Nicholas Royle is the author of five novels – *Counterparts, Saxophone Dreams, The Matter of the Heart, The Director's Cut* and *Antwerp* – as well as one collection of short stories, *Mortality* (Serpent's Tail, 2006). He has edited twelve anthologies of short fiction including *A Book of Two Halves, The Tiger Garden: A Book of Writers' Dreams, The Time Out Book of New York Short Stories,* and *Dreams Never End* (Tindal Street Press).

Gerard Woodward was born in London in 1961 and studied art and anthropology. He has published four poetry collections: *Householder* (1991), which won a Somerset Maugham Award; *After the Deafening* (1994); *Island to Island* (1999); and *We Were Pedestrians* (2005). His first novel, *August,* was shortlisted for the 2001 Whitbread First Novel Award, and was followed in 2004 by *I'll Go To Bed At Noon* (2004), shortlisted for the Man Booker Prize, and the third in this semi-autobiographical series, *A Curious Earth* (2007). His first collection of short stories *The Caravan Thieves* was published this year.

Special Thanks

The editors would like to thank the following people for their advice and support throughout the project: Tom Spooner, Tim Cooke, Libby Tempest, Deborah Rogers, Andy Darby, Lin and Jon Shaffer, and Hot Chip.